Independence

a Significance Series novel

SHELLY CRANE

Independence

a Significance Series novel

SHELLY CRANE

Printed in paperback and available in Kindle and E-book format through Amazon, Create Space and Barnes & Noble.

Printed in the United States
10 9 8 7 6 5 4 3 2 1

More information can be found at the author's website
http://shellycrane.blogspot.com

ISBN-13: 978-1494803797
ISBN-10: 1494803798

This Book is Dedicated To The FANS!

The last book of the series... Bittersweet doesn't really cover it for me. And SO much has happened to me personally this year.

I'm dedicating this book to the fans that have been with me from the beginning. The ones who ask me how I'm doing and not just when the next book is due. The ones who've sent me mail and tweets and email saying how much you love the books. Without you, this book would not be.

To the Hellcats, Michelle Leighton, Amy Bartol, Georgia Cates, Rachel Higginson, Angeline Kace, Quinn Loftis, Lila Felix, and Samantha Young, you girls have made this year bearable. And you rocked the Indie world's face off. I couldn't be more proud of you or happy to bask in your glows. I love you!

Your presence
is cordially requested at the marriage of

Maggie Camille Masters
&
Caleb Maxwell Jacobson

At the home of the groom's parents
No shoes allowed
7:00 p.m.
September 20th

One

Maggie

"Lynne, listen." I knelt down beside her and tried not to glance at the scar glaring from her cheekbone that was a constant reminder of what had happened. I had been in her shoes before, just weeks ago, and it was still fresh in my brain. "For some reason, the powers are taking their time figuring out what they want to be. Caleb didn't realize his until… well, you remember. And you and Kyle will learn what your powers are, too, soon enough. I'm sorry that we were all too wrapped up to really even pay attention to you guys."

Kyle and Lynne had ascended on the roof of the palace and mutualized right after. Everyone had been so focused on what was going on with us and worrying about the bigger problems, that we hadn't had time to dwell on the fact that neither of them were getting a feeling for what their ability was going to be. Or the fact that Lynne was human and had gotten the tattoo on her wrist.

"No," she said quickly. "I don't want the spotlight. It's just that Kyle…" She sniffed in a way that showed me she'd been crying way before she came to see me. "He's upset about it. I just know it. How could he not be, right?"

I smiled. I knew this one firsthand as well. I felt my cell buzz in my pocket, but ignored it. "Caleb and I went through the same thing. I felt like he'd been cheated because he was an Ace and I wasn't."

"Yeah," she said and nodded. "That's how I feel."

I knew it was mere minutes before Kyle would come and find her. She was so upset, there was no way Kyle couldn't feel her. "Don't worry, Lynne. Kyle is a big boy. I promise you you'll both get your abilities when you're ready and it'll be something great. And Kyle isn't upset. I'm in his head, remember?"

"Well, then get out of it!" she screeched and stood. She blushed all the way into her hairline. "His brain is private now."

I pursed my lips so I wouldn't laugh at her. "I just mean that I'd hear him if he was upset. He'd be broadcasting it out if he was."

"Whatever," she grumbled and wiped her cheek furiously. "This whole thing has turned me into such a chick."

I laughed just as Kyle bolted through the palace roof door. He practically flew to her and gripped her arms. "What's wrong?" He looked around for threats and found none. He looked between us and then finally focused on Lynne. Hearing her thoughts, he grimaced. "Lynne, it'll be fine. I told you that already."

Her mouth opened and then closed. Then she said quickly, "But it-"

"Uhuh," he said to cut her off and put his finger over her lips. I smiled at the sudden death glare she was giving him. "I have complete confidence in my kind. The abilities will come when they're ready. And I have faith in our new Visionary." He smirked at me. "She's a goody two shoes that's making the universe a very happy and giving entity. Teacher's pet."

"Bite me, Kyle."

He laughed. "See?" He turned back to Lynne and his smile changed. It was the one he saved just for her. "She's totally harmless and on board. So, can't you be?"

She sighed and chewed the inside of her cheek. "I'm on board, too. I'll chill out."

"Really? All the way on board?"

"Choo, choo," she joked wryly and he grinned, taking her face in his hands. Then his thumb swept over the scar and he let his breath go slowly. "Good," he muttered, and I heard his guilty thoughts. He thought he let her down. He had been so upset about Rodney that he wasn't able to heal her cheek and knew she'd be stuck with it forever, because of him.

"Stop," she whispered harshly. "Stop, Kyle." She gripped his face, too. "It wasn't your fault. You didn't cut me."

"But I should have been able to heal you."

"You lost your cousin," she whispered back. "Stop this."

He thought about it before smiling sadly. "Right back at ya."

She groaned at being caught in his trap before laughing softly. "Fine."

When she reached up on her toes to kiss him, I was outta there. I skipped down the stairs, my steps light and curiously worry free. Just yesterday, we'd learned that Haddock was my real father, and then Jen and Bish had imprinted... finally!

But today, I just felt better. I felt like there was so much more to solve, but that we'd be OK. I hadn't felt that sense in my bones in a long time and I craved it. Things were falling back into their right place.

Lynne had found me on the roof. I was trying to call Beck before she interrupted with her cute little tirade. I tried Beck's cell several times, but always got voicemail. And Beck, who was driving up to the mountains with Ralph, was furious with me in the only way a best friend could be as I checked message after message from her that said, "How could you not tell me you were going to freaking London! Why haven't you called me all week?" And of course, my favorite. "When am I going to get the juicy details of you and college boy? You better call me back before I get postal on your cute butt!"

I smiled thinking about that. I missed her. She was my slice of normal pie and I could have used an extra helping.

I heard his thoughts around the door just a second before his arms closed around my waist. I was pressed, but went willingly, to the wall with my back and then it was all warm lips and closed eyes and soft, but needy hands.

Poor Caleb. Maria had taken it upon herself after our big reveal with Jen and Bish to come and sleep with us to give them some privacy. Caleb grumbled about needing our own privacy in his mind, but it was just one night, right?

So when I felt his fingers teasing the skin just under my shirt, to soak me in as much as I was him, I knew he was making up for lost time. The hand in my hair gave me goosebumps as it massaged and swept through my hair gently. I shivered, causing him to groan. I pulled back just a bit and looked up at him.

My Caleb.

He smiled cockily and happily back down at me.

Why, Mrs. Jacobson, are you blushing?

Flushing is more like it, I corrected and smirked my own smirk.

Well, I have it on good authority that our room is finally vacant of transients and squatters. Wanna come and...nap with me?

His grin was absolutely not about a nap. I bit my lip and nodded for him to lead the way. He laced our fingers as we made our way down the hall. We reached our room and he kissed me again as he fiddled with the door lock. He swept deep in my mouth. I held on to his collar to keep him there and to hold myself up.

But the loud giggling made us pause. Caleb pushed our door open to find Bish and Jen there. They had their shoes off, their legs hanging off the edge of the bed and they were lounging on their backs looking at each other. Before I could stop myself, I heard their thoughts. They were talking about learning to drive, remembering and laughing.

They looked up and Jen smiled sheepishly. "Sorry. Mom and Maria are napping in our room."

"What about your room?" Caleb asked Bish, anxious to evict our guests.

"They never gave me one," he answered smoothly.

"Well..." Caleb searched for any semi-polite way to tell them to get the heck out. I chuckled under my breath and grabbed his collar once more. He rested his hands on my lower back, his forehead to mine.

"We won't get a moment's peace until we get back to the States," I told him. "And then still not. Beck is going to drive me crazy for at least a week. Then Gran is going to start the wedding stuff, I just know it."

Caleb nodded and silently told me I was right.

"Sorry," Jen said again, but plopped back on the bed with no intention of leaving. Bish joined her, closer this time.

He whispered, "I'm not sorry." Then he kissed her once, pulling her to his chest and they lay still as if to go to sleep.

"Want to go back to the roof?" Caleb suggested in a low voice that held promise.

"Eew," Jen groaned. "Get out before you start the sexy voice, little brother."

"*Our* room," he retorted and smiled at me. It was his *I'm happy no matter what we're doing* smile.

This was the smile he saved just for me, for when no one was looking.

I smiled back and started to lead him back to our roof when Haddock met us at the door.

"Maggie. Caleb," he addressed and fidgeted. I, of course, couldn't hear his thoughts so I had no idea what he wanted. "I was wondering if we could talk…before you all leave."

"About what?" I said gently. I wasn't angry with Haddock and I didn't want him to think he owed me anything. I closed the door so Bish wouldn't hear him. He didn't know about this, after all.

But Haddock said, "When you leave tomorrow to go back to Tennessee, I'm coming with you. To your town, I mean."

"What?" I blurted loudly. "What do you mean?"

He stood a little taller. "I may not have been your father this whole time, and I know you have Jim, that's great, but I lost you once and didn't even know I had you to begin with. I have no intention of doing that again."

I closed my eyes and tried to breathe normally. So, Dad and Fiona, and Caleb and me, and Bish and Jen, now Haddock.

One big, happy family.

"Whatever, that's fine," I said politely and tried to smile. "We'll see what we can work out, but I'm not telling my father…um, Jim. You know what I mean. I'm not telling him about all of this."

"Understood," he said and smiled. "See you at dinner."

I remembered the text in my pocket. I pulled my cell out and tried not to shoot daggers at Haddock's back as he walked away. My phone was very full now with all the clan's phone numbers. I told everyone to keep in touch with me and if anyone else imprinted, to let me know as soon as possible. Caleb and I were determined to keep on top of things with all the Aces.

Meanwhile, I examined my text. Caleb was muttering something about Haddock being a troublemaker, but stopped as soon as he felt my thoughts slam into him.

I reread the text message five times while Caleb held on to me. When he pressed my face into his neck and said, "Ah, baby. I'm *so* sorry," I knew the text from Beck's mom was real.

Beck & Ralph were in a car accident in the mountains. I tried to call u several times. They fnd the car, but no one was inside. They suspect they went looking for help &… They called off the search today. We're having the funerals on Sat. Pls, come home.

I felt my knees begin to shake.

Caleb leaned back and took my face in his hands. "We'll leave, right now." I could feel him pushing all of his comfort and love into me, into my skin with his touch. I couldn't remember a time I was ever so grateful for him than in that moment. I felt my lip quiver and bit into it to stop it. He looked at my lip and back up to my eyes with a pained expression. He could do nothing to fix this situation for me and feeling helpless wasn't something Caleb liked very much. Neither did I for that matter. "Maggie…tell me what to do," he said, anguished and swept my cheek with the side of his thumb. "What can I do?"

I lifted and wrapped my arms around his neck. "You're doing it." I sighed and tried to calm down. "You're doing it."

When he finally spoke, it was soft and in my ear, as if he were easing me along. "I'll go and tell Dad that we're leaving now. They can come later on. Why don't you…sit with Jen and Bish for a minute, until I get back, OK?"

I nodded. He took me there in a haze. I'd been so wrapped up in everything going on lately – granted, it was huge, life-altering things, but still – that I had barely been able to speak to Beck much lately.

Rebecca. I never even used her real name, and she never used mine.

I felt a flood of guilt, remorse, and loss. It was then I felt Caleb's warmth and comfort leave me. I heard his groan and turned to him. Bish had me by my arm and Jen was with him, too. Caleb was trying to leave me there…but he couldn't. He wanted to. He wanted to let me have a minute with my brother in my time of mourning, but Bish would understand. Bish could be the one to tell everyone we were leaving…that I'd lost my friends.

I needed Caleb.

We both moved at the same time and wrapped our arms around each other. I heard Bish say something about Dad and a plane. I just focused on the soft, plaid pattern of Caleb's shirt with my eyes and fingers.

In that moment I felt like the girl I used to be. The girl who felt abandoned and alone in a world full of people and things. But I wasn't that girl. I looked up at Caleb's face as we stood in my room at the foot of the bed. His face spelled out his need to make my hurt go away.

No, I was not alone anymore.

But my friend was still gone.

Two

Caleb

SHE WAS still shaking. I knew there was nothing I could *do* to make it better. Her friend died. But this…just feeling her body shake and my shirt wet because she'd been crying for the past twenty minutes…

Each minute that ticked by was a knife in my gut. I eventually picked her up and we lay on the bed together and waited for word on us going home. I stared at the ceiling as I let my fingers dance what I hoped was a soothing rhythm across her bare shoulder. She tangled our legs and gripped my shirt in her fingers.

I tried to keep my suspicions to myself and not let them seep out to Maggie, but it was very much a possibility in my mind that this was retaliation. The Watsons had lost Marla and Donald to our hands. Would they still risk coming against us just for revenge? If they killed Beck and Ralph and I was the one who brought Maggie into this mess…

I groaned angrily and shifted a bit. Maggie lifted her head slightly to look at me. "What are you so angry about?"

"Nothing, baby," I assured. "I'm just...sad for you."

"You're mad, I can tell." She yawned and scooted up closer to be by my head. "I'm too exhausted to make you tell me though."

I found myself chuckling. "Don't worry about me. I'm worried about *you*."

"I'm...all right." She sniffed and it broke my heart. "I just wish I could've seen her one more time. She was so mad at me before...and then we came here and..." Her eyes looked up to mine. "But they did say they never found the bodies. So maybe there's still hope, right?"

"Yeah, absolutely."

I really wanted to believe that.

She licked her lips and continued. "Maybe I can find them. Maybe..." Her face fell. "I'd have to touch her to get a vision though, wouldn't I?"

I started to say something, I'm not even sure what, when a knock banged on the door. I sighed. "What?" I asked loudly.

Jen poked her head in. "Hey," she said slowly. It was obvious she was walking on eggshells. I gave her a face to tell her to stop it. She had to know Maggie would hate that. She straightened and opened the door. "Our flight's booked."

"You're coming, too?" Maggie asked. "I don't want to cut your trip short."

"It's just one day. It won't matter. Are you OK?"

Maggie sighed. "Why is everyone so worried about me? You guys lost your cousin not even a week ago."

"Yeah," Jen agreed and sighed, too. "We did. Still."

 12

"I'm…" Maggie shook her head. "How are you?"

"I'm…" Jen shook her head, too, and shrugged. They both chuckled a little sadly. Maggie got up from the bed to give Jen a hug. They hugged hard for a long time. Jen nodded to her. "This week has been… bittersweet."

"I'm sorry I couldn't save him," Maggie whispered and I felt a painful ping go through my chest.

"Maggie, stop it," I told her and lifted myself from the bed.

She wouldn't look at me. Jen looked between us.

I repeated softer. "Maggie, stop it."

She finally looked up, her eyes glistening. "He saved us. He saved us and I didn't save him!"

"It wasn't your fault." I took her from Jen, but she kept going as if I hadn't spoken.

"And now Beck…I couldn't save her either. And Rodney's significant! She's all alone because I couldn't save him!" Her chest started to quake and I held her to me. She pushed me back a little, but I held onto her. "No! Don't comfort me. I caused all this." She looked up at me with questions in her eyes. "I can't believe you're not mad at me for letting him die."

"Stop, Maggie," I said and took a deep breath. "Stop this."

She wasn't going to stop so I yanked her to me. She tried to push me off and I just held on tighter. She wasn't this kind of fighter. It took no time before she was burying her face in my neck instead of pushing me away. I held on to her just as tightly as she was me. "I'm so sorry," she cried.

I took a deep breath to hold back my own emotion. Hers, plus mine, plus knowing things were probably going to get worse, was killing me.

She took my face in her small, cold hands and looked into me. "I'm. So. Sorry."

"Baby," I pleaded. "This wasn't your fault."

"You're only saying that because of the imprint. It won't let you be mad."

"I'm saying it because it's true," I said, hard and unrelenting. "Beck isn't your fault. Rodney…isn't your fault." I fought the clog in my throat. "Maggie, things happen. Some things just happen sometimes and no one is to blame and no one could have stopped it."

She didn't look completely convinced, but I felt her fingers move a little on my face. She let them slide away and then looked at Jen. "Is Bish packing?"

"Yeah," she answered. "He's got Maria helping him." She smiled. "Those two get along pretty well so far."

"He adores her," Maggie confirmed. "And vice-versa." She looked at me and cleared her throat. "We should probably pack, too."

"All my stuff is here," I said. "I moved it all from upstairs. I'll start putting stuff in the suitcases."

She nodded and I turned to do just that. She and Jen spoke for a second before Maggie closed the door. She stayed there a bit and waited. I'd known that she was putting on a front the past few days. She was trying to be happy and strong for everyone, but with Haddock, Rodney, and now Beck, it was just too much for her. But she was acting like she didn't want my comfort at all.

Was it her idea of self-punishment because she blamed herself, or did she honestly think I was upset with her and just couldn't face my anger because of the imprint?

I glanced over at her to find her watching me as I threw a wad of t-shirts into the duffle bag. "You all right?"

She nodded. "I'm fine, Caleb. Just…" She shook her head. "I'm just ready to get there. See Mr. and Mrs. T."

I nodded at that. "I'll get you there as soon as possible. We'll go to your Dad's straight from the airport, and then I'll take you to Beck's."

"Thank you."

I decided to let the awkward behavior between us go and not mention it further. She needed to process what was going on. I could wait.

So we packed up everything in silence and I tamped down on the protective vibe racing through my veins. I dragged our bags and let her carry her purse and my hoodie for the plane as she walked in front of me.

We were almost down the hall when Jonathon turned the corner, running into Maggie. He gripped her arms to keep her upright and even though he was just being a gentleman, I saw red at the sight of his hands on her skin.

Maggie quickly pulled back and I wondered if it was because she felt my annoyance or she felt the angry buzz her skin makes when someone touched her that wasn't me. I frowned. And she didn't even want *me* to touch her right now.

She jerked her gaze to me. "That's not true."

Crap. I forgot to block her. "Yes, it is," I argued softly. "This is stupid, Maggie. You don't need to punish yourself."

"I'm…not."

"You're not?" I asked and she paused before shaking her head and refusing to look at me. I let our bags fall from my fingers to the floor and went to stand in front of her. "It wasn't your fault. None of this was."

Jonathon just stood there, his eyes moved back and forth like he was watching a volleyball game. I ignored him.

"Maggie."

"You can't say that Beck and Ralph aren't my fault," she said and finally looked up at me.

"Yes, I can. Because it's mine." If my beautiful little Maggie wanted to play martyr, two could play that game.

"No," she said, confused. "How could it be your fault?"

"Because I touched you and made you mine." I felt my jaw clench at the truth of those words. Maggie's life hadn't exactly been rosy since I'd dragged her into my world.

"Don't say that," she pleaded. "Don't start this again."

"Don't start what? Don't start saying that if it weren't for me that you and your family would be safe and normal like they used to be?"

"Caleb…" Her lips quivered again and I knew I'd won. I stopped everything and pulled her elbows so she'd come into my arms. Her skin was soft and sweet smelling and gulp inducing. I took her chin in my fingers and made her look up at me. I wrapped my other arm around the small of her back to keep her there.

"Maggie Camille," I breathed and felt her breath catch. "Stop this right now. It's no more your fault than it is mine. Stuff happens. It sucks, it sucks so bad and, baby…I'm dying for you. I wish I could stop this, but I can't." I let my thumb sweep across her bottom lip.

She sniffed once before wrapping her arms around my neck. I exhaled as her skin touched mine and gripped her to my chest tightly. I felt good for bringing her down from the ledge. It was my job to protect her, even when it was from herself.

I could feel her breaths on my neck and had to hold myself back as I always did. I opened my eyes to find Jonathon still standing there. I ticked my head toward the hall to tell him to get lost. He cleared his throat and did just that.

I leaned back to rest us against the wall, but it was the stairwell door instead. I heard my "Crap!" but it was too late. I held her tighter as we tumbled back to the floor and landed on my butt with her in my lap. She was giggling before I could even get what had happened. I chuckled, too, and smoothed her hair back. I toyed with a piece between my fingers. It was so stinking soft. "Whoops."

She laughed and put her hand on my cheek, shifting to straddle me on the floor. "Silly boy," she said softly.

I gripped her hips and tried to remember that she needed me because she was upset. But Maggie on my lap… My imprinted body was done with being the good guy in this department. It wanted her. All of her.

She sobered a bit then and licked her lips. "I'm sorry."

"You don't have to be sorry, baby. That's the point." I took her face in my hands. "It was a tragedy, not a vision that you could stop."

I saw a flash of worry and the vision of Bish and Jen play through her mind before she said, "I know."

"You're overwhelmed by everything. I understand. Just don't push me away when all I want to do is be here."

She leaned forward and pressed a kiss to my chin. She looked up at mc from under her lashes and I barely suppressed my groan. She leaned forward to kiss me where I wanted her. I let my hands travel to her hips, tugging her a tad closer, and then told them to stay.

Stay, hands, stay right there.

The kiss was over too quickly for me, but I knew that Maggie was still hurting. I rubbed her soft arms, letting her be calmed and eased back into reality, until she was ready to go.

I helped her stand and we turned the corner only to run into Jonathon again. "Dude?" I said in annoyance.

"Wait," Maggie said and I saw it all play out in her mind. She took Jonathon's arm and peeked around the corner, all business.

She was the Visionary and she was so freaking good at it.

Then I saw who Maggie was waiting for. Rodney's significant, the girl who Maggie had talked to and learned what she was, came around the corner with a book in her hands. She was fully engrossed in her reading and didn't look up. Maggie stopped and pushed Jonathon in front of her. The girl looked up just in time to see him, jumped back to avoid the collision and giggled in embarrassment. But Jonathon, the ever-clingy guy, grabbed onto her arms to keep her from falling.

The imprint started with bursts and shivers as I watched in Maggie's mind, and we held onto each other and remembered our own imprint. The day I damned the girl I wanted so badly and got the love of my life all in the same moment.

The day she became my girl.

I whispered how amazing she was into her ear. She had to have grown tired of my saying it, but I couldn't stop. Maggie was torn between a fulfillment of watching her subjects follow their destiny, and the sadness going on in her own life. I held her tighter and felt her gratitude.

"I'll always be here to hold you together," I told her with conviction.

She turned and pulled me down to her. And as I let her control me and my lips, my hands found their favorite spot. Her hips. And I told them to freaking stay.

Stay, hands, stay right there.

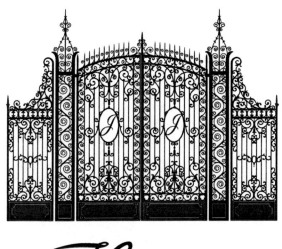

Three

Maggie

I SNUGGLED into Caleb's hoodie as we sat on the plane. We hadn't even taken off yet. Bish and Jen were in the seats in front of us, and Fiona and Dad were in the seats in front of them. Peter had purchased us all First Class tickets and I felt bad about that, but not bad enough to actually feel it. I was too busy feeling guilty over Ralph and Beck.

But good things were happening around us. Maria stayed with Peter and Rachel so Bish and Jen were, for lack of a better phrase, all over each other. It was gross and sweet all at the same time. She was turned in her seat toward him and kept sweeping his hair back as they talked. She was telling him about her job and trying to avoid any talks of houses and what they were going to do. For now, they'd stay with Peter, but soon… I didn't want to think about it either. Bish didn't have any money, it wasn't a secret, but it was Virtuoso tradition for the groom to buy his wife a house, to have a place to take her home to after the wedding.

I sighed and pushed it away. Then I *looked* away when Bish took her jaw in his hand and kissed her. Deeply.

I buckled up and turned into Caleb's side. I fully intended to sleep the whole way. I needed all the rest I could get to be ready to meet up with Beck's parents. Caleb lounged and lifted the armrest so I could lay against his chest. His fingers brushed my neck repeatedly as he tried to fill me with his calm.

I slept so good it was unreal.

When I opened my eyes, we were back in Tennessee. I rubbed my face and squinted at the woman who insisted on blaring the news so loudly. Caleb and I made our way past Bish and Jen to Dad. He and Fiona were just as new as Bish and Jen, but less obvious. My dad had always been sweet to my mom, but at home. I couldn't imagine him as the PDA type, so it didn't surprise me that they just held hands as they made their way out of the seats. I smiled at him and he smiled back. Man, life was different. I was headed home with not one, but two sets of newly imprinted significants, and we'd left another new set at the palace.

Things were turning around for the Virtuoso and turning upside down for me. I tried not to think about it too much. I didn't want Caleb to feel even more guilty.

When we made it back to Dad's house, I stumbled in my shock as I went inside. Dad had removed all of the things that my mother had used to make it a 'home'. Pictures were off the walls and replaced with ones of just us, without *her*.

The frilly lamps and silly knick-knacks were thrown out. All that was left was a normalcy that I was grateful for. Dad really had moved on, and just in time, it seemed. It would have probably been awkward for Fiona to come home to a house filled with the face of another woman.

I looked at him. "You were pretty busy while I was gone, huh?"

"You're not upset, are you? I saved you a few things, put them on your bed. And this…" He pointed to the large mirror they'd found at the antique place together. "I thought you might want that…for yours and Caleb's place."

"Thanks, Dad," I hummed. "No, I'm not upset. I think it was about time."

He hugged me sideways with one arm, but that wasn't enough. I hugged him around his middle like the little girl I used to be and squeezed. He gripped me in that knowing way and held me tightly. He whispered, "I'm sorry about Rebecca, baby."

I nodded. "I'm gonna go see her parents now."

"Want us to come?"

"Nah," I insisted. It was going to be hard enough to face them without an audience. "You can just come with me to the memorial tomorrow, all right?"

"That's fine. Whatever you want."

"This'll give you two time to settle in anyway." I glanced at Fiona as she stood off to the side, regal and quiet. "We'll sleep at Caleb's tonight." I didn't add anything further. I didn't want to get into intimate details about…that.

"And I'm just here to get some stuff," Bish spouted quickly. "I guess I'll stay with Jen at Peter's for a while."

"Don't faint when you see the place," I told him. "It's massive."

He didn't smile, but he did come and give me one of his big bear hugs that I had been missing. "Maggie," he sighed, at a loss for words. His mind was literally blank of anything comforting to say. I shook my head at him to tell him it was OK. He kissed my cheek and said, "We'll see you later, won't we? At Peter's?"

"Nah," I said and looked at Caleb. "I thought we'd stay at your apartment, if that's all right?"

He nodded and gave me a look. "Of course."

I looked back to Bish. "That way you can get settled in, too, without anybody else to distract you."

Once again, I left it at that.

"If that's what you want," Bish countered. "We'll come tomorrow, to the memorial."

"Sure." Caleb still had our bags in his hands. I realized we didn't even have a car here. Caleb's bike was at Uncle Max's. I swung my gaze to Dad. "Can we leave our stuff here and get it later?"

"Of course."

I nodded. "OK. I'm ready when you are," I told Caleb, the ever-stoic bodyguard. I jiggled the key ring he'd given me in the front pocket of his hoodie. It clanked against the star bracelet that he'd replaced from the 25 Hour Skillet crew and reminded me that no matter what happened from now on, I had people who loved me and cared about whether I was happy or not.

I let that thought hang there as Caleb led me out the door with his hand on my lower back. I heard Dad and Fiona talking to each other in their minds about me; poor me, sweet me, me who'd been through so much. What about poor Beck? Poor Ralph? They were the ones paying for my mistakes.

My Converses smacked on the pavement as we made the short trek to Beck's house. Caleb was quiet and I was thankful as he held my hand. I didn't want to talk about it, not really. I just wanted her to be alive and she wasn't, and it was my fault. Gosh... I thought about what Beck would say at hearing me talk like this. She'd tear me a new one for sure.

I laughed at the memory of her yelling at me when I cried about her being grounded when we were twelve. She had gotten caught and I hadn't. I wanted to turn myself in, confess all, but she scoffed and made out like I was being a complete idiot. "Now why would you do that? Then we'd both be in trouble instead of just one of us! That's makes no sense, Mags."

But I felt so guilty that I wound up telling on myself. They may as well have printed up 'Wanted' posters for me because my conscience plagued me everywhere I went. So naïve, so simple, so easy...such a different time in our lives.

Caleb's thumb rubbed gently across my fingers, bringing me out of my memory. I looked up to find his sympathetic face watching me. When we came up on Becks' house, I saw her car in the driveway. They must've taken Ralph's. The ache in my chest got almost unbearable as her parents' silhouettes could be seen through the window.

Caleb stopped me and turned me to him. "Wait."

"I'm gonna lose it, Caleb," I told him, my voice shaky. "I'm not going to be able to-"

His warm lips were on mine, halting anything else I might have said. I wasn't exactly kissing him, but he sure was kissing me. He wrapped me into his chest and kissed the breath right out of me. My hands were trapped between us. I curled my fingers so I could feel productive in the *hanging on for dear life* department. The harder he kissed me, the deeper I fell.

I knew what he was doing. And as grateful as I was to him for trying to fill me up with calm instead of sorrow, I was now being wracked with a need for Caleb that seemed suddenly desperate. I forced my hands out from between us and curled them around his neck. My tiptoes pushed me up to meet him of their own accord.

"Hell, Maggie," he murmured against my lips. His hands became paws as he gripped me closer to him.

The hoodie was suddenly very warm. It was strange. I'd never felt like this before. It was as if my body was done with being on the backburner to my responsibilities. It didn't give a darn what was going on around us, it just knew that Caleb was here, he was touching me and he was mine.

It was too much, but I couldn't stop myself. I was on autopilot and my imprint was driving. I felt completely out of control.

Caleb brought his hands up to my face and exhaled harshly against my cheek as he pulled back a little. "It's OK," he soothed and rubbed with his thumbs. "It's OK. It's been like this for me since the beginning and it's totally normal. Our bodies are just...tired of waiting to be together, that's all."

"You've felt like this the whole time?" I asked, my voice barely a whisper.

"Well...not exactly like this, but it's been pretty bad at times," he answered wryly.

"The boxer briefs incident?" I said and found myself smiling.

He laughed and chewed the corner of his lip. "Yep. Top of the list."

"So what does this mean?"

"Remember when I said most significants are married within a couple of weeks? Well it's been a few weeks already, babe. We can wait, but it's not going to get any easier."

He was trying not to grin. "Oh, you seem *so* broken up about it," I teased.

He laughed and gripped my hips tighter. "Not really broken up about it, no. The fact that you finally want me almost as much as I want you does feel kinda nice though."

I rolled my eyes good-naturedly and we both seemed to know that our little 'calming session' was over. I looked at Beck's car once more and whispered, "Thanks, babe."

He smiled at the 'babe'. "I love you and you can do this. I'll be right behind you, remember? I'll always be here to keep you together."

I wrapped my arms around his middle just like I had my father and let him squeeze me and kiss my hair. A part of me almost hated being so dependent on him, but he was right. He always kept me together and I needed to cling to that, not push it away.

After I felt like I had taken all the time I could, I turned to go inside, but found Mrs. T coming outside with the trash. As soon as she saw me, she started to cry. She opened her arms for me and, like the little girl that I felt like, I ran to her.

She cried and I cried, but eventually we parted and I said I'd be back the next day. When I was walking away, I couldn't help but touch Beck's Dodge Neon…and was smacked with a vision.

Caleb rushed forward. I held on and watched as Beck and Ralph made the mountain pass, laughing and singing to the radio. They got to the last exit before taking the highway when the car broke down. Ralph was furious. He was saying there was no way that they were out of gas because he'd just filled up in town. But they were bone dry and not a person or house in sight. The pass wasn't used very often unless you had a summer house up there or something.

They were alive!

So, they started walking. As the days dragged on, they ran out of water and food and eventually, lost their way. They were in a small alcove or cave on the mountainside in the valley. Ralph was worse off because he had refused to take the last bit of water, giving it to Beck instead. As I looked at the vision, and saw Beck's face, dirty, sad, defeated and beautiful as she brushed back Ralph's hair, I knew there was still a chance for me to save her.

I glanced up at Caleb, who nodded, having seen the vision. He was ready to go, too. Ready to take me to save my friends.

Just like that I joined hands with Caleb and we ran all the way to his uncle's house. We bypassed Dad's house because he would try to stop me and Bish would try to go with me. No one else was dying or being hurt for me. This was my mess and my fight.

Well, and Caleb's by association.

He laughed at my thought.

We had no clothes to change into and nothing with us, but as we jumped into Caleb's uncle's black SUV, I didn't care. I just wanted to get there. We were hours away and then still had to try to find them.

Caleb said we would stop for some supplies on the way as he flew in reverse down the driveway and then zoomed down the street.

We did just that.

About an hour into our drive, we stopped at a little gas station for some water bottles and food. More than enough food, because Beck and Ralph would need to eat once we found them. And we would find them.

We drove for hours. Caleb blared the radio and sang along, toying with my fingers in my lap. He did anything but talk about Beck and I was grateful. I kicked my shoes off and pulled them into the seat under me. I pulled the hood up on his hoodie and snuggled in for the long ride.

However, my vision had been vague. So when we reached the last gas station before heading into the backside of the mountain, we stopped to fill up and get another gas can to fill up as well, just in case. We knew it was the last gas station because the sign that stated so was bigger than the freaking store was.

He gave me his debit card and wrote the code on my hand. I smiled and tried not to laugh. Now that's love. Your bank card and pin code.

I slipped back on my shoes and went to the bathroom while he pumped. I was getting us both a drink when I heard him.

Grab a couple of honey buns, too, babe. I've got a hankering.

I laughed at him in my mind. *Then I better grab about ten then, 'cause I ain't sharing.*

Aho! Well, you better get ten more 'cause I ain't sharing either.

Fine! I will!

I heard his laugh. *Will you grab me a couple sticks of beef jerky, too, pretty please?*

Of course, my love.

I did that and grabbed a few honey buns, along with some crackers and Gatorades, too. My arms were loaded down when I flung it all onto the counter. The attendant's raised brow was not in jest and I cleared my throat in apology. He swiped everything with annoyance and stuffed it into a bag. I swiped the card and punched in the code.

When he handed me the receipt I grabbed our spoils and met Caleb outside, where he had pulled the car right up to the door. I hopped in.

"I texted your dad and mine to let them know what was going on," he admitted. "Didn't want them to worry."

"Thank you," I said in relief. "I hadn't even thought to do that." I pulled his beef jerky out and handed it to him along with his huge can of Arizona sweet tea. I laughed and pointed to the can. "See? It's fate that you go to Arizona."

He chuckled a little, but it was reserved. I sent him a questioning look. "It's nothing. I mean…it's something, but you're not allowed to know it yet. We can't talk about the future right now, remember? You're not supposed to know until the wedding."

I smiled good-naturedly and nibbled my honey bun as he plowed through two long sticks of jerky.

About an hour later, he pulled off the side of the road. I saw in his mind that he wanted to sleep. "We're sleeping here?"

"No hotels, babe."

"I know…but…"

He gave me a sympathetic smile. "I know, but we can't look for them in the dark. We'll sleep here. It's not in the valley yet, so we may have a little traffic, but no one should mess with us. First thing in the morning, we'll get up and go find her."

"Nobody will mess with us, huh? Ever seen *The Hills Have Eyes? The Chainsaw Massacre? Psycho!*"

He laughed. "Yes, but I'll murder anyone who comes near you, do you hear me?" I nodded with a smirk. "You trust me, don't you?"

"Of course."

He took the keys and got out, hopping into the back seat. He locked the doors and beckoned me to him by waggling his fingers. I climbed over the center console and almost made it before my Converse slipped on the leather. I fell, a giggling heap, into his lap.

He chuckled, all husky and amused, as he helped me up only to place me on his lap, one of my legs on either side of him. He smiled and reached over to remove my shoes one at a time. Slowly. He let them fall with a thud to the SUV floorboard and never took his eyes off me as he pulled my socks off, too.

I stopped giggling at the intimate gesture.

That part of me that I had discovered earlier, the part that was all of a sudden so attuned to Caleb's body and every movement, was wide awake now. He pushed my hoodie down from my head. I understood why the store clerk had been so weird now. He probably thought I was going to rob him or something. Caleb smoothed my hair back and let his fingers barely graze my neck. I gulped.

"You all right to sleep here?" he asked, his voice low. "We can lie down in the back if you want, but…"

"No," I said. I felt my eyes go wide at the rasping of my voice. He noticed, too, and sucked his lip into his mouth. I watched. "I want to stay right here."

"OK. Whatever you want."

I laid my head down in the dip of his shoulder and neck. I inhaled and exhaled harshly. He smelled amazing. The scent caused me physical problems. My body was rethinking some things. It wanted Caleb in all ways and it was making it hard for me to keep my head on straight.

Rationally, we were going to get married anyway, right? That was a fact, but I wanted to keep to the Ace's tradition. And I wanted to keep to *my* tradition. It wasn't religion or old fashioned-ness or parents sheltering me or any other reason. It was just *my* decision. But as I felt Caleb's fingers graze the top of my hand, I shivered from that small touch alone because I was wound so tight and attuned to him.

My heart hitched, my lungs beckoned me to take another whiff of him, my fingers curled into his shirt without even asking me first.

He leaned his head against mine. "Welcome to my world, Maggie."

I sighed. "I can't believe it's been like this for you the whole time."

"Believe it." He chuckled, the movement shaking his chest and me on it. "It's Heaven and Hell."

He turned the radio on and *Where I Belong* by Switchfoot began to play.

I sat up a bit and looked into his face. "We're going to find them, right?"

He cupped my face and promised, "We won't stop until we find them."

I licked my lips. "Thank you for being so…you."

He smiled. Not a smirk, a smile that was real and full of the love that was my constant. He leaned forward to kiss me and pulled back after one small taste. He licked his bottom lip. "I know," I groaned. "I taste like honey buns."

"Baby," he told me, his eyes lidded and dark, "you always taste like honey buns."

Then he went in for the kill.

We both groaned at the same time, our mouths opened to each

other's at the same time, and I gasped while he sucked in a quick breath. I put my arms around his neck while he pulled me closer with his hands on my hips.

They slowly moved away from my hips and he gripped my bottom to lift me to him even more. I gasped in a good way and loved that he hadn't asked for permission. This was a first. A *good* first. I was Caleb's and he was mine. I didn't plan on asking for permission either, so when I found that his breath caught every time I lifted using my knees, I kept doing that.

The windows began to shake and rattle a little as I felt my control slipping, but we ignored it.

Soon, he was pulling the too hot hoodie from my body and tossing it in the seat next to us. I was only wearing a white tank underneath and the suddenly cool air made me shiver with goose bumps. He took my hand and kissed the pads of my fingers, the inside of my wrist, and then the inside of my elbow.

I closed my eyes, my lips parted on their own.

He kept going and eventually made it to my bare shoulder. He pulled the thick strap down and kissed me there, too. When he bit into the flesh there softly, I almost accused him right there of lying to me about me being his first girlfriend, because he was way too good at this. But his imprinted body knew me inside and out. It knew exactly what to do to drive me insane for him.

So I felt it out to see if I could do the same to him.

As if on instinct, I leaned forward to nibble under his chin. It was coarse and scratchy, but in a very good way. He leaned his head back on the seat and let out a smothered moan as his hands gripped me tighter.

"Hell, Maggie," he repeated his earlier sentiment.

Why was it so hot when he said it like that?

I moved my attention to the spot under his ear and he made a completely new noise I'd never heard before. It fueled me, spurred me on. So I took his earlobe into my mouth and bit down gently.

The noise had more than doubled by then. I felt powerful. For once in my life, I felt like I was out of control in the most controlled way, and I smiled against his skin.

Four

Caleb

She was doing this thing with her tongue. I couldn't handle another second of it. I was about to lose it in every way. I moved my face to connect with hers once more and then her tongue was mine. But that was worse. Oh, man, so much worse.

This was beyond making out, or kissing, or…whatever else you wanted to label it. And my body was singing for it. But she was upset about her friend, and her body had finally just gotten calmed down enough after all that drama to start feeling her need for me in full force. It wasn't right to let her do this.

It pained me, but I took one last long pull from her mouth and then released her. I still gripped her in my hands, but her mouth was free. I started immediately so she'd understand that this wasn't rejection. "Baby, there's a line. A very fine line, and we are straddling that line right now. If we cross it, I won't be able to go back. You feel so good. Your body, your lips, your skin…all of it. I'm drowning in you. So, please, we've got to just hold on a minute."

She hesitated and I barely breathed waiting for her words. "What if I don't want to stop?" she asked breathlessly.

My heart skidded to the pace of a dead man. "Maggie…"

"I know." She squeezed her eyes tight. The war waging in her was waging in me, too. I could practically taste it in the air. "I know I've always thought that I'd wait. And you said your kind waits until marriage, too. I just… I feel… We're going to get married anyway, right? This isn't puppy love. I *know* I'm going to marry you, so I don't think it matters when we both…want to."

I stared. It was all my muddled brain would do. Then finally, "It's just too much for you right now. With your body…reacting to the imprint so strongly and your friend and all the stuff that happened in London. I just think we should wait. My number one issue with the scenario though, is the fact that we're out in the mountains, looking for your lost friend, and we're in the backseat of my uncle's SUV. I refuse to be a cliché teenager." I tried to smile, but she seemed deflated. "Baby, I don't want that for our first memory together, do you?"

"No, I don't," she sighed. "So the tyrant is protecting me…from myself?" she asked softly.

"It looks that way," I chuckled. I pressed my nose to hers and exhaled. But if she was ready for more, so was I. "But there's plenty we *can* do, lots of things that straddle the line." Her eager, glazed eyes had me pulling her tighter once more.

"Show me," she demanded eagerly and kissed me again, her lips soft, but demanding.

So I did. My fingers dug into the jeaned flesh of her backside and thighs, and I showed her exactly what I meant. I inched the innocent strap on her tank top a little lower on her arm, and as I melded our minds, I realized how amazing our ease with each other was. Maggie trusted me with every inch and piece of her and that was a very satisfying thing.

A long while later, she was snuggled into my chest, a satisfied little purring kitten. I let my fingers tangle in her hair and rub her scalp. I thought she'd go right to sleep...afterwards...but she was still wide awake. I started to get worried and went digging in her mind to make sure she wasn't upset, that she didn't think I'd gone too far. But when I found her replaying it all in her mind as a hazy, dreamy movie, I knew it wasn't that.

I had effectively taken her mind off Beck for a while, and that's what I had wanted. Mission accomplished. I grinned smugly and satisfactorily.

The tap on our window made us both jump. Maggie covered her arms and chest though she was still wearing all of her clothes, as she had been the whole time.

I sighed and rolled down the windows when I saw the blue flashing lights. "Officer?"

"Kid, you've got to know that parking and making out isn't allowed, especially this time of night."

"We're trying to sleep, not make out. We're on a road trip."

"Is that so?" he said slowly and tapped his flashlight to the window. "The fogged up windows beg to differ."

Maggie huffed, just barely. I looked at him and felt the chagrin on my face. "OK, there may have been some making out, but now, we're sleeping. We're heading into the valley tomorrow."

"What for?"

"Our friends came up here and are lost."

His brow drew together. "You mean the two they just called the search off for?"

"Yes, sir."

He grimaced. "I know it's sad to see something like that happen to your friends, but accidents happen sometimes. I won't stop you, but I think it's best if you go home and be with your families. You won't find those kids out here. We scoured every surface."

Maggie spoke up. "And I thank you for looking, but I'll always wonder if we don't at least look once."

He nodded. "I'll be up and down this highway all night." He pointed. "Sleep. No more hanky panky."

"Yes, sir," I said and chuckled silently at Maggie's pink cheeks.

He left and I couldn't stop the laugh that escaped. She gave me a pouty look and pushed my chest playfully. "Not funny."

"Oh, it's hilarious."

"Oh, my gosh," she whispered in a groan. "So embarrassing."

"Are you OK?" I asked, but smiled. "With everything."

"You mean…everything?" she said coyly and smiled, too.

"Exactly."

"I'm perfect," she whispered. "Better than fine. I know I was kind of…crazy before. I'm sorry. I felt a little out of control, and you're right, I just feel so strange about everything and this *thing* in my body…just wants you." She shook her head. "Thank you for not taking advantage, for knowing me inside out, and understanding that I'm such a girl sometimes."

I chuckled. "I love that you're a girl." She smiled and waited, knowing I had more to say. "I know the pull of our bodies is crazy, but my first priority is to protect you. I'll never hurt you in any way."

"I know." She smiled, thinking about the events of the night. "I like to straddle the line with you, though."

I growled my words, "Oh, we're going to do more line straddling soon. It's a fact."

She giggled and man, it was sexy. "Caleb Maxwell." She shook her head.

"Maggie Camille," I whispered and let her burrow in once more. This time, we slept.

I woke to a nuzzling at my neck. I moved my hands to find Maggie under them and still in my lap. She lifted her face and smiled before lifting her arms over her head and stretching.

Hell…

I gripped her sides through her thin shirt and watched her as she looked around. And I saw the change come over her. She saw where we were and remembered what we were doing there. The afterglow was over, but that was OK. It was time to get to work.

I lifted her off my lap and set her to the side to help her put her socks and shoes back on. She watched me, biting her thumbnail, and smiled softly until I was done. "Ready?" I asked her, knowing the answer.

"Ready."

We climbed up front and I sped down into the valley. She handed me another jerky stick and tore into a honey bun. Her eyes peeled the hills apart.

The hours passed as we drove. The terrain was beginning to get ridiculous, even on the road. The cabins that Ralph had been heading up to were all the way through the valley and up the mountainside. The SUV handled it just fine, but I had to pay attention extra hard on the thin roads, which didn't let me look around much. Even I was beginning to get discouraged.

When we came up on Ralph's car, Maggie was just done.

I screeched the car to a halt and Maggie was out of the car before the car was barely stopped. I growled, "Maggie."

I knew she was worried, but the girl was crazy if she thought I was going to let her hurt herself.

She ran and I jumped out to follow her. She threw open the passenger door and her face crumpled when she found no one there. I reached her and put my arms around her from behind to keep her from running any further. "We knew they had abandoned the car. We need to go further in."

"I just thought maybe…they had tried to come back."

"We won't stop looking," I promised. "Come on."

She obliged easily and let me put her back in the passenger seat of the SUV. The tyrant in me was front and center. I took deep breaths as I jogged back to my side and climbed in. I drove around Ralph's car and bounded through the open gate that led to the new road. Maggie was quiet and that was all right. I turned on the radio again and gripped her hand as we kept looking.

She squeezed my fingers in silent thanks. She leaned forward on her elbows and let her eyes sweep the terrain and trees. I heard my phone beep and pulled it out of my front pocket. It was letting me know cell range was now gone.

Great.

We needed to be careful or we'd end up stuck out here ourselves. At least I had told our fathers where we were. And I hadn't even checked their return text messages from that. I was sure they weren't pleasant, especially Jim's, but I was the Champion of my clan now. It wasn't like I needed anyone's permission to take the Visionary on a quest that she'd gotten a vision for.

I winced, thinking about Jim. The man already struggled to like me. I was sure this hadn't helped the situation any. But Maggie was what mattered most. Not being down with the in-laws wasn't unheard of by any means.

I glanced over at her. She was so focused she wasn't even picking up anything I was thinking. She had no idea what I had planned for the house that was to be her wedding present. I was going against everything the Virtuoso had done before me. I was sure my family would be upset and appalled, but the one thing Maggie had taught me was that I had to do what was right for me, right for us.

I knew exactly what I was going to do, it was just the manner of executing the plan without heads rolling that was tricky.

By the evening, I had to refill the tank. It was all we had left and I hated to say it, but I had to tell her that if we hadn't found them by the morning, we had to head home. She nodded in understanding, but was frustrated. She'd gotten the vision for Beck, so why couldn't we find her?

We got out and walked for a while. She called for Beck and I called for Ralph. We searched along the bush and hedge line for any kind of place that people could hide in…or in this case, fall asleep in from exhaustion and hunger.

When nightfall came, I took Maggie back to the car as she cried softly. She felt like a failure and I had no idea what to tell her. Her ability was to get visions as the Visionary, so why would she get a vision for Beck only to never find her?

This time we lay in the back as I folded the seats down. I laid my hoodie down and climbed onto it, beckoning her to me. She nuzzled her face into my neck for comfort, but also as a way to hide. I sighed, but said nothing as I stroked her hair. I was starving. The beef jerky was gone and we wanted to save the drinks and crackers for when we found Beck and Ralph, but it was looking more like *if* we found them.

I saw it when she saw it. The vision smacked into her with enough force that she flew onto her back. She sat up and saw the cave behind her eyes in her mind. She started to go and I knew she was being led by some other force, just like she had been before. I didn't say anything. I just followed close behind as she ran.

I began to get worried when it had been ten minutes and she was still hustling along the dirt. She began to stumble over the rocks and things. "Maggie," I complained, but she kept going.

"I can't stop," she said softly and then gasped as her body swung her to make a sharp right. Then we were looking right at a bright red shoe peeking out of a small cave. We both took off toward it.

"Beck," Maggie sighed as she knelt down to the prone forms of her friends. "Ralph," she barked and shook his arm. "Beck!" Maggie's hand touched Beck's cheek and she patted it gently.

When Beck's eyes flew open, I sighed and thanked the big guy. Maggie didn't squeal or laugh or say anything at all. She just lifted Beck's head to rest on her knees. And then she told her over and over again that everything would be OK, that they were fine now, that we were taking them home.

I told Maggie in our minds that I was getting the car and ran all the way. The bumps and bangs on the SUV had me cringing as I bounded over the rocks, hills, and bushes to get back to them, but I'd apologize to Uncle Ken later.

A million bad things were going through my head as I slammed the car to a stop and got out to go to Maggie. Was Ralph even alive? And Maggie's vision…she only showed them alive, it never said they would make it. If Maggie's friends didn't make it, I could only imagine the amount of guilt Maggie would bury herself with.

I pushed that to the side and knelt down next to Maggie. She was exactly as I left her and when I touched her arm to get her attention, she jolted a little. "Baby, let me have her," I told her. She gulped. "Let me take her."

She nodded and I lifted Beck into my arms and ran as quickly as I could to the backseat with her. I laid her down gently, settling her legs in the seat with her, before running to the back hatch and lifting it open. I went back to Maggie and saw her wet face as she stroked Ralph's hair.

Hell.

"He's alive," she said to stop my thoughts. "Barely."

She backed away and I reached down to heft him over my shoulder. Dude was a freaking tank. I grunted all the way before slamming him as gently as I could into the back. Maggie climbed in the back, too. I wasn't surprised. She immediately began opening a water bottle and trying to pour some into his mouth.

See if you can get her to drink, Caleb. Please.

I opened the other door on my side and looked down at Beck's face. I reached for one of the bottles and saw her eyes open. She tried to sit up so I helped her. She drank and drank and drank. She wiped her mouth with the back of her shaky hand when it was drained and asked where Ralph was. I pointed to Maggie in the back.

That must've been what she was waiting for, because when she saw Ralph taking small sips from Maggie's bottle, she lost it. She gripped my arm so she wouldn't fall over and was wracked with sobs. I slid onto the edge of the seat and put my arm around her. I was glad that Maggie was too focused to be reading their minds right then. I did not want to live the nightmare that they had lived. I was sure it was nothing but absolute hell.

She cried, but there were no tears on my shirt. She had nothing in her system to produce them. I closed my eyes and was thankful we found them, and apparently, just in time. They were safe now, and Maggie was now safe from her own guilt...I hoped.

Beck looked back once more over my shoulder and watched for a second before leaning forward and whispering to me. "Did I imagine all that glowing light when you found us?"

Crap. "It was a flashlight," I tried.

"No," she insisted and shook her head. She gave me the *'no bullcrap'* look. "No, it wasn't."

Double crap. How was I going to explain the energy ribbons from

Maggie's gift to a human? So I took the coward's path and changed the subject. "You lie down back here." I shifted to ease her back down gently. She sighed, letting me know she knew something was up and knew I was playing the deflection card. "So what happened?"

Her lip started to quiver. I leaned down and put a hand on her head to hopefully, offer her some comfort. I felt a little sting go through my arm. I realized it was my body warning me that this girl didn't belong to me and I wasn't supposed to be touching her. She wasn't Maggie. I pushed it away and tried to keep up my comfort of Maggie's best friend. She started slow. "We ran out of gas. Ralph had just filled up about an hour before that so I knew something was wrong. The gauge said we were empty, but that wasn't possible. Our cells didn't work. We waited and waited and then decided to try to find someone or something when night came and… and we knew no one was coming for us. But then we got lost and couldn't find the car again."

"It's OK," I soothed, but under my breath, I was cursing Marcus. I *knew* he had something to do with this. Knew it. "Shh. Sleep, all right?"

She nodded and let a breath go that said she was exhausted.

"Babe," I called quietly back to Maggie before rounding the back and sitting on the edge of the trunk. "How's he doing?"

"He drank the whole bottle down." She smiled in relief. "I think he'll be all right."

"OK, well…" I hated this next part. "We can't take them to a hospital… or home, you know that right?"

She sighed and nodded. "I know. The Watsons can't know that they're alive."

"We'll find a hotel in town and then we'll go back to my place tomorrow. Figure out what to do from there."

"Are you going to be OK with that? All of us invading your space?" She bit her lip. "I mean, I've never even been there."

"Are you kidding? Of course I'm fine with it. I would like to have you there all alone, but…" Even I heard my voice go all husky. She scooted out from under Ralph's head, who had passed back out, and met me at the back. I helped her down and wrapped my arms around her. "You in my space is what I've wanted from the very beginning."

"Thank you," she whispered. I felt her body jolt as she tried to hold in a sob. She was breaking my heart all over again. "For being so sweet to my friend."

"Of course, baby. Of course." I put my hand behind her head and pulled her to me. She tried to stop me.

"No, Caleb, I'll start crying again. Let's just go-"

"Resistance is futile." She fought her smile and rolled her eyes at me. I smiled and beckoned her back to me with my fingers. "Come here."

She sighed dramatically, but her fingers told the truth when she gripped my back and laid her cheek on my chest. I knew we had things to do, but she needed this right now. She needed my touch to refill her and calm her so she could be there for her friend with a clear head. I combed my fingers through her hair before pulling the hood on my hoodie she was still wearing up over her head. "It's cold. Ok, let's go. You all right?"

"I'll be fine when these two are safe again." She closed her eyes tight. "She almost died. I thought she *was* dead."

"We'll find Marcus, don't you worry about that," I promised and felt the rumble go through my chest. "And when we do, I'll end this like I should have done a long time ago."

She looked up at me. I expected her to be appalled, but she nodded. "And I'll be right there beside you."

I didn't argue or agree. I just held her chin between my thumb and fingers and kissed her once. Then I ticked my head toward the car and climbed into the driver's seat to find us a hotel for the night.

I couldn't tell anyone that we'd found them or that they were alive. Not yet. That sucked worse than anything right then, remembering Beck's mom's face. She deserved to know the truth, but for now, it was our little secret to bear.

As I backed out to turn around, I saw Maggie reach back to grip Beck's hand and then took her hoodie off and laid it over Beck's torso before gripping her fingers again. I cranked the heat higher and tried not to think about Maggie being cold in her camisole.

When Maggie finally leaned over to put her head on my shoulder and fell asleep, I knew that it was done. The night had ended as well as it could have and my Maggie was spent. Her gift had saved her friends.

I just hoped that we could write off all the weird stuff from Maggie's gift with Beck as just a hallucination. If not, well, we were going to have a problem.

Five

Maggie

BECK WAS trying as hard as she could. She leaned hard on me as we made it up the stairs to our hotel room. Caleb was lugging Ralph behind us in a similar manner. They were better after munching on crackers and downing some Gatorade, just tired.

There could be no hospital visit. We didn't know how closely the Watsons were keeping an eye on things. But it was without a doubt them that did this. Caleb and I both knew it in our guts.

And we weren't taking any chances.

So we lugged them to the hotel and watched them carefully to make sure they were all right. They were talking and walking...sort of. We assumed they would make it with a lot of rest. We put them straight to bed. It didn't matter that they were dirty.

They were asleep within a minute flat. But the sweetest thing ever?

Ralph searched for her with his hands until he found her in the sheets and when he did, he heaved with all his strength to pull her into his chest. I felt all the relief and everything just hit me like a sledgehammer as I watched my two best friends cling to each other in sleep. I felt my eyes well.

Then Caleb's arms were around me from behind. He moved my short hair out of the way and kissed the back of my neck. "It's over, baby," he whispered, his lips moving on my skin with each word. "You found them. You did good."

I nodded and turned into him. He pulled me right to the bed, our clothes on and all, and laid me in the covers. I kicked my shoes off as he kicked off his. He climbed in with me and wrapped me up just like Ralph was doing to Beck.

She was safe, and he was safe.

I sighed into Caleb's chest and went right to sleep.

I was awakened with the sound of the shower. I peeked up to find myself alone in the bed. Beck and Ralph were still passed out in the next bed. More like sprawled like the dead. I smiled.

They were safe.

I woke with the blanket up to my chin and an unnatural warmth in the room. We never turned on the air when we came in last night. I threw the blanket off and went to turn on the air, to stir the stale room and make it easier to breathe. The steam pouring from under the door wasn't helping things.

I checked both Rebecca and Ralph's breathing – ridiculous, I know – and then stopped at the bathroom door. I thought about knocking. I thought about just bursting in. With my hand poised on the old brass knob, I remembered *straddling the line* with him. I felt my cheeks pink with pleasure and a blush, too. I couldn't lie about that. It was all so new, but so welcomed, and my body was calm and inviting it.

So I compromised. I knocked gently, but opened the door without waiting for an answer. I heard him say, "Hey."

"Hey. Couldn't sleep?" I went to the mirror and wiped it with a hand towel.

"Nah. Dad texted me and woke me up. He's…kinda pissed."

The frosted glass was obscuring my view just enough to keep me from making him out behind the door. I could tell he was washing his hair though. "What for?"

"Well, apparently, running off with the Visionary into the mountains alone isn't what is proper of the Champion of our clan." His voice was mocking. He was pissed at his dad, too. I hated that. I hopped up on the counter.

"I'm sorry. You did it for me."

"I'm not complaining. He just can't understand sometimes, especially over the phone, that I'm not a fifteen year old boy anymore that needs to be fed the rules of our kind at every turn. We weren't sneaking off on a getaway, we were rescuing your friends."

"I'm sorry," I muttered again.

He poked his head out of the shower curtain. "Don't be. You're the freaking Visionary. You can do whatever the hell you want to." He grinned. "By the way," he started and closed the curtain to finish, "there are only two toothbrushes. You wanna share one and they can share the other?"

Share a toothbrush with him? I'd never even thought about that before. Did married people share toothbrushes normally? His mocking voice belted over the waterfall, "Don't over think this, baby." He poked his head out once more. "My tongue has been in your mouth. Your tongue has been in *my* mouth. We've already shared fluids. It's not a big deal."

"I know," I said and scoffed like I hadn't been worried at all. "I know that." He chuckled and shut the door once more. I unwrapped one of the cheapest toothbrushes I'd ever laid eyes on. I brushed my teeth and then wiped off the sleep and mascara gunk from under my eyes. "So what's the plan for today?"

"We'll leave as soon as they're ready and head back to my place. *They* need to see us there. They would expect us to go to my apartment. We'll just sneak them in and then figure out what to do from there. I don't know how far their plan goes. If they are watching us or just toying with us, you know?"

I grumbled, "When are they going to learn that they shouldn't mess with a Jacobson?"

He chuckled again and then the water shut off. "Hand me a towel, babe?"

I grabbed one and tossed it over. He came out seconds later, dripping and grinning as he watched me. He was waiting for me to freak out like I'd done in the palace. But something had changed in me. My body was taking over in a new way. I wasn't on defense anymore. I was on *offense*. And he had better watch it or he was going to get tackled.

I walked to him across the damp floor and rubbed the hollow star on his shoulder with my thumb. "What's this one for?"

He glanced at it and back down at me. "Uh…rebellion?" He grinned. "I wanted to get more tattoos, matching the whole moon and filigree theme for our families. Dad wasn't happy about that. Even though my own body put a tattoo on me." He rubbed his wrist. "Oh, well. He got over it. Mom was on my side with that one. He doesn't fight with Mom for very long."

"I bet," I said and laughed, remembering the way Peter smacked her behind at the beach house. "I'm sure your mom can be pretty persuasive."

He ticked his head to the shower. "You going to get in?"

I nodded. "I left the toothbrush on the sink."

Once again, if he thought I was going to cower and tell him to scram, he was wrong. I pulled my shirt off as I walked to the shower and took the rest off after I closed the door, tossing it over the top. I saw him in my peripheral and he stood there for a long time. He was thinking about the change in me. He didn't really understand it; why the imprint in my body was all of sudden so intent on…whatever it was trying to do, but he was intrigued. He was thinking about our wedding night, about how he thought I was going to be scared and incredibly nervous. He had been surprised in the best way in the car last night.

He wanted us to go forward. Always moving forward.

Our bodies were tuned to it, latched onto the idea of being completely comfortable and satisfied in the other. I had been so wrapped up with the Visionary stuff that I had fought that off somehow, and when all that seemed to fade away to a manageable amount, my body said, 'Uhuh, we're back in business.'

I smiled and poked my head out the shower door just like he had done. "Don't over think this, baby," I repeated back to him and raised my eyebrows at him before shutting the door. He laughed and I heard the faucet water turn on. Soon I was done and putting back on those grungy clothes.

As soon as I opened the bathroom door, Caleb looked my way from the window. "All scrubbadubbed?"

I nodded. He walked to me slowly and put his arm around my back. His face was inches from mine and the way he was looking into my eyes made my breaths increase. He started softly, not quite a whisper. "I'm glad that you're not nervous. I'm glad that you're ready." I didn't blush. Yay, a point for me! I smiled to encourage him. It must've, because he cupped my face. "The last thing I wanted was for you to be scared. I expected it," he admitted, "but I didn't want that. So to know that you're just as ready as I am…" His chest rumbled and his grip tightened a bit. "That makes me very happy."

"I could never be scared with you," I realized. That was it, wasn't it? That was what had changed? I finally came to the realization that Caleb would never, ever hurt me under any circumstances and had risked himself over and over for me to prove it. In London, the hell we endured was just another stepping stone.

He nodded to everything he was hearing in my mind. "I'm so glad it finally sunk in." His grin was all masculine and smugness. It was sexy and cute and endearing all at once. "These hands," he squeezed them both on my face to make his point, "will never touch you without being gentle. Unless that's not what you want, of course." His eyebrow lifted waiting for me to balk, but I just waited. "These arms will never hold you back, but I'll hold you as tight as you'll let me. I can't wait for you to be all mine. You belong to me in every way, Maggie. Mine." I nodded in his hands. He leaned closer and whispered, "Say it."

I didn't wait a beat. "I belong to you." And he belonged to me.

He grinned. "You're daggum right you do." He pulled me closer and up to meet him. When his tongue swept into mine, I could taste the toothpaste. I giggled into his mouth at the thought. He chuckled, too, and I swung my arms around his back. His hands pulled me closer and I was just settling in when we heard one of the sleepers groan.

I licked my lips as he pulled away. I glanced at the clock. It was after eleven in the morning. I turned around to find Beck looking at me. She was pale. Her eyes were filled with tears. She croaked, "It was real? It wasn't a dream that you came and saved us?"

I fought my own tears at that. "No, it was real." I got on my knees and laid my head next to hers on the pillow. "How do you feel?"

"Like I got intimately acquainted with a meat grinder."

I smiled. "I can imagine." The clog in my throat was very much present. "I'm really sorry."

"What are you sorry for?" She sniffed and then glared with a second wind. "And how did you find me anyway? And what the Hades were you doing in London with college boy and why the freak didn't you tell me?"

I laughed. "There she is." She tried to smile at me. "I'm sorry about all that, too."

"We'll get answers later. Right now, I have to pee like nobody's business." She groaned again and tried to sit up. I reached to help her stand and saw Caleb in my peripheral. He was standing at the foot of the bed with his arms crossed, watching us. He smiled when my eyes met his. She snapped her fingers in front of my face. "Hello? Help a sister out?" I slung her arm over my shoulder. "Geez, I know bathroom duty sucks, but come on."

"Shut up," I laughed.

I set her on the toilet and turned on the faucet, per her request. Then I waited as she finished, again per her request. I asked if she wanted to shower and she said it was pointless without clean clothes. Her clothes were pretty destroyed so, I agreed. I helped her back to the bed where Ralph was awake. He sighed at seeing her. It made my heart flutter. "Becks."

"Hey, sweetie," she crooned and put her hand on his cheek. "You're OK," she observed.

"*You're* OK." He sighed. "God...I have never been so worried in my life. The last thing I remember was you...and you wouldn't wake up. Then I woke up and you were stroking my hair and then..." He shook his head. He pulled her close and kissed her lips. "I love you."

She smiled, but her cheeks weren't dry anymore. "It took almost dying for you to tell me you love me?"

"I'm sorry," he said sincerely.

"I love you, too."

"That's all I could think about out there. That I was going to die and you'd never know that I've been in love with you this *whole* time. I've loved you since fifth grade, Becks."

I felt arms go around me from behind. Caleb's rumbling voice was at my ear as he spoke to them. "We'll be back. We'll get some breakfast and let you talk for a minute."

They didn't even look up. Caleb pulled me from the room and took me to the café down in the lobby. I started to grab a drink carrier and fill up some coffee cups, but Caleb shook his head and only grabbed two cups. He sat me down and then brought me a huge pile of pancakes and sausage, and one for himself.

"You don't think they're hungry up there?" I asked curiously.

"Oh, they're hungry all right," he said sarcastically.

I got his meaning and kicked his boot under the table. "Eww."

He laughed. "I can't help it if I see what you can't because you're so innocent and pure of heart." I couldn't help but grin at that. "Maybe they'll be hungry for pancakes in a little while."

"You and your innuendos, mister." I shook my head in mock distress. "You're going to ruin me."

"I plan to," he suggested low before taking a big bite.

I smiled as I bit into my sausage and then gasped as something ice cold went sprawling down my arm. I stood on instinct and the older lady was obviously embarrassed. She reached for my napkin and began to blot the orange juice off my arm. "Oh, it's fine. Don't worry."

"I am so sorry."

"Really, it's OK."

"I am so clumsy!" she exclaimed. "Harold!" she yelled at someone. "Help me."

The man – Harold, I presumed – came and looked over the situation. I was dry at this point. "Really, I'm fine. It was just a little juice. It's OK."

"I told you I'd get it for you, Arlene," he chastised. "You don't need to be up and around, honey."

I smiled at his endearment for her. She patted his arm and then looked at us. "Ah, you must be newlyweds."

"No, ma'am," Caleb answered and gripped my hand. "Not yet, but soon."

"Well, you better get on the move, boy," she joked. Caleb, always the gentleman, chuckled good-naturedly and smiled.

"Yes, ma'am. I'm working on that."

"My Harold and I," she said affectionately and looked up at him, "we've been together for forty two years."

"Wow," I said in awe. "That's really awesome."

"The key is compromise and love, no matter what. There's always a little wiggle room to work with when you're both in it 'til the end."

I nodded. Her husband's thoughts made their way to me as he watched her. He was worried about her. She had some cancer that even he in his own mind wouldn't name. I tried not to frown or make a face, but my heart was breaking for them.

I joined the conversation she and Caleb had started while I'd been snooping, unintentionally. He was asking why she thought we were newlyweds. She smiled and patted his cheek. "Because you look at her the way my Harold still looks at me." Then she looked at me. "I'm sorry I spilled my juice on you. Y'all have a nice trip."

Harold said his goodbyes, too, and helped her away. "It's OK. Thank you," I found myself saying. Caleb was watching me. He knew what I'd heard from the man's mind. I waved him off. "I better get used to it, right?"

"That doesn't make it any easier for you," he argued. He watched them go. "They were nice. And normal. And human." His gaze swung to mine. "Normal, human people who lived together and loved each other for forty two years. If they can do it, we have absolutely no worries."

"I was never worried." I hugged his middle. "Never."

"I can't believe how calm you're being about the wedding," he mused. "You know, the wedding will probably be this coming up this weekend." He waited. "My parents and Gran are eager for it." Pause. "They'll make it as soon as possible." Another pause. "Our whole family, in my back yard, watching us..."

I laughed. "Ok, now you're just *trying* to scare me."

"I can't believe it," he said again and smiled. "I guess we'll see your true colors when I get your up there in front of everyone and you're shaking in your bare feet."

He led me back to the table and we finished our food.

"Caleb, I told you. My body feels so completely different now. I'm ready. I am not going to be nervous."

"Good," he murmured and rubbed my foot against his under the table.

Six

Caleb

MAGGIE HELD the cups of juice and I carried the take-out pancake boxes. We climbed the stairs and I watched her jeans as we went up.

I stared a hole in those jeans.

If she felt the heat of my stare, she didn't say anything. If she heard my thoughts, she didn't say anything about that either. I heard her laugh and decided to leave it at that and not go in her mind to see what she was laughing about. It was probably about me…staring a hole…in those daggum jeans.

She outright laughed and turned on the last step. She was on the step above me so we were perfect height to match. "I get it," she joked. "I've got good jeans."

"It's true, but it's what's in the jeans that's making me crazy," I told her.

She smiled and leaned forward to kiss the end of my nose. "You're going to be impossible this week, aren't you?" she said breathlessly.

"Yes, ma'am," I growled.

"Behave, Jacobson," she scolded and smiled. She leaned in and kissed my lips. Then she turned, her smile firmly in place, and knocked on the door. Beck answered, barely. The girl was running a few cylinders short and it was showing. She was beat. She sat down on the edge of the bed and accepted the plate from me. She inhaled and groaned. "Pancakes! Are you freaking kidding me? I could kiss you!"

"But you won't," Maggie said and pointed with a cocked brow.

"Not right now," Beck said laughing. "I'm in no position to fight *sleep*, let alone a whole other person. You're safe for now, college boy."

Maggie rolled her eyes and gave her the juice. Ralph was already scarfing his down, waiting for nothing or no one.

"Ah," he groaned through a bite, "even *I* could kiss you. I'm starving."

I laughed. "I'd rather neither of you do any kissing, if that's all right."

"Boo," Beck complained, but never looked up as she tore into the plate.

Maggie sat on the bed, her chin in her hand, and watched the two eat with a concentration that was motherly and cute. I stood by the wall, leaning against the old maroon wallpaper, and watched Maggie watch them. We were going home today. To *my* home. Maggie had never been there before and I was *oh so* ready to have her smell and voice crawling through my space.

She finally glanced my way and smiled crookedly. Then she rolled her eyes and looked back to Beck. So she *was* paying attention to my inner monologue. Good to know.

As soon as Beck was done, she did what I had been waiting for her to do. She asked to call her parents.

"Beck," Maggie started slowly. "I don't think you can call them. We're..." She shook her head. "I'm sorry. It's complicated."

"What's complicated?" Beck said and glared at her. "Why are you saying I can't call my parents? Of course I can. What the blazing hell is wrong with you, Mags!"

She reached for the phone. Maggie reached for her arm. Then the proverbial crap hit the fan.

Maggie had a vision, and she, Beck and I watched it all play out behind our eyelids.

It started with a dark street and we watched as a dark head waited in the bushes like a coward. I knew immediately it was Marcus, but felt Maggie's confusion because we couldn't see his face. She didn't want to believe it. She wanted to think we'd been wrong all along and that Marcus was out of our lives forever, but it wasn't going to happen that way.

He half turned as he saw a car coming. He ducked. As soon as the car passed, he crept out and stealthily went around the backside of a car. With gloved hands, he leaned down on the asphalt and swung around on his back. He pulled the pocket knife from his front pocket, flipped it open, and actually grinned like the bastard he was when he nicked the fuel line.

He didn't slice it. No, he wanted it to drain slowly so as not to alert them that there was a problem. He turned and looked at the dawn creeping up over the street. Beck and Ralph would be leaving soon. In his mind, he was determined. He was going to ruin our lives and this was just the beginning. He'd start with Beck, then he'd move on to Vic, taking our best friends and knowing we'd blame ourselves. Then he was moving on to Bish and Jen, Maggie's father. I saw the gun in his mind as he imagined catching them off guard.

It was the vision that Maggie had seen for them. I felt Maggie's gasp all the way from across the room. Then Marcus pulled his hood up over his dark face and whistled as he walked down the street like he belonged there. Like he hadn't just tried to take the life of Maggie's friend. Like he wasn't trying to ruin my girl's life.

I seethed. I fisted my hands against my sides and it was literally a chore to stand there and not go and hunt down that selfish....

Maggie was trembling as the vision faded away. I pushed from the wall and gripped her arms gently, but quickly moved my hands to her face so she could get the full contact of my skin. I held in my groan, but she sighed a harsh and loud breath against my neck. Her eyes strayed to Beck, who was wide-eyed and backing away.

Crap, no, don't do that, Beck.

I let Maggie go, reluctantly, but stayed right at her back as she raised her hands in an *it's OK* motion for Beck. "Beck, it's still me."

"What. The. Hell. Have you done. To my best friend!" she bellowed in choppy, emotional spouts. She was yelling at me. Her eyes blazed her anger at me over Maggie's shoulder. Maggie put her arm out to the side as if to shield me. It was cute, but this was not the time to think about that. I figured this was one of those keep-my-mouth-shut-kind of moments. Maggie would have to field the questions on this one. Apparently, I was the enemy.

"You...you made me see things..." Beck tried and then stiffened. "And I knew I saw something happening before! I told you I saw the air glowing or whatever."

"Beck, I can explain."

"Please do. Start with what college boy did to you to make you a freak."

"Hold up," I heard myself say before I could even think. "She is not a freak. Don't call her that. She saved your life with the ability she has and you owe her, if nothing else, to listen to what she has to say."

Maggie leaned back against my chest, almost sagged, while Beck stood stunned. I spared Ralph a glance, but he was still in shock and did nothing but stare at Maggie like she'd grown two heads. Dang…this was exactly what I *never* wanted to happen to Maggie; her human life and our new Ace life colliding.

"Well?" Beck demanded and stomped her foot. "Get on with it." She sat on the end of the bed and crossed her arms. "This ought to be good."

Maggie looked back at me helplessly. She didn't know where to begin. So I pulled her to sit on my lap as I sat on the bed opposite Beck. I began at the beginning, the day we met. I told her everything. I was the Champion of my clan now and I knew the consequences of telling humans about us. The only reason I was the Champion was because my father had told Maggie's father, and now here I was breaking the rules once again. And I'd do it a million times over if it would take the heartbreaking look off of Maggie's face.

I told Beck all about the imprinting, what Marcus had done to Maggie then, about California and what had been going on while they were visiting us, and what happened in London. And I told her why Maggie hadn't told her anything was because it was forbidden. We were breaking ancient laws right then and she needed to cut Maggie some slack. She was an amazing leader of our people with an amazing gift that saved people. It had saved Beck and Ralph's life.

She sat there and stared me down until I was done. It was then that she looked at Maggie. Her stubborn lip trembled, but she stood, slipped her shoes on and nodded her head to Ralph for him to follow her.

Crap.

He eased out of the bed and they both shuffled uneasily to the door. She looked back once and then shut the door behind her without another word. I turned Maggie fully on my lap sideways and prepared to take the brunt of her anger, of her being mad that I caused all this with my touch those short weeks ago.

After everything we'd been through, it seemed like an eternity.

"Maggie, I am so sorry."

She shook her head and I knew then I was probably never going to see an enraged Maggie directed at me. She was too sweet to blame me. She smiled and shook her head again, but that morphed into a bunched nose and upturned lips before the tears came. I wrapped my arms around my girl, but before Maggie's arm could even make their way around me, the hotel door was banged on with excessive force.

Maggie gasped and leapt from my lap, jerking the door open. Beck flew into Maggie's embrace and they both cried and laughed at the same time as they swayed back and forth. "I want to be mad at you," Beck admitted and glared at me over Maggie's shoulder. "And I really want to hate you."

"Beck," Maggie protested and leaned back, "don't."

"Let me finish. I want to hate you, but I can't because…I've never seen Maggie so freaking giddy before. But I know you did this to her, whatever *this* is, and I want to hate you so badly for taking my friend from me."

"He didn't take me, Beck. I'm right here."

"You're only here because you have to be. Otherwise, you would have never told me any of this, now would you?"

"No. Of course not. Would you have believed me?"

"No!" Beck shrieked. "I barely believe you now."

"Ok, then. There's reason we've kept our distance these past couple of weeks. But I had no idea he'd go after you." Maggie's eyes filled. "Beck, you'll never know how sorry I am."

"I know." Beck sighed and looked at the floor. "Mags, I know, OK? You don't have to feel guilty because some egomaniac with a God complex cut our fuel line. What you should feel guilty about is thinking that you could keep this from me." They both looked up and stared at the other. "The only way you could have ever kept all this from me was to either lie to me every day or let me go. Were you going to slowly let me go and we'd drift apart, not being friends anymore in a few years, with me just thinking life had gotten in the way? That it was just how normal friends ended things?"

"No. I just didn't know what to do. I wanted to keep you, but I have to keep Caleb."

"If you loving him means losing me, you should've chosen me! I had you first!"

"It's not that simple," Maggie ground out. "I love him, yes, but we have to be together. We have to touch and…" She shook her head. "You know what? No. This isn't some hos before bros situation, OK? I shouldn't have to choose. I was going to do what I had to do to still be friends, but it *is* normal, Beck. To drift apart, to not be so dependent on each other anymore. When you find the person you're going to marry, they become first. Everyone else is second to that, as they should be. You don't think that if you and Ralph got married that he'd always come before me?"

Rebecca snorted. "We're not talking about me, we're talking about you!"

Maggie just sighed. I decided to take that opportunity to butt in. "We need to check out soon. You can finish this fight at my place."

"Oh, we're done," Beck said sarcastically. "We'll be waiting in the car."

They left. I couldn't see Maggie's face, as she was turned away, but I suspected tears. Her mind was as blank as an empty chalkboard, but when she turned, her face was drawn in anger, not sadness. "How dare she?" she asked.

"Maggie-"

"No, how dare she!" She turned to look fully on me. "She's acting like I fed her to the wolves instead of saved her life. I protected her! I've done everything to keep her, even argue with you over it, and she has the nerve to make out like she's the victim?"

I felt that go straight through my chest. "And you feel like the victim?"

"No," she said quickly and then looked at me. *Really* looked at me. "No, Caleb. I don't think there's a victim here at all. Yes, she's Marcus' victim, but not mine." She practically ran across the room to put her arms around my middle. She squeezed. "Don't be thickheaded here, Jacobson." She smiled with truth. "I always wondered why Beck and I were friends. We were absolutely nothing alike. She's crazy and rash and rude and can be downright snobbish sometimes. But she's always been there for me. If she can't be here for me now? Now when I've found you, my husband, then we're not really friends anyway, are we?" She moved closer, letting her thighs touch mine. "I'll always choose you."

I nodded. She cocked her head to the side. "Why didn't you just read my mind? You would have seen the answer there."

"I'm trying to give you space. We can't be in each other's mind all day, every day, for the rest of our lives. There needs to be *some* mystery there." She smiled at that. "Plus, I thought you might want some privacy while you talked to Beck. Especially since you were fighting about me."

"You mean if I wanted to have thoughts of regret, you were going to let me have them in private?" she said wryly and scowled up at me.

I didn't hesitate. "Yes."

"My, my, how the tables have turned," she said playfully, but then frowned. "You're doubting me? Really?"

I got a full dose of the feelings of the very limited times when Maggie had felt inadequate, like she didn't deserve me, like she wasn't what I needed. It hurt like hell in my chest to be on the other end of that, to feel her ache as she sat there and thought that *I thought* that I was ruining her life. Beck was important to her, I knew that, and now she had to choose between her and me. And she was going to choose me, every time.

There wasn't a doubt in my mind about that.

But I hated it to hell and back that she *had* to choose because Beck was human and humans freaked when they realized something hokey was going on. Seeing your best friend give you a vision was pretty hokey.

I sighed as I took her elbow in my hand and pulled her to me. My body screamed at me to take away her hurt. When my fingers touched her skin, she jolted with the hit of calm I gave her. I pushed everything I had into it and pulled her into my arms. She didn't resist. I hoped it was because she wanted me to hold her and not just because her body wanted my comfort.

But when she settled in and started to play with the buttons of my shirt, I got my answer. I had to stop doubting this girl. This amazing girl who loved me even after she lost her friend because of me.

For the first time, I really did feel like a tyrant.

She reached up on her tiptoes and pressed her face to mine. She didn't kiss me, but let our cheeks and noses touch. I smiled, realizing she was doing what I had done to her so many times when I waited for her to kiss me. She had to make the first move in the beginning, those few short weeks ago. Seemed like an eternity ago now.

Now, as she turned the tables on me, I gave her a ghost of a kiss. I barely let my top lip touch her bottom one before going back for another soft touch that killed me to do. But I enjoyed her reaction as she pushed forward to take more, which I denied by leaning back a little. "We should go," I whispered. "Still a couple hours away from my place."

She groaned, "You did that on purpose."

"Uh huh," I answered and tightened my grip on her elbow. "I'd rather not have nips and pecks here when I can straddle the line with you as soon as we get home."

She sucked in a small breath and let her feet fall flat to the floor. Her eyes were wide as she agreed with a nod and scooted quickly to get her purse from the bed. I chuckled huskily in amusement and enjoyment.

This girl was going to be the death of me.

Well, that was fine. They could write, "Died a happy man" on my coffin.

Seven

Maggie

THE CAR ride was possibly one of the most awkward I'd ever endured. It was more awkward than the time I caught my parents having sex... before church, and we all had to ride together in that strangely hot, too small car to God's house.

But as we walked into Caleb's apartment, and Beck pushed through us without so much as a 'thank you' to Caleb for letting them crash there, I would have relived that awkward moment with my parents any day.

We had to creep. Beck was wearing Caleb's hoodie and Ralph had on Caleb's hat and whoever's sunglasses had been left in the SUV. They went first and waited for us. Caleb and I waited a few minutes before we went, too. Then Caleb unlocked the door, looking around for anything strange, and let them in. And there we were.

Ralph looked back at Caleb and me with a sympathetic look. "Sorry about her. Thanks for letting us stay here, man. I'm still not quite sure what's going on though." His questioning eyes glanced to me and back to Caleb.

"We'll….talk later," Caleb promised and sighed as he tossed his keys into a VOLS cup on the hall table. "You two can take the last room on the right."

Ralph saluted and jogged to catch up to Beck, who was the one who slammed the door, I had no doubt.

As Caleb locked the door behind us, I looked around his walls. I made my way to the fireplace and was impressed with the place. It was nice for a college kid, but the accommodations were definitely more along the lines of a bachelor. There was nothing on the walls. In the living room, there was a couch, an end table and a lamp. End of story.

He did have a couple of photos on his mantle. One of Maria and one of their family. Caleb looked so young there. I picked it up and rubbed my thumb over his photo face. No dust. I eyed the mantle and found no dust there either. So, Caleb had a maid.

"I do," he answered from behind me. "Her name is Rose and she comes once a week."

I put the picture back gently, straightening it just as I found it before turning to him. He was leaned with his hip on the arm of the green couch, watching me. But I noticed his lip as he chewed and sucked on it; his nervous tick.

He was nervous that I was here. It gave me pause, but something else took precedence over that.

I was in Caleb's home. Finally.

I grinned before tackling him, both of us falling back onto the soft, green pillows of the couch. He laughed in surprise before I covered his mouth with mine. My knees were bent and his legs were still dangling over the couch arm, but he didn't mind as he pulled me up his body further with his hands on my sides.

I pulled back and held myself up on my elbows. I was already winded, but managed to say, "I love your apartment."

He smiled. "You've only see one room so far."

I shook my head before he was even finished. "Doesn't matter. It's yours. You live here. It's your home."

"It's *your* home," he countered. He shook his head slowly and reached up to push my hair back. He let his thumb rub my temple as he spoke. "I have wanted to bring you here ever since…the beginning." His mind ran with images of us at the stop light, him talking to his parents about me, picking me up the next day at my Dad's house. "And now you're here. In my space," he said, his voice gravelly and sexy. "Gah…I love it."

"I love it, too."

"And I love you in it." I just smiled down at him at that. "You being here is like a missing puzzle piece finally coming together with the rest." I nodded and reveled in the feel of his hands in my hair. He reached up to kiss the corner of my mouth. "Do you want the tour?"

"Not right now I don't," I countered and let my weight fall on him once more. Our lips met spot-on, as if they knew right where to go. Caleb's hands both went under the hem of my tank and gripped the skin of my sides. It was like, the more skin he was touching, the more intense our connection was. My mind pushed right into his and he put up no fight.

But as soon as I started to see the energy ribbons behind my eyelids,

I heard a faint knock in the back of my consciousness and then the door opened. I lifted up to see over the couch as Kyle and Lynne came in without waiting. I gasped and glared at him as he lifted his arms in an annoyed manner.

"What the hell are you two doing here?" he asked. "And making out, no less. Uncle Peter is going nuts worrying about you both." He looked to the hallway and paled. "Beck?"

I jumped up and straightened my clothes. "We found them, but couldn't take them home. I had a vision."

Caleb grunted in annoyance beside me. "And I called Dad and told him we were fine."

Kyle had to drag his eyes from Beck, who stood bored in the hallway entrance, arms crossed. "Well, he's just worried about you. He said you should have called him again by now, so I decided to come and see if you were here, though I never actually expected to find you here."

I saw in mind *exactly* what he'd been expecting. His house was still crowded from the meeting, and family in and out. He thought he'd get some alone time in with Lynne. In Caleb's apartment. *Alone.*

Lynne smiled even as the boys stared angrily at each other, and came to stand next to me. She laced her arm through mine. Beck moved further into the room and cocked her head at me. Or Lynne, rather. "So, you've replaced me? And with this blonde cute-as-a-cookie chick at that? Is that why you don't care about being friends with me anymore?"

Lynne jolted at the implication and looked at me. I said, "No, I didn't replace you. What are you, five? Besides, you were the one with the ultimatums and accusations. I saved your life, if you remember."

"Yeah," Beck sneered, "how could I forget, freak."

"Hey!" Kyle yelled, startling us all. "Don't talk to her like that. She's the V-"

"It's OK, Kyle," I waved away his help and Caleb's as I saw his mouth open to say something, too. "Beck's just having a hard time." And she definitely didn't know anything about the Visionary stuff and I wasn't inclined to clue her into it yet. She was already walking away as I said it. I heard the door slam again.

"So, *anyway*," Kyle continued in annoyance, "you need to come back and let Uncle Peter know what's going on."

Caleb sighed and licked his lips before saying, "Well, I'm the Champion now, not Dad." Kyle sighed, too. "I'm the Champion and I saw what needed to be done and did it. I have to do what's best, not worry about whether Dad will be angry, even if it means he's left in the dark."

Kyle twisted his lips. "Yeah. I kind of forgot about that. Sorry."

"It takes some getting used to," Caleb agreed. "Even I forget half the time."

"No you don't," I called him on his bull crap. "You never stop thinking about it." I left Lynne to stand in front of Caleb. He looked so vulnerable and open right then. "But the thing you don't understand is that no one has doubts that you can do this but you."

He took a deep breath. He glanced over at Kyle. Kyle took that as his cue to say something smart, in typical Kyle fashion. "Yeah, what she said. But you can keep your bossy pants off when we come visit, 'cause I ain't following orders, bro."

Caleb cracked a wry smile. "Speaking of which," he crossed his arms, which was very distracting for me, "what the heck are you doing marching in my house when the door was locked?"

"So I had Aunt Rachel make a key." He shrugged. "What's the big deal?"

"The big deal?" Caleb laughed. "This is my house! And Maggie lives here now. What if you had walked in on something?"

Kyle grinned devilishly. "I thought I had."

I bit my lip, but still blushed. Caleb laughed and punched Kyle's arm. "Shut up, man." He came up behind me and put his arms around me.

"Besides," Kyle continued and accepted Lynne into his arms as she came back to him, "I thought I was going to live here once upon a time, remember?"

"You still can," I interjected. Caleb nuzzled the side of my neck and grunted his disagreement of that.

"No offense, but I'm not interested in bunking with the leader of our race, thank you very much," Kyle spouted and mimicked Caleb's position by wrapping his arms around Lynne from behind. He nipped her neck. "And I think we'd rather live alone anyway."

"Kyle," Lynne complained and slapped his hand, but she leaned back into him further and slung her arm around his neck. "Oh, my gosh, you're so crass!"

"You like it, babe, don't lie."

She grinned. "OK." She giggled. "I like it."

"I know," he groaned and bit into her earlobe.

I felt my lips part in shock of their brazenness. Yes, Caleb and I could be accused of being a little clingy, and I was never afraid of PDA, but those two were going above and beyond.

Caleb thought so, too, and said, "All right, hit the road." He shooed them with his hand. "We just got here. I want Maggie to myself."

"But we can't stay the night?" Lynne whined. "We wanted to be away from Kyle's house tonight if we could. No offense, Mister Champion, but your family is driving me insane."

"What's wrong?" I asked. I loved the Jacobsons and couldn't imagine being annoyed with them.

"That granny won't stop making inappropriate sex talk!" Lynne spouted. Caleb, Kyle and I burst with laughter. "What?" she said, vexed. "It's true! She's so nosy and always asking me if I'm being careful. I'll have her know I'm a proud V-card carrying member."

I laughed harder. "Oh, my gosh, Lynne! Stop!" I gripped Caleb's arm for support. "How could you not like Gran?"

"Oh, I like her just fine, but she's a ball buster."

Caleb and Kyle were falling all over each other laughing.

Kyle and Lynne eventually accepted defeat and knew they couldn't stay there with Beck and Ralph already taking up the guest room. So they started to leave. Lynne hugged me hard and said we should do something seriously girly soon, like shopping and coffee. I agreed.

They were on their way out when Kyle reached for Lynne's hand to tow her out the door, and that's as far as they got.

They both gasped, but Lynne was the one who spoke. "What is that? Kyle!" she screeched in fear.

He pulled her close and smiled in adoration, taking her face in his hands. "It's OK, babe," he breathed in reverence. "Just hang on to me."

I felt Caleb's arm pull me into his chest, but I couldn't look away from the magic of what was going on. I saw it all as it transformed and realized their abilities just as they did. They had some kind of affinities. Lynne's was water and Kyle's was air. My mind immediately went back to Captain

Planet, a show I used to watch when I was a kid.

Lynne was freaked. She had no idea how to go about using it or where to even start. All Kyle could think about was all the pranks he could do with his gift. I started to speak, to think of something brave and inspiring and...leadery to say.

Lynne's eyes met mine right before her gaze jerked to the hall and she gasped. It all happened in a rapid succession that was almost too fast to follow.

Lynne's ability fired without her consent as she panicked, breaking the fire sprinkler above her head on the wall, and blasting Beck with a downpour of water, who had chosen the worst moment to mosey into the hall.

I felt in Beck's mind as the water that a scared Lynne dispelled pelted her skin. She screamed and fell back into the wall dramatically, more mad than anything else. I lifted my hand to stop the water spraying out, damming it back. Beck gave me a look of disgust at my act. I started to rush over, but she screamed for me to stop. I heard her thoughts, but tried to play it off as her being freaked by what happened.

No such luck.

"Don't touch me!" she screamed and scrambled to the room. She slammed the door. I ran after her and tapped on the door gently, but she told me to go away.

I felt torn. Lynne was now my responsibility, as were all the Aces. She was going through something supernatural that I'd already been through and it was my job as Visionary to 'deal' with it. Beck was being...Beck. Hopefully, she'd understand soon.

"Lynne," I said distractedly as I came down the hall and willed Beck to come out. I came out of the hall to see Lynne crying hysterically into Kyle's neck and him trying to soothe her. Caleb, in turn, was trying to calm her down as well. She was mumbling that she didn't mean to, that she was sorry.

I went to her side, but didn't try to take her from Kyle. I knew that would be a bad idea. So I just touched her shoulder and tried to tell her that it was all right. Beck was fine and everything else would be, too.

Soon.

But of course, Beck's dramatic flair won out again as she stormed down the hallway with Ralph in tow. She glared at me and said, "Don't even bother asking if I'm OK. I am so far from OK with all of this! We're leaving. I refuse to stay here in this house with you and him!" She pointed at Caleb and then Lynne. "And her! I'm done. We'll stay in a motel or something until I think it's safe for us to go home."

"Beck, please," I tried futilely.

"No!" she screeched and jerked her arm away from my outreached hand. "No, Maggie."

She never called me Maggie. This was bad. This was so bad.

"I'm sorry," I said lamely.

She scoffed. "Now you're sorry that you've lied and picked him over me?"

"No," I answered truthfully and silently said goodbye to her. "I'm sorry that I hurt you."

She would never understand Caleb and me. She would never be OK with what I could do. She would never get used to the fact that I was growing up and away from her and we couldn't be silly high school friends forever. Things changed. It hurt, but I didn't know what else to do at that point but to let her go since that was what she wanted.

She once again slammed the door on her way out and I stood there as if waiting for something further to happen. It didn't.

Caleb lifted my chin with his fingers. "I'm sorry."

"If we were meant to still be friends, we would be, right?"

He shrugged sadly. "Yeah. That doesn't make it suck any less. This is the reason that I keep Vic at a distance."

I nodded and screwed my lips up. "It's a good plan."

"I'm sorry," Lynne told me in a whisper. "I didn't mean to. I didn't know what I was doing."

"It's OK, I promise. She was mad before you got here. It's better this way with Beck." I nodded to reassure myself more than anyone else that this was right. "It is."

"I'm sor-"

I effectively cut her off by pulling her to me. She was ridiculously tiny. "Remember what it felt like when we realized that things weren't... normal?" She nodded like a child. "Well, we had our significant and all the stuff going on in our minds to help us understand. Beck doesn't. She's human and I'll just have to accept that she's...never going to fit in my world anymore." I shook my head and refused to look at Caleb, who was pouring on the sympathy next to me. Kyle took Lynne's hand again, which didn't surprise me. She was still pretty upset and he would want to draw that off of her with his touch. "But you ascended," I reminded her. "That's amazing, Lynne."

"Yeah," she agreed and sniffed before looking up at Kyle. They both smiled slowly at the same time. "Yeah."

I sighed. "Stay," Caleb and I both said at the same time. We all laughed. "Just stay the night. You may as well, now."

"I'll go order some Chinese," Caleb said and kissed my forehead before sprinting to the phone.

Twenty five minutes later, and a couple of stories about Gran and her inappropriateness down, the delivery arrived and we sat on Caleb's couch side-by-side and watched a movie.

Of course, it was a horror flick.

No one cared that I was a chicken when it came to gore on the screen, but Caleb promised to keep me safe. It was *so* normal. We ate right out of the take-out boxes with our chopsticks. I had beef and broccoli, and shared with Caleb. He had General Tso's Chicken and shared with me, feeding me bites sweetly from his own chopsticks.

I tried to remain calm, normal and serene until the movie was over, and laugh and let everyone think that I was fine.

Kyle and Lynne retired to the guest room as soon as the movie was over and I blocked them out. Not only to give them privacy, but I didn't not want to be privy to their thoughts as they mutualized and that was exactly what they were going to do.

I told Caleb I wanted a bath and he rummaged through drawers to find a t-shirt and boxers for me. I took them in my hands. It was his *Imagine Dragons* shirt. I gave Caleb a smile as I went to the bathroom attached to his room and shut the door. He said he needed to make a few phone calls to his dad and his work, so he'd be busy for a while.

So I blocked Caleb, hoped he didn't notice because he was on the phone, and I took that opportunity as I sank down into the hot, bubbly water of his huge garden tub to break loose. To break loose over my friend. My friend who had been with me through everything. Who was spoiled, carefree and shallow, but mine. The girl who was angry with me because I hadn't told her about my mom\Chad drama and she was a glutton for it. A glutton for drama and mayhem and gossip.

But when I needed her to be my friend most, to look past anything else and just look at me, she walked out without looking back.

Right now, I was breaking down with hurt and loss. First, I thought I lost her when she went missing and now, she walked out, and I lost her again.

I leaned my head back, the white bubbles up to my chin, and let the tears come. The steam made the air thick, so I sniffed more than I would at a normal cry-session. I let my arms float beside me and stared at the pretty glass ceiling of the beautiful bathroom.

My body grew tenser with every breath, and the shakes of my chest got worse with every minute.

I barely heard the door click open as Caleb came inside. I sat up, taking my knees to my chest, and knew there was no way to hide my cry-face. "Did you finish your calls?" I tried for nonchalance.

"I haven't called the center yet, but I talked to Dad. I've got it under control. Don't worry about it."

I nodded. "Well, go call the center. I'm fine."

He took his phone out of his pocket and placed it on the counter. Then his wallet followed soundlessly. With bare feet, pants, and shirt, he climbed into the tub behind me.

"Caleb, what are you doing?" I asked, though I knew.

I knew exactly what he was doing.

He pulled me by my arms for me to rest in between his legs as he settled into the back of the tub. The water rose almost to the rim. I decided to let him do what he came in here to do and sank into his chest, turning a little on my side, letting my fingers hook in the collar of his soaked shirt.

He pressed his lips to my temple and spoke firmly. "It's not her fault, babe. She just doesn't understand. She'll never really understand, but she'll come around one day."

"But aren't you glad that she's gone?" I asked and felt my breaths shudder to hold back the sob. "As the Champion, aren't you supposed to keep the Ace secrets safe, not pass them around to your girlfriend's friends?"

"Fiancé," he corrected. "And yes, that's my job now, but when it comes to you, I'd do anything you asked me to. I'll break any law, any rule, any sanction if it meant that you were happy."

I sniffed. "I'm sorry. I didn't want you to have to do that for me, but she…"

"Shhh," he calmed, running his hands up and down my arms in the water. "Shhh."

His calm and warmth soaked into me and I pushed everything else away but us in that tub. I let all my anger and sadness blow through me. I cried while Caleb held me tight and I soon calmed. It was hard to stay upset with Caleb's calm keeping me from it, but I was grateful.

"You're crazy, getting in the tub with your clothes on," I admonished softly and laughed. "But thank you. I'm sorry you couldn't make your call."

"There are things more important." He kissed my temple. "Besides, I'd have to call the manager because the center is closed. It's kinda late anyway. I'll call her tomorrow. It'll be fine."

I saw the woman in his mind. She was an older, very pretty, but slightly heavyset black woman about Gran's age who ran Caleb's main office when he was away. I winced. He'd been away since he met me. I was wreaking havoc on his life, wasn't I?

I looked up to see his scowl as he listened to my inner monologue. I smiled and touched his cheek. "There's no one else I'd rather be wreaking havoc on."

He laughed in a rumble and growled, "You're daggum right." Then he sobered as he looked down at me. He rubbed my nose with his and stayed close. "Better?"

"As better as I can be."

He nodded. I leaned forward, pulling him to me with my hand on his face, and kissed him, solid and good. We stayed like that until the water turned cold.

Eight

Caleb

I WOKE to the tune of Maggie's heartbeat going nuts.

I jerked up and pulled the covers back a bit to inspect her. I turned her to face me and finally saw what she was dreaming about. I sighed.

She was dreaming about walking down the aisle and seeing my bare feet. And she had a gorgeous grin on her face.

It didn't matter that there wasn't going to be an aisle to walk down, I grinned back at my sleeping girl and scooted out gently so as not to wake her. The sun was barely peeking through the curtains, but I wanted to get up and get ready. I had big plans for us, and Maggie, though she didn't know it yet, had a big night with Gran and Mom.

Wedding stuff.

I was worried that Maggie would feel overwhelmed and not ready for it all, but from the look on her face just now, I guess that worry was unfounded. So I went to shave. I wanted to last night, but after we lazed in the tub forever, I just wanted to go to bed, hold my girl, and forget everything else.

Of course, Kyle and Lynne in the next room were having none of that. Maggie slept peacefully in my arms, but I was worried about her and couldn't fall asleep. Therefore, I was forced to listen to those two and their freaky-deakyness for what seemed like forever. Lynne was a giggler, I'll tell you that. And Kyle, well…

Just gross.

"I see you had an interesting night."

I turned to look at her as I pulled my shirt over my head. She was all sprawled on the bed like she belonged there. God, did she ever belong there. She smiled. "You're dressed already?"

"Yep. Get up, gorgeous. I've got plans for us."

"Oh, yeah?"

"Mmhmm." I swooped in, hovering over her on my arms, and kissed her easily. She combed out my hair with her fingers.

"You need a haircut."

"I thought you liked the shag?"

"I love it, but it's going a little overboard, surfer boy." Her mouth grinned. "Besides, don't you want to look amazing for our wedding photos?" I stilled and waited. She just continued to smile up at me like she had no secrets at all. Finally she laughed. "I know you're planning to hand me over to your mom and Gran tonight. You did manage to fall asleep for a few minutes last night and I felt like being nosy."

I felt my smirk. "You little sneak."

"Mmhmm," she agreed and ran her hand through my hair again. "I'll get dressed."

"Did you see everything?" I asked her softly. "Did you see where we're going?"

Her brow scrunched in confusion. "No. Where else are we going?"

"Get dressed. I'm glad we washed your clothes last night before bed. We should, uh," I started and waited a breath, "bring some of your stuff here."

She tried not to think about the house I was supposed to buy for her, but she couldn't help herself. I saw the struggle in her and glanced her way to see her with her knees drawn up as she chewed on her thumbnail. There was a little smile sitting on her lips. Her hair was tussled and it hadn't escaped my notice that she hadn't even tried to fix it at all when she woke. She was *that* comfortable with me, here, in my home.

It made me grin like a fool.

"I love that grin," she confessed and tilted her head a bit. "What does that mean?" she asked, pointing to my shirt. "What's with all the ducks?"

"You don't know?"

She shook her head. "And what's with the pink duck?"

"I'm not telling."

She laughed and I soaked it up like a sponge.

When we emerged from the bedroom, Kyle and Lynne were just coming out, too. I avoided eye contact and asked Kyle how he got here. He said he drove my truck since I had his Dad's car. I told him I was taking the truck back and we were leaving. I tossed him my keys. He tossed me mine and hovered them in the air using his ability to keep them just out of my reach. I lifted an annoyed eyebrow at him. I heard Kyle's chuckle as I jumped to grab them, but I just grabbed Maggie's hand and towed her out the door, yelling for Kyle to lock up when they left.

Maggie giggled all the way down the steps from my apartment at me, but I just kept on going. I dialed the center to see who was there. I told her I was on the way and she said she'd be waiting. "Thanks, Honey," I told her and hung up. Maggie gave me a 'What the?' look, but I blocked her from my mind and fought to keep a straight face.

"So, this is your truck," she said coyly. She drew her finger down the front end. "Does she have a name, too? I'm surprised Lola puts up with you cheating on her like this."

"Ha. Ha." I grinned and opened her door. "As a matter of fact, she does have a name." I took Maggie's hand and helped her into the side door. Even I had to admit, it was a big truck. "And Marlana isn't jealous. She knows how to share."

I shut the door, but could still hear Maggie's laughter as I walked around to my side. I hopped up inside and actually felt a sigh of relief. It had been forever since I'd driven my truck. Maggie had never even been in it. I glanced over to see her watching me. One of her feet was up in the seat under her and her head was tilted to the side.

My mouth said, "You are so gorgeous."

She smiled and looked down at her shoe, then back to me. "You're so good at that."

I grabbed her around the thigh and dragged her to me. "What's that?"

She lifted her hand and let her fingers smooth down the side of my face. She sucked on her bottom lip, but still managed to smile. The girl had no idea how gorgeous and sexy something so simple could be. Then she said, "You're so good at making me feel like I'm the only girl in the world."

I chuckled softly. "Didn't you know? You are."

She closed her eyes and pressed her nose to mine. "That sounds like good wedding vows to me."

"You'll get to read my vows soon enough. You've still got them, right?"

"Right in the obsidian box you gave them to me in." She leaned back just far enough to give me a look. "Really, that was just mean. You can't give a girl your vows and tell her not to read them." I just shrugged smugly. "I'm supposed to write my vows to you, too, right?" she asked nervously.

"Yeah, but we don't read them out loud at the wedding." She gave me a curious look. "The vows are for us. We read them, by ourselves, the night before the wedding. No one else hears or sees them."

"So what are we going to say at the wedding?"

"We won't say anything." I felt myself grin. "It's not a traditional wedding, Maggie. The wedding is, from what I've been told, a showering of blessings. The wedding isn't for us to pledge our love for each other. I think it's pretty obvious that imprinted couples love each other. And it's blaringly obvious that you're head over heels for me." She giggled. "It's for our family to give us the best start possible by being there on our first day as a real couple."

"That sounds beautiful. Your mom, she…" A picture played in Maggie's head from when Mom showed her wedding day. "She showed me their wedding day with everyone surrounding them." She looked me straight in the eye. "I can't wait." She grinned gorgeously. "Caleb, I can't wait. Let's get married tomorrow."

I laughed and cupped her cheek. "I can't believe you went from finding the idea of marrying me ridiculous to begging me."

"I'm begging," she whispered. "I've waited long enough to start my life."

I nodded, feeling those words to my bones. "We'll tell them tonight that we want to have the dedication this weekend."

"Well, you are the boss now."

"Technically, you are," I countered.

"I'll let you be boss for the day," she said cheekily, laughing when I grinned in challenge.

"Stop distracting me, gorgeous. I'm trying to take you somewhere."

She laced her arm through mine and leaned her head against my shoulder. "Take me anywhere."

My veins practically sighed inside of me. I kept a hand stuck between her thighs and put the truck in reverse, cursing Kyle for his horrible parking job. I put us in forward. Her mind was a peaceful haze of all sorts of things, but the most important thing to me right then was the fact that she was willing and eager to go anywhere I wanted to take her. She didn't need to know where it was, or why we were going there, she was just happy to be with me.

After we drove for a while, I pulled into the parking lot and barely suppressed my grin. This was it. My girl was here and I was about to lay all of my cards on the table. I kissed her forehead and hoped that I had her pegged as well as I thought I did.

I parked in the back of the lot and opened the door, pulling her out my side of the truck. Her eyes held a curious suspicion, but she never said a word. When I swung the door to the community center open, I felt it when her understanding hit her.

She turned to look at me just as I was bulldozed right in the guts by eighty five pounds of sixth grader. "Caleb!"

That alerted everyone to our presence. I looked around the faces and most of them were kids I'd seen before, but a few new ones hung back, unaware of who I was.

"Caleb!"

I turned and smiled. "Honey, hey."

Maggie scoffed and laughed. "This is Honey?"

"This is my Honey," I joked and accepted Honey's kiss on my cheek.

The older woman laughed. "Don't get cheeky, Caleb."

"How's everybody doing?" I asked. They all answered at once, jumping up and down and trying to get my attention.

Then one question was louder than the rest. "Who's she?"

I smiled and saw Maggie's nervous smile in return. I quirked a brow at her.

Kids intimidate you?

There's so many of them.

There's only eight here tonight, babe.

And they all look like they want to murder me for taking you away from them for so long.

I shook my head at her. "Guys, this is Maggie. Now, I know I haven't been in for a while and I don't know what Mrs. Honey told you, but Maggie and I are…getting married."

"Eeew!" the kids rang out.

That made Maggie laugh. I laughed, too, and pulled her to me. "It's not eeew."

"Does that mean you aren't going to be our teacher anymore?" Will asked.

"Well…" I glanced at Maggie. It was time. "Actually, I'm not going anywhere."

That got her attention. I waited for her disappointment or worry or…. something. See, she knew I wanted to be a teacher, she knew I wanted to go to Arizona and start up the centers there, too, and she knew I didn't want to work with my father, but she never thought I was actually going to go against him. She didn't try to wonder about what we were going to do one day for jobs or houses. My family had so many traditions and I hated – really hated – to be the one who broke them, but if I was going to lead our people and be the Visionary's mate, along with being myself, then I had to do this.

I had to make my own choices and live my own life. And that didn't include working for Jacobson Buildings and Things.

I'm sorry I didn't tell you before, but I just wanted to show you first. To let you see what this was all about. I looked at the kids as they waited. *These kids…some of them have no one. No family that cares or can afford to keep them out of trouble. Some kids, this is all they've got. And some kids just have a hard time with math and I can help them with that. I want to-*

Are you kidding me?

I stared at her. She was good at keeping her mind blank now. So good at keeping her every thought private from me.

I'm sorry. I should have told you, but…

You think I want you to work for your father?

I jolted. *Don't you?*

I want you to do what makes you happy.

But with this job there's…traveling all over the state and maybe even the country if I have my way. There's no guarantee of steady incomes and schedules. It's seasonal, sometimes good, sometimes bad. It may fail all together. I…

"Have y'all missed Caleb?" Maggie asked, never taking her eyes from me.

"YES!" the kids said.

"Do y'all want him to stop coming in and helping you?"

"NO!"

I will follow you to the ends of the earth, Caleb Jacobson. You have to know that by now.

Woman, you are about to get kissed in front of all of these kids if you don't stop being so amazing.

They love you. She smiled and picked up a painting from the table. "Who did this?"

"Me!" Molly said and grinned. "You like it?"

"Yeah, I do!" Maggie agreed through a laugh. She sat down at one of the tables and picked up a green marker. "And green is my favorite color, so the fact that you drew a green times-table is awesome."

Molly and some of the others sat down with her and they loved her immediately. I stared at the back of her head as she interacted with my kids. I felt the weight lifted from me. I had been worried that she'd want me to be happy, obviously, but would want me to not upset the family by not following tradition. I thought she was going to try to talk me into doing both, but letting someone run the centers for me.

But these were *my* kids and it was the only thing I ever wanted to do.

I should have known my Maggie would understand.

"So you leave for a few weeks and come back engaged to this girl?" Honey asked, her hands on her hips.

"Now, Honey," I admonished. "Maggie is great."

"So am I, but you ain't going to marry me, are you?"

"I would if you'd say yes."

She slapped my arm and glared at me as I laughed. "What do you know about being somebody's husband? You're just a baby, yourself!"

"I know that I'll do anything I have to. I'm not *that* young, Honey. I love her, that's why I asked her to marry me. I can do this."

She pursed her lips. "Does she have a bun in the oven?"

I scoffed. "Absolutely not."

"What does your mamma say about this?"

"That she can't wait," I told her softly. "My dad, especially. They've all fallen in love with her."

She sighed. "Well, you've made up your mind, now haven't you?"

"Yes, ma'am."

"Well, now. What are we gonna do now?" She gave me a pointed look. "Do I need to start looking for a new job?"

"No, ma'am. You're safe. By the way, where is everyone?"

"Just running a little late," she told me. "Sage and Violet are on tonight. They're going to do multiplication piñatas with the kids."

I laughed. "I can only imagine what multiplication piñatas are."

Violet and Sage came in minutes later with bags of supplies for the projects. Violet was the same age as me, and not only was her name colorful, but so was her hair. It was a different color every week or so.

Sage, her boyfriend, was just as colorful in personality. It was hard to keep track of all the kids and helpers, but this office was my *main* office. This was where I spent most of my time.

I went and introduced Maggie to them and before we knew it, we'd been there for three hours. I hated to leave because Maggie was having so much fun, but Gran would skin me alive if she didn't get Maggie tonight.

As I opened the door to let Maggie walk ahead of me, she lightly punched my gut as she walked down the stairs. "Jacobson, you are in so much trouble."

"I figured," I joked and walked right up to her. I looked right down at her and watched her as she tried not to smile. "I take it you like my kids."

"I love them," she said softly and toyed with the hem of my shirt. "I know you're worried about telling Peter-"

"That's my battle," I insisted and kissed the end of her nose. It was almost dark in the parking lot now and I found myself looking around for anything out of place.

She pulled my face to look at her. "I can hear their mind if someone wants to mess with us."

"We don't know that," I insisted. "The Watsons may be human now, but what if your abilities don't work on them anymore? We have no idea what they're capable of yet."

"I have a pretty good idea," she muttered and thought of Beck. "Being cowards."

"No Watson talk tonight," I commanded softly. "We can only talk about things like...weddings." I grinned.

She grinned, too. "We better go or Gran is going to kill you."

"And Dad, too. This is my first meeting." I left off the part that mattered most. That it was the first meeting that I was the Champion for. And it was going to be my show, my deal, mine. It was just my family, but I was scared crapless.

Maggie put her arms around my neck, reaching on her tiptoes as far as they'd go. "You'll be great." She kissed behind my ear. "Besides, what could go wrong, right?"

I knew something was wrong the second we pulled up to Dad's. When I opened the door, Dad was there next to Bella, who wagged her tail and stared at me expectantly. Dad, however, did not wag his tail. In fact, he glared. "You're late."

"I'm right on time," I corrected and re-checked my watch.

"Pushing the limits doesn't make a good leader. Setting a good example does."

"I was showing Maggie the center. I think that teaching kids is about as good as an example as I can set."

"Maybe," he conceded. "We've been worried about you two. They've been talking about some things on the news today."

"What kinds of..." Maggie trailed off as she read it in his mind. "Mom?"

We both took off down the hall. I towed Maggie behind me because I still hadn't shown her how to maneuver the maze of halls. We reached the kitchen where Mom and Gran were watching the TV on the counter. We listened intently as they described the bus accident that happened on the highway. They listed the ones on the bus who'd been injured.

My heart pumped painfully as I watched helpless-as-all-get-out as

Maggie heard her mother's name as one of the ones taken to the hospital. For the second time in just days, we had to wonder if someone else Maggie cared about had been hurt by a Watson.

Nine

Maggie

"THE HOSPITAL said she's fine," Dad assured me. "They called and said it was just a scratch on her arm. She got three stitches. It's not a big deal."

I sighed. I may not like the woman much, but she was still my mother. "Good." I switched the phone to my other ear. "Are you OK?"

"I'm fine," he answered. I heard Fiona asking him if he wanted something to drink in the background. He told her, "No, thank you," and then told me, "All right, well, I heard you have a big night ahead of you." He cleared his throat. "So I'll guess I'll let you go…get to that."

"Can we come for dinner?" I blurted out. "Caleb and me?"

"Of course," he answered brightly. "I'll invite Bish and Jen, too."

"Great. It's a date."

He laughed. "Have fun tonight. I'm glad you've got a woman to help you with all the wedding stuff."

"Help?" I scoffed. "Do you really think Gran is going to let me have the reins on anything, Dad?"

He laughed again. "Well, you're probably right. Still."

"Yeah. Still."

"Love ya, baby girl. See you later."

"Love you, too, Dad." I hung up and turned, bumping my nose right into Caleb's chest. I was glad that he was so close. I slipped my phone into my pocket and let him wrap me up. "She's fine."

"I know. I heard," he said. "But are *you* fine?"

"As a fiddle."

He chuckled. "*Fine* as a fiddle?"

"Yep," I sighed and gripped him tighter.

"Baby," he said, his voice husky. "I've got to go, but now I don't want to leave you."

"I'm fine," I said with certainty. "I promise."

He paused and thought. He was thinking of a way to get out of going. I shook my head at him. "This is your first meeting as the leader of the Jacobsons." I felt my lips smile with pride. "You have to go. Show them who's boss."

He laughed reluctantly. "That would be *you*, gorgeous. I thought we went over this?"

"So I can come, too?" I remembered our *friend* that needed to be found and dealt with. "We need to figure out what to do about Marcus."

"Next time, sure. I'll handle it, I promise. This time? Wedding stuff." He pointed to the floor. "And you're staying right here."

"OK," I said easily. "Well, have fun."

"Doubtful," he grumbled. "It'll all be formalities and tradition and...

things like that. I won't be gone too long. We're taking it to Kyle's tonight since all the girls are here getting things ready."

"Getting ready for this weekend, right?" I said, biting my lip to tamp down on my excitement.

"Yep. Just a few days now." He cupped my cheek. "Then you'll be Mrs. Jacobson, and I'll be Mr. Visionary."

I burst out laughing. He laughed, too, and kissed my smiling mouth. "I love you."

"I love *you*," he insisted in a rumble.

When he bent to kiss me again, I welcomed it, but Gran had other plans. "Stop that right now and get your butt outta this house!" We both looked at her, Caleb's hand still on my cheek. "I mean it! Get gone!"

He sighed and gave me a sullen look. "I'll pick you up in a little bit."

"I'll be here," I told him and managed to pull him down to kiss him right before he was dragged away.

Gran swatted his butt and shooed him away out the door. "Now, we can get down to business." She rubbed her hands together like a villain. I felt my eyebrows rise.

"Shouldn't we wait for Rachel?"

"Oh, she's coming with Jen. They'll be here in a little bit." She smiled, showing teeth. "Now, let me show you something."

She took my hand. It was impossible not to notice the cool and wrinkled feel of hers. We went upstairs to the bedroom where she slept. She looked back at me and then to the trunk at the end of the bed. She started to kneel down and I rushed to help her. While gripping her elbow, I went down with her to my knees. She gave me a smile that said what she was about to show me meant a lot to her. I waited with silent patience.

"This," she started and pulled a box out of the chest, "was mine."

The white top came off the box and she rummaged through the silver tissue paper to reveal a swath of red material. I knew immediately what it was.

Her wedding dress.

I pulled it from the box gently and held it up. It was a long dress with a small train, I assumed, because the fabric just kept going and going. "Gran, it's beautiful."

"I know," she said and laughed. She touched the side of the dress, rubbing it in her fingers, and I saw in her mind as she remembered wearing it and feeling as beautiful as a woman ever felt. Grandpa Ray watched her and his mouth fell open as she came to him. It was almost enough to giggle about, but Gran was so wrapped up in her memory. She smiled, though her eyes watered.

I touched her arm. "You looked amazing in this dress, Gran."

She nodded. "My grandmother made it for me. And now I want you to wear it."

I felt my chin fall in shock, but before I could say anything, I heard a gasp. I turned to look and saw Jen and Rachel in the doorway. Rachel was smiling and looking at me funny. I would have been worried had I not been able to read her mind, but she was thinking about how beautiful I was going to look in it. The funny look was because she was trying not to cry. I glanced back at Gran and saw a tear run down to her chin. When I looked back at Rachel, she wiped under her eyes. I flicked a look at Jen and saw her sniff.

Oh, boy. This had to be stopped.

"No crying allowed!" I said and laughed. "Come on, guys. You're going to make me cry." Rachel chuckled, but Gran gave me a hilariously snooty look. "Besides…" I braced myself. "I can't wear the dress, Gran."

Her face fell. I rushed on so she didn't burst into tears. "Because Jen's going to wear it."

Jen smiled in that way that says someone is being silly. "We can both wear it. You can wear it for your dedication and then I'll wear it to mine. It's no big deal. We can have it altered if we need to."

"No, I mean I want you to wear this to my dedication." She frowned in confusion. "Because I want you and Bish, and Dad and Fiona, and Kyle and Lynne to get married with us." They all sat there very still. "I know that's not tradition."

"It's never been done," Gran said. "Especially since Fiona is part of another clan."

"I know," I said and took a deep breath as I spoke softly, "but all these rules and regulations and traditions…I mean, no offense, but that's what got your kind in so much trouble in the first place, right?"

She sighed. "It's just hard to change things when you've done them a certain way for so long. And I'm human like you, and it's hard for me, so I can only imagine how hard this will be for Peter and the council."

"The council isn't present at a wedding though, are they?"

"No, but it has to be recorded through them." She pinched her chin and smiled. "Oh, well. The old coots can deal with it, I guess. Especially since it's coming from you."

I bit my lip. "I'm not trying to cause problems," I assured her. "I just think we should make our own traditions now." I looked at the infinity symbol on my wrist. "This has to mean something. Us going to London and breaking the hold of the council has to mean something. Caleb finding me, me being human, and everything that has happened since that didn't make any sense…it all has to mean something."

"It does, honey," Rachel insisted and gave me a half hug. "It means that you're right where you're supposed to be. I think it's a wonderful idea. A great way to show the council and the whole race that when you say you're going to change things that you mean business."

"I hope so," I said softly. "So, Jen is wearing the dress. It's only right."

I held it out to her and she smiled as she touched it. "Oh, gosh. You showed me this dress when I was a kid, Gran. I dreamed about wearing this dress." Her lip trembled.

I never thought I'd get the chance to wear it.

Rachel put her other arm around Jen. "No more dreaming now, baby."

Jen put her arm around her mom's waist like a child would and tried to keep her tears in check. The room held a vibe that had a bittersweet happiness to it. It soaked the air with it, making me want to cry with them. Jen was finally getting what was always promised to her as a little girl. What she knew was going to be hers was taken and withheld. Then Maria happened and she took that little blessing with stride, knowing she'd never have the chance to have a child otherwise. And now here she was, on the cusp of everything she ever wanted, and it was hitting her all at once…with this dress.

She smiled and didn't try to wipe the tear as it fell. Her fingers reverently fingered a nonexistent pattern on the fabric and she wondered what Bish's face would look like as he watched her come to him while wearing it. She hoped it made her look beautiful enough to make up for all the drama and trouble she was bringing into his life with this family and her kind.

"Bish is happier than I've ever seen him," I told her. "Jen, he's head over feet in love with you and everything that's attached to you. He has been ever since he first saw you. Don't worry about him. Bish isn't in the habit of letting inconsequential things bother him."

"I guess," she said noncommittally and sniffed. "I just know how hard it's been for *you* to come into this life."

"Well, I'm here to help him. And my situation was a little different," I said wryly and remembered the fuss everyone made over me for being the first human in a very long time, along with the first imprint.

She laughed at my scowl. "Yeah…I guess it was a little different."

"Just a little," I played along. I put the dress all the way into her arms because she had still not taken it from me. "It's your right to wear it. And I want to share my day with you, if you want to."

"Of course I do," she said, like I was crazy for thinking otherwise. "I know you still don't really understand exactly what the dedication wedding is for, but I do, and for you to ask me to share that with you and my brother is… I'm honored."

"*I'm* honored." I let her hug me to her. "Don't worry about anything," I told her and when I felt her breath catch a little, I realized I had inadvertently brought up the unavoidable future. The vision I saw of Bish and Jen played in both of our minds and I leaned back. I mouthed, 'I'm sorry.'

She shook her head and mouthed, 'I trust you.'

'I won't let anything happen to you. Or Bish. I haven't forgotten, I promise.'

'I know.'

I saw Gran watching us curiously. Jen wrapped her arm around me and said, "Sister stuff."

I felt my heart skid a beat or two at that. She squeezed me. "So Fiona, Lynne, you, and me. What a pretty bunch of ladies we're going to be," she joked and flipped her hair. "They should rename Saturday *Diva Day* 'cause that's totally what it's going to be."

I laughed along with Rachel and Gran, even though I knew she was trying to take her mind off the vision. I took a steadying breath. I refused to let the vision come to fruition. I refused to let something so beautiful and needed for our family and our race end so pointlessly by a jackass with a God complex. That bastard had ruined enough already and I refused to let him take one more thing from me or this family.

"Did someone tell a knock-knock joke?"

I turned to find Maria.

And Bish.

And my goodness was the man glowing from the inside out.

I smiled at him and he smiled back. I went to him, expecting him to be different now somehow. Like the way Beck had called me a freak and ran, he would be different since he'd seen me in all my Visionary glory in London and had finally found his way into Jen's life the way he wanted… and now things wouldn't be the same. But I was proven wrong when he lifted me into a bear hug. I sank into it and felt not just relief, but a sense of rightness wash over me.

I peeked back to see his face, to see if he was feeling the same thing as I was. His face said he was and then I heard him.

She looks so…happy and…free. I feel kinda terrible about everything

I did.

"You're my brother," I justified. "It would have been weird if you hadn't been worried about me."

"Yeah, but…all the things I said to Caleb. If you had just given me a couple minutes alone with the guy, I would've laid him out."

I chuckled. "I have no doubt. But it's over now."

He touched my cheek. "You have no idea how beautiful you look when you're this happy. I know it's because of him."

I blushed and pressed my lips in a line. "It is."

He sighed and moved back. "How was the memorial?"

"Oh, uh…fine."

"I'm sorry."

"It's OK," I hurriedly said and looked back at Gran. "Are you going to go shopping with me? I'm gonna need a new dress."

"Heck no!" She sized me up. "I'm gonna make you one, pretty girl. And Fiona's and Lynne's, too."

"There's no way you can make them all in-"

"Are you doubting me?" She cocked her little eyebrow and waited.

"N-no, ma'am," I stuttered.

"Good." She looked past me to Bish. "Out, beefy. The women folk have work to do."

Bish laughed and pointed to himself. "I'm *beefy*, I suppose."

"Well, no one else in this room has his arms stuffed into his sleeves like sausage casings, now do they?"

He laughed. "No, ma'am." He turned to Jen and I thought he'd do a simple wave and tell her goodbye since he definitely didn't seem like the type for PDA, but he shocked us all when he walked up to her and held her chin as he placed his lips on hers. She smiled softly up at him as he said, "I'll see you in a bit."

She nodded. He took Maria's hand and turned back to me. "We'll go hang out with Dad. You're coming for supper tonight, right?"

"Yeah," I answered. "As soon as Caleb's meeting is done. We'll meet you there."

He nodded once and smiled at us as a whole. "Later, ladies."

"Bye," Jen said softly and watched him go.

We all stood around for a few more seconds before moving. When I finally looked over at Jen, she was fighting tears. Rachel took her and hugged her hard. "Mom," Jen whispered. "I don't have to wonder what it feels like to be like you and Daddy anymore. I *know*."

"Jenna, I've always hoped you would, baby." She sniffed, very ladylike. "I always tried to believe it for you. Bish is…"

"I know," Jen said and laughed. "He's amazing."

I felt my nose wrinkle. "OK, let's all try to remember that he's my brother."

They laughed and then *Radioactive* by the Imagine Dragons rang out through the room. Rachel took her phone from her pocket and answered it. I gaped at her. "Hey, baby…No, I'm OK. Jenna and I were just talking about…finally being a significant." She smiled at Jen. "Yes, I promise. I'm sorry I scared you." I heard Peter in Rachel's mind as he said something about her '*pretty tush getting it later*.' I couldn't stop my gasp. Rachel giggled and then said, "Peter, Maggie's in the room with me." He laughed in a slightly embarrassed way and said to tell Caleb and me to come over tomorrow and that he'd see her later. "Okay. I love you, honey." He said he loved her, too, 'something fierce'. I smiled at her, but looked away. She cleared her throat. "I guess you got that, huh?"

"Come over tomorrow? Yeah."

"He was just calling to check on me, said my heartbeat was fast."

"I can imagine," I said dryly.

Gran interrupted. "All right, enough, you two. I know my son is as McDreamy as they come." Gran smacked me on the butt. I stared at her, open mouthed. "We've got work to do. Strip."

"Strip for what?"

"I'm going to measure you for your dress. Strip!"

Rachel saved me…sort of. "You can do her measurements with her clothes on, Mamma," she chastised.

"Oh, I know I can." She pointed at me. "But look at her face! Ha! I just wanted to see her face pucker up like that." She continued to cackle at my expense and I let her because Gran was…Gran.

We spent the next two hours getting measured and looking at dresses online that we liked so Gran could get some semblance of our tastes. She said she'd do Fiona's later. As soon as Caleb came back, we left for Dad's.

"Come in!" Fiona chimed and swung the door open wide with gusto. I led the way with Caleb's hand on the small of my back. I was pleasantly surprised by the place. Fiona had apparently been putting her own touch on things. "Oh, gosh, Maggie. I swear you get prettier every time I see you."

"Thanks," I said and tried not to be awkward, so I went right in for a hug. And that's how Dad found us.

"Baby girl," he sighed. My feet propelled me until I was practically strangling the man. He chuckled a little into my hair. "I'm so glad you're as happy to see me as I am to see you." He leaned back and kissed my forehead. "Bish and Jen are in the den. Hey, that rhymed."

I laughed. "I'm glad you're still you, Dad."

"I'm stuck this way now." He smiled and opened one arm to Fiona, who went willingly into his side. Maria ran in from the kitchen and took his other arm. He seemed so natural and comfortable with them both. I felt my chest ache with happiness for him. "Thank God."

"Agreed," I said. "I'm gonna go see Bish and then I'll help in the kitchen."

"Oh, will you?" she said sweetly. "I'm a horrible cook. Your father told me you're so good with Mac-N-Cheese."

I laughed. "Then he lied to you."

She turned to him laughing as we walked out to the den. I opened the hide-a-door and Caleb plowed into my back as I stopped. My eyes bugged. Bish had Jen up on the piano as he stood between her knees. And the man must've been starving because he was devouring her mouth right there on the Baby Grand.

Ten

Caleb

"Yikes," I muttered and turned, gripping my hair in my fists. Dude had my sister up on the piano kissing the sense out of her. Significants or not, she was still my sister. I did not want to see that crap.

I felt Maggie's hands on my back. She must've turned away from the debauchery, too. I shivered in disgust and tried to think of something else. Maggie giggled, making me turn to face her. "And just what is so funny?"

"Oh, come on. It's funny!"

"Not. Even."

"You know we're worse," she said and nipped at my chin. "You know it's true."

"But I devour you in private," I said low.

"Hey," Bish said and we turned to see his face, full of chagrin. "Sorry.

We didn't hear you come in."

"I'll remember to make more noise next time," Maggie said easily.

"Definitely more noise," I agreed sardonically.

Jen laughed softly. "Shut up." She sighed, tucking her hair behind her ear and whispering, "You know."

"Yeah," I agreed and squeezed Maggie's hand. "I also know what it's like to be the brother and have to watch it though. Bish, I totally understand now, dude."

"Yeah," Bish said and took a deep breath. "Look, Caleb, I know we started off on the wrong foot. And I know that was my fault. I understand now what it's like to need each other and feel so weird and just...helpless to what's going on inside my skin. I'm sorry I gave you and Maggie such a hard time–especially you. It's no secret that I never liked you."

"Yeah." I laughed. "Yeah. No sweat, man. I understand."

"Is everyone ready for supper now?" Fiona peeked her head inside and smiled. "I made pot roast."

"Yes, ma'am," I answered and towed Maggie to follow me.

Dinner was easy flowing and natural. The chatter and talk was as normal as ever. You'd never know there were so many people with 'gifts' sitting around the table, let alone the leader of her race and the Champion of the clan. And so many people with gifts on the way. But, either way, it was normal. It made Maggie smile and be happy to know that things could go back to the way they used to be. For the most part.

Then she sprung the idea of us all getting married together on them. Fiona sputtered a little about tradition and rules, but eventually came to the conclusion that things needed to change and this was a good way to start. When she told Fiona that Gran was going to make her dress, that sealed the deal. She started to cry. Maggie was thinking how it was good to see her dad comfort Fiona so effortlessly and not worry about us watching. He had always been a good man even with Maggie's mother. She was just too stupid to see what she had.

When the doorbell rang, I assumed it was Kyle and Lynne coming to hang out. Bish said he'd get it and ran to do so, but I sat stunned as I heard the thoughts through Maggie of the person on the other side of the door. She gave her dad a look in warning before she got up from her chair and made her way in to stare at the woman who had ruined her life.

Maggie's heartbeat banged like an angry drum. I wrapped my hand around her wrist and my fingers on her pulse kept time with it. She went to meet Bish at the door to confront her mother. Her clueless father still sat at the table, wondering what was going on. I couldn't even imagine the crap that was about to go down when Fiona met Sarah. Or rather, when Sarah met Fiona.

I held Maggie's hand as we turned the corner. And there she was in all of her home-wrecker glory.

"What are you doing here?" Maggie asked. No one could mistake the ice in her voice for anything but.

She lowered her head. "I was coming to see you again and the bus I was on got in an accident. I was in the hospital. The hospital called your father, but he wouldn't come see me!" She blubbered and peeked her eyes open and up to make sure we were watching. It was pretty pathetic. "And he didn't tell you I was there because I know you would have come to see me. So I thought I would come see you for myself."

"Why do you think I would have come to see you? Or that Dad

would have?" Maggie asked.

"Why wouldn't you?"

"Oh, I don't know," Maggie started softly. Too softly. "Maybe because you ruined Dad's life and then ruined mine? Maybe because you lied to everyone? Cheated on Dad, and then lied to Haddock about being pregnant?"

Her mom's eyes bulged. And then moved on to the size of lemons when Jim came around the corner with Fiona. He stopped in his tracks, clearly not aware of who it had been at the door. Maggie's mind reminded herself that Jim didn't know about him not being her father and that she needed to rein in her anger before she let something slip.

He glanced down at Fiona, who was a smart girl and had figured out what was up, and then looked over at Maggie's mom. "Sarah, what are you doing here?" he asked quickly.

I saw Fiona flinch when he said her name. I winced for them all. This situation was delicate at best. He reached up and touched her arm, rubbing his calm touch into her skin. "Sorry," he whispered.

"Sorry?" Sarah yelped. "For what? This is my house!"

"It's not, Mom," Maggie told her. She sighed and her shoulders slumped. She was done before she even started this fight. I moved to her back and put my hand on her side under her shirt. I saw her take a deep breath as my calm hit her. "Mom, you can't just keep showing up here."

"She's right, Sarah," Jim spoke up and moved to stand in front of Fiona a little when Sarah glared at her. "You don't live here anymore. I put a couple boxes of your stuff out in the garage. You can take them if you want."

She seethed. "You can't keep me from my own daughter. She's still a minor."

"Not for long," Maggie muttered under her breath.

"If Maggie wants to see you that's between y'all, but as far as this house and me, you don't belong here anymore."

"I thought you weren't seeing anyone," she sulked.

"I wasn't…you know what? That's none of your business anymore, Sarah." He spoke softly in chastisement. "What are you doing here?"

"I told you." She flipped her hair and grimaced. "I came to see you because you wouldn't come to see me." She lifted her sleeve to show her arm. "See! I got four stitches in that wreck."

"Wow," Bish said bitterly. I had almost forgotten he was there. We all turned to look at him. Jen was at his side with both of her hands on his arm. Her lips were pinched in that way they did when she was angry about something. Bish continued with, "Four whole stitches."

He looked at her angrily for a few dragged out seconds before pulling Jen with him as he left the room. That's exactly what I wanted to do to Maggie. Her heart hurt because of this woman. I squeezed my fingers around her side a little tighter to remind her I was right there.

"What are you here for?" Jim asked once more.

Maggie's mom sighed. "Look… I gave Maggie my great aunt's platinum bracelet for Christmas when she was fifteen and I want it back. She gave it to me and I think she'd want me to have it."

Maggie scoffed. Then she left. I closed my eyes and waited. I knew exactly what she was doing, as I'm sure they all did. She came back not even seconds later and put it in her mom's waiting palm. "Now leave me alone."

I did take her from the room that time. I couldn't stand there and watch that anymore. I didn't have to drag her in the slightest as she let me tow her. As soon as we passed the threshold for the kitchen, I turned and engulfed her in my arms. "That woman," was all I could say.

"Yeah," Bish agreed and I swung my gaze to the side to see him sitting at the table with Jen in his lap. She was comforting her significant as I was comforting mine. "That woman."

Maggie peeked at him. She opened her mouth to say that she was sorry about her, that it wasn't Bish's fault that she didn't speak to him… again. But she closed her mouth and didn't even try.

"It's OK," he told her and patted Jen's leg, asking her to let him up. He came to Maggie and ruffled her hair. "You were always the cute one anyway."

"I don't understand her," Maggie told him. "It's not you, Bish. It's not."

"I'm done worrying about it." He stood a little taller and breathed deep. "What about-"

He stopped talking when a pale Fiona came back into the kitchen. She leaned on the doorjamb like she couldn't hold herself up anymore. My sweet Maggie sprung to action. "Fiona, look." She pulled out the iPhone I bought her and moved her finger around until she found the page she was looking for. "See? Isn't this gorgeous?"

In her mind, I saw that it was a website of the dresses they'd looked at earlier that day. She was showing Fiona one of them. I blocked it out in case it was the one Maggie was going to wear. Fiona seemed grateful for the distraction, but still noticed when Jim came back in. He didn't pretend that things weren't awkward, he just jumped right into it. "Well, glad that's over. Who's ready for pie?"

That night on the way home in the truck, Maggie was back to her normal self. She hadn't even thought about *that woman* in over half an hour. "So it went well with Gran today?"

She smiled and ticked her finger back and forth. "Uh, uh, uh." I laughed. "How did everything go with you?" But even as she asked, I felt her poking around for the answers, and I let her instead of saying anything.

She saw Dad and me driving to Kyle's, him fidgeting and freaking out about me taking over, me freaking out and fidgeting because I was taking over, everyone smiling and being weirdly nice to me…because I was taking over.

Every time someone patted me on the back or gave me that *you can do this* look, I felt this odd swell in my chest. Everyone believed in me so much. No one was worried that I was going to screw anything up but me.

So I stood before my family and started the meeting the way every meeting was started, by placing the object on the table before me and calling the meeting to order. *The object* was what my father had given me at the Reunification in London when he'd been forced to step down. The object was something the Champion of each clan held and kept on him to prove at any time that he was aware, ready, and willing to be and do anything necessary to protect his people. Keeping the object on you and calling the meeting to order with it was to serve as a reminder to the Champion of his promise to do all of those things.

The object for our clan was an old cog wheel.

Even as she watched it all in my mind, I reached into the pocket of my jeans and rubbed the coarse metal with my fingers. She watched as I took note of all the happenings of the family. All the things they wanted to talk about and discuss. She watched me as I leaned back in my seat and took their ribbing good-naturedly about being the man of my house now, about being the big man on Jacobson campus as soon as I started work at the firm with the rest of the family…the wedding night.

Dad stopped that as soon as it started, but they still got in a few jokes about it before that. I just laughed it off.

Then we got down to business about Marcus and the search.

I gripped Maggie's fingers and squeezed them gently. Then I told her what we'd concluded. "We're going to look for him. Go a couple of us at a time and search for him everywhere we can think of. Dad has already searched the compound and the houses and he's not there. Neither are the rest of them. We have no idea where they are, but I won't stop until we find him."

"I believe you." She gulped and downcast her eyes. "I just hope it's not too late."

"It won't be," I assured her. "I believe in you completely."

"But I've had no luck coming up with a solution to the vision. I know they needed to go ahead with the bonding or they would have gone mad, I know that, but what if we're just playing right into fate's hands about this? What if we can't stop it?"

I looked right before swerving through two lanes of traffic and pulling over in the emergency lane. I ignored the honking horns as I threw it in park and took her face in my hands. "If you believe in me, then believe in yourself, too. Because I'm going to work just as hard as you to make sure that that vision doesn't come true."

She nodded. "I want to just have faith that it'll all be OK. I want to so badly. I'm going to try."

"We're going to find Marcus and anyone else from the Watson clan who wants to come play, and then we're gonna kick their aces." I grinned, silently pleading with her to let me calm her. "See what I did there?"

She shook her head. "You are so cheesy."

"You like my cheese."

"I like you any way I can get you," she said sweetly, but her pleading eyes begged me to make it all OK.

I pulled her chin up slowly, pressing my lips to her lips once, and then moving to her chin, just once. "Don't spend another minute worrying about whether you're good enough or not," I whispered against her skin. She sighed and inhaled deeply. "You were born for this, for this task, for this life, for me."

She pulled back just enough to see me. Her eyes were more focused, like she truly wanted to believe it one hundred percent. "I was born for this," she repeated and nodded. "For you."

"Absolutely," I said, but it sounded sort of growly. The corner of her mouth rose, letting me know it was indeed growly and she loved it.

"Take me home, Jacobson."

I felt a rumble go through my chest.

I pulled back onto the highway and made lickety-split time back to the apartment. Kyle and Lynne were still there. We said our goodnights and went straight to bed. Even though neither one of us fell asleep right away, I enjoyed her fingers as they danced across my skin distractedly. She was thinking about what she needed to do, about how she could find the bastard who kept ruining her days. But no matter where her thoughts drifted, she always came back to one thing.

Me. Her. Bare feet. Red dress.

"I made coffee!" Lynne chimed as I came into the hall. I squinted at her.

"You are seriously chipper, Lynne."

"Yeah," she said and cocked her head to the side. "It's my thing."

"I guess it is," I agreed and chuckled as I took the cup she offered. "Where's Kyle?"

"Shower. Where's our Visionary?" she joked in a syrupy voice and smirked.

"Shower. Kyle better not be stealing all the hot water." I swigged the coffee she made and almost choked on it.

"What?" she barked. "I make great coffee!"

"It's just hot," I lied.

"Hey!" we heard Kyle down the hall. "Turn off the water! You're freezing my-"

"Maggie's in the shower," I cut him off. "You don't live here and she does. Be grateful that I let you use the shower at all."

"Wow," he complained. "What a little diva-boy you're turning out to be." He slammed the door and Lynne gave me the stink-eye for messing with her significant as she grabbed the cream cheese from the fridge.

"Bagel?" she asked and placed one on a plate before sliding it across the counter to me.

"Thanks. Did y'all go grocery shopping?"

She licked her finger clean of cream cheese. "Just got a couple of things."

"We're getting married this weekend," I said pointedly. "You can stay 'til then, but after that-"

"What about the house you bought for Maggie. Won't you be going there?"

"It's complicated."

She stopped and stared. "But Kyle told me it's a big deal. It's like," she waved her fingers dramatically, "the only way you can marry her. You did buy a house for her, right?"

I stayed silent. When I finally swung my gaze over to her, she was slack jawed. "Oh, stop, Lynne. I have it all under control."

She forgot my problems just like that and sighed. "I can't wait to see where we're going to live. Kyle's been keeping it secret, of course, but he said it had a pink breakfast nook just for me."

"A pink breakfast nook," I said dryly. "Really?"

She scoffed. "Pink is the color of rebellion."

I laughed. "OK, Lynne. OK."

"You told him about the breakfast nook?" Kyle said as he pulled his shirt over his head and kissed her cheek. "You can't tell him these things." He leaned on the counter beside her and bit into her bagel before speaking with his mouth full. "He's married to the leader of our race and we're not supposed to tell you anything about the house before the wedding."

"Oh, please. He's not going to tell anyone. Besides," she said and I saw the evil twinkle in her eye, "he's got his own secrets. Don't you, Caleb?"

"Shh," I said as I heard Maggie's thoughts saying she was almost dressed. "I told you, I've got it under control."

Maggie came out and I smiled at her. She was wearing a baby blue tank top with that necklace her dad gave her, the one with the jumble of charms on the end. And those jeans again, the ones that made it impossible to not stare at.

Yeah. Those.

She walked to me easily and kissed me on my dimple before wiggling herself in between the counter and me. "What's up?" she asked us.

Seven times two plus fourteen minus three times five is one twenty five.

The square root of one eighty four is thirteen point five six.

She looked at me over her shoulder. "Why are you doing math?"

"No reason." Eighty nine divided by six is fourteen point eight three.

"What are y'all talking about out here?" she asked, but secretly she knew.

"Nothing," Lynne said and quickly grabbed a cup. She poured the liquid first and then asked, "Coffee?" She shoved it into Maggie's hand.

"Um, sure." She sipped it and I cringed at tasting it through Maggie. I had to taste that horrible mess twice. "Ugh," she complained before she could stop it. "I mean…mmmm."

Lynne sulked while we laughed. "Aw," Kyle said and pulled her to him. "I hate coffee anyway so you never have to worry about that with me."

My phone buzzed with a text. I pulled it out while Kyle and Lynne's sickening banter went back and forth. It was from Dad.

Your mom said to bring Maggie to Gran for a dress fitting. You can come help me at the office while she's doing that.

I sighed. It was time to tell him that I had no intentions of being an architect. I wanted to wait until after the wedding, but I wasn't sure I could anymore. I relayed the message to Maggie and she turned to Lynne and told her that she wanted her and Kyle to share our day, so she needed to go to Gran's with her. Kyle's eyes bulged at the idea, but oblivious Lynne squealed and hugged her emphatically.

Kyle asked me if I was sure I was OK with sharing the day with them. "Of course," I said. "No better way to make a statement that things really are going to change."

"I guess."

"Unless you don't want to," I told him.

"Are you kidding?" He threw his arm around my shoulder. "Dude…" he smiled and shook his head, "we've only been talking about this since we were twelve."

"Yeah," I smiled. "When you had a crush on that chick from the Constantine clan."

He pushed me and retreated while he laughed. "You did not just bring that up!"

"Oh, yes I did." I made a girly face and fluttered my eyelashes. "Kyle, oh, please show me your muscles again!"

"You are so dead if you don't shut it, dude," he laughed his words.

I ran to the other side of the counter where Maggie was to get away from him. "Oh, Kyle!" He charged, but I dodged as Maggie giggled in between us. "I love your hair. It's so cute. Take me the roof, Kyle!"

He reached around her to me and I felt how his strength had increased since his ascension, but so had mine. I yanked him around and pushed his back to the wall. He punched my gut just enough to make me "oomph" and then wrapped his arms around my stomach to tackle me.

The girls giggled at us as we wrestled in my kitchen. It had been too long. He actually felt like my cousin again.

Later, I dropped Maggie and Lynne off at Kyle's to see Gran, and he and I went in to Dad and Uncle Max's office to 'work' for the day. Kyle was ecstatic, I was not. I sighed as we climbed the stairs and waved to Rick, the building guard, waved to my aunt Sue who worked as one of the office secretaries, then the rest of our family who worked there. Dad and Uncle Max were working on something when I knocked. He looked up and smiled in elation. Man, I hated to ruin that.

I sighed. Here we go.

Eleven

Maggie

I HAD to give it to her. Even with Gran's older hands and shaky disposition, she only managed to stick me with her pins three times. It was hilarious how Caleb checked on me the first time, and by the third, he was grumbling about Gran taking it easy.

Then he called and asked if Bish could come and take Lynne and me to the apartment since his dad had swamped him and Kyle both with paperwork. So that's what we did. I also got Bish to take me by Dad's to pick up some of my stuff. Dad and Fiona were gone and I was happy about that. Dad would be all depressed at seeing my stuff leave the house.

I decided since I had a little time without Caleb that I'd see about making dinner. So, I called Rachel and got a recipe and instructions for something easy, and made Bish stop by the store for me to get everything that I needed. Lynne told me she wanted her and Kyle to go out and do something. I just wanted to have a night in with Caleb.

Bish dropped us off and he and Jen went to Peter's. I left my huge bag of clothes on the chair in Caleb's room, because I had no idea what to do with them, and went to take a shower. Though wearing Caleb's clothes made me feel like I was being hugged by fabric, I wanted my cute clothes back.

As soon as we heard the key in the knob, Lynne was gone to meet Kyle and I waited at the stove while I stirred.

Caleb came up behind me. "You cooked supper?" he asked and sniffed the air over my shoulder from behind. "Smells good."

"It's your mom's Shepherd's Pie," I explained and turned to him. "She gave me the recipe and a few pointers."

"I'm sure it's awesome," he murmured and kissed my neck before making his way to my lips. "Did you get anything else done today?" He grinned. "Wedding wise?"

"Gran finished fitting me for my dress," I said and sighed. "It's so unbelievably beautiful."

"I can't wait to see it on you," he replied in a husky tone. "For now, I'll settle with fruit shorts." He squeezed my hips in his hands. "Bananas tonight, huh?"

"Yeah," I breathed as he inched closer. "I heard they were your favorite."

"To be absolutely honest, Maggie," he stopped when there was no more space between us, just cotton and denim separated all of him from all of me, "they are my favorite."

And then supper was forgotten.

His tongue found mine and commanded it as he lifted me and carried me right to his bed. When he pressed my hands to the comforter above my head without even taking off his shoes yet, I sighed at getting what I wanted. I wondered if mutualizing felt the same for everyone. For me, it was like I was drowning and had suddenly breached the surface. My body sang all over and goose bumps crawled over my skin as I let him into my mind to consume me from the inside out. He kept his lips on mine as we let ourselves be taken over. The energy ribbons, ever present and ever ready, moved around us. It seemed strange to have them in this new place, the glow from them illuminating his stuff in ways I'd never seen.

When they died away, along with the intensity, he rolled and pulled me to lay on his chest. My whole body rose up and down as he tried to catch his breath. He combed my hair with his fingers. "Well, your plan worked." He chuckled. "Being all domestic and then wearing those shorts. Daggum banana shorts…" He chuckled again.

"You caught me." We grinned at each other. "So, how was your day with your dad?" I gave him a pointed look. "Everything work out?"

"I didn't tell him. I want to tell him and Mom together, and she was running errands all day. We'll go over there tomorrow. I need to help Dad interview the new security guy anyway." He gulped and I felt for him. Poor Randolph. "Don't worry. It'll be OK." I nodded. "So, it really did go well with Gran? She didn't push you into something you don't like, did she? I know how she is."

"She was great." I lifted my head to look down at him. "That woman can work a needle and thread."

He smiled. "She used to make me gloves when I was a kid. I was always too embarrassed to wear them though."

I scoffed. "She made them with her bare hands and you wouldn't wear them?"

"They had Frosty the Snowman on them, babe. Frosty the freaking Snowman."

I tried not to laugh. "Didn't you like Frosty the Snowman when you were little?"

"Not when I was fourteen." I did laugh then. He smiled waiting for me. "She makes stuff for everyone. That's her thing."

"I wonder what my thing will be," I mused and chewed my lip while playing with the button of his shirt. "I haven't even thought about what my major's going to be yet."

"They don't offer classes in *Gorgeous Leader of Her Race*. Sorry. You're stuck with something crappy, like Biology or Business Economics."

I giggled and climbed up his chest to kiss his dimple. "You want to eat the perfectly good dinner I cooked now? Maybe watch a movie with me?"

"You read my mind." He sat up with me and took my face in his warm hands. "Thank you." Then he kissed my lips. "If I can come home to this every day, I'll be the happiest man alive."

I smiled and led him to the kitchen. We ate and watched bad reality TV. We made fun of the people and laughed. The last thing I remembered was being carried to bed, Caleb's scruffy chin rubbing my cheek, before being surrounded with his usual warmth and falling back asleep peacefully.

"Dad! We're here!" Caleb yelled as he opened the door. "Bella!" She came bounding around the corner before plowing into him. He knelt down and crooned to her. "Oh, my goodness. Look at my girl. You're so big."

I just watched with amused fascination. "Does your apartment complex not let you have dogs?"

"They will, but I just usually leave her here because I'm always at school." He straightened. "And then *someone* had to take up all of my time this summer, so…" He grinned and pulled me to him. "But…maybe soon she'll be able to come with us."

He was giving me house hints. I stared up into his blue eyes, but he left it at that. I nodded, letting him know that I definitely wanted Bella to be with us. I scratched under her chin before following Caleb.

"All right," he said and stopped me. "Let me show you the trick with the hallways." He pointed to the floor in the corner. "See the tiles?" I nodded. They were all mixed up and different colors of greens and browns that seemed to have no pattern. "Ok, see the corner, the tile is cream over there? And in that corner, the corner tile is green? The cream tiles take you to the west side of the house, for my room and the living room. The browns take you to the back end of the house, like the kitchen and dining room. The green tiles take you in circles."

I was skeptical. It didn't look that complicated. It didn't look like it was a trick except for the fact that the halls were winding and seemed to be everywhere. It looked confusing, but that seemed pretty elaborate. So he took me on a tour of the green corner-tiled hallways and to my surprise, we wound up right where we started. "But I didn't even realize we were coming back around. That's so weird."

"Yep. Dad's a genius."

"Why yes, yes I am," Peter joked. We turned to find him laughing at us. "Thanks for noticing."

"Hey, Dad."

"Hey, son." He beamed at me. "Are you going to just stand there or give your father-in-law a hug?"

I laughed. "I like the sound of that."

"I like it, too, sweetheart." He pulled back, but kept his arm around my shoulder as he made his way down the cream corner-tiled halls. Caleb trailed behind us with Bella at his side. "So, what is it you've come to tell us?"

"Um..." I peeked at Caleb as we landed in the den. He looked curiously at his dad.

"I could tell something was wrong yesterday, Caleb. I assumed it was something Maggie wanted to discuss with us, about her human friends, perhaps." It was his turn to look confused. "I guess not by the looks on your faces."

"Where's Mom, Dad?" Caleb asked gently and took my hand to sit on the couch with him.

I heard Peter call to her in his mind and she told him she'd be there in just a minute. "She's coming. Is everything all right?"

"Everything's fine. We just want to talk to you about something."

Peter nodded and looked pensive. There was a crystal bowl on the end table. Peter swung his fingers back a forth a little, causing the bowl to slide back and forth with his ability, following his finger's movements across the table as he tried to figure out what we were about to tell them. Rachel entered and, after hugs and glasses of tea, Caleb got down to the matter. He explained it all, about what he wanted to do, about how he wanted to expand the tutoring centers and he wasn't interested in joining the architecture firm. Peter listened while Rachel looked warily between the two of them. Peter's silence was weird. It was almost as if he wasn't thinking at all and his thoughts were just on pause, unable to process.

He finally started to, and I heard his answer before he said them. "Caleb, you know I've always admired your initiative. Starting your own company like that all by yourself was brilliant." Heavy pause. "But I always assumed it would be a temporary thing. I always assumed and wanted you to come work with me at the firm. To find out that you don't want that is pretty surprising, son. This is the first I've heard of it."

"I know," Caleb answered. "To be honest, if Maggie hadn't come along I would probably have gone to work with you at the firm." He rushed on. "Not that it's her idea or her fault that I'm not, it's just that she gave me the courage to do what I want to do. I'm not all by myself in my decision making anymore and she has faith in me that I can do it."

"So do I." Peter cleared his throat. "I have faith that you can do it. That was never in question. It's just that…working at the firm is tradition, and an honor to carry on the legacy our family built. I just…thought you'd *want* to be a part of that."

"It's not that I don't want to work with you, Dad. It's just that I want to do this more."

Peter thought. Rachel and I stayed quiet. This was something the boys had to work out. Eventually, he spoke quietly. "You're a man, Caleb, and I can't tell you what to do. I'd be lying if I said I was thrilled about it, but I'll stand behind you like I always do. You've never let me down before. If this is what you want, then I think it's what you should do."

Caleb sighed, a weight lifted and a burden released. "Thanks, Dad."

"No matter what I said, you were still going to move ahead with your plan," Peter mused and opened his arm for Rachel to come into. She scooted over and they looked at each other for a few seconds before he looked back at Caleb. "Am I right?"

Caleb smiled wryly. "Yes, sir."

Peter nodded and smiled. "I figured. You've always been a little bit rebellious. That star on your shoulder." He gave him a pointed 'fatherly' look. "Joining the swim team instead of going out for football, leaving during Kyle's graduation party when everyone was waiting for you." He sighed and laughed soundlessly. "I guess…it all worked out for you."

"Yes, sir," Caleb whispered and pulled me to kiss my temple. "It did."

And I love that star tattoo.

He grinned down at me. "I know."

Something hit me then as I stared up at the grin I never wanted to be away from. We only had two days left until the wedding.

Two. Days.

And I hadn't even written my vows out for him yet. I hadn't even had time to *think* about them, let alone put pen to paper. He kept smiling as he let me have my mini freak-out.

I turned to Rachel. "Thanks for the recipe. I actually cooked something edible for once."

She giggled a little. "You're so welcome. You can come over later on and I'll teach you a few things if you'd like. My mother was an excellent cook. And Jen tries, but she's always pretty preoccupied with work and Maria."

"That sounds great."

Peter smiled at me and asked, "Have you thought any about what you're going to do for school and such?"

Caleb leaned back further, laying his ankle over his knee as he settled back into the couch with me pressed to his ribs. "I told you this, Dad. She's coming to school with me this semester."

"And that's what you want to do?" Peter asked me. "You want to go to U of T?"

"I do. I didn't think that I was going to be able to go to college, so for you to work that out for me...thank you. I'm very grateful."

"Not a problem. It was my pleasure to do it. But since Caleb was reluctant to tell me that he didn't want to work with me, I was just checking to make sure that this is what you wanted."

"It is. Thank you," I said sincerely. "I can't wait."

Jen and Bish came around the hall corner. "Can't wait for what?"

"College," Peter answered for me. "Our Maggie is starting the end of next month."

I smiled. Our Maggie. Bish grinned at me, too, and shook his head. "It ain't all it's cracked up to be, kid."

"Don't rain on my parade!" I playfully scolded as Jen sat on the couch and he leaned on the back with his arms. "What are you guys up to?"

They looked at each other and then back to me. "Well..." she started.

Bish continued, "We went apartment hunting."

I felt Caleb stiffen next to me, and then the math started again. What in the world was wrong with him lately? I gave him a questioning look.

Everything's fine, gorgeous. Just stay out of my head.

He smirked on top of his command. Gosh, it was so cute. I turned back to Bish to try to figure out why Caleb would care that they were apartment hunting as Bish continued. "So, we think we found a place. Just a matter of…nailing down the details."

And coming up with freaking two thousand dollars in deposits.

Jen's head moved up to look at him as Peter and Rachel talked about their first house together. *Sweetie, it's fine. We'll-*

No, it's not fine. If nothing else, since I can't buy you the house that I'm supposed to, I'm going to come up with the deposit on my own.

She sighed. *If that's what you want.*

It's what I need. *Jenna, I've got to be able to take care of you if for nothing else, my own peace of mind. My chest…aches knowing that I can't give you what I'm supposed to.*

She gulped. *I'm sorry. I never wanted you to feel-*

He touched her cheek gently and shook his head. *It's not something you should apologize for. I wouldn't change anything that happened. I just…let me take care of this, OK? Then my chest will give me a break.*

She tried to smile. *OK.*

OK. He kissed her once, softly. He leaned back up just as Peter was finishing and no one but Caleb and I were the wiser.

"So," Peter clapped his hands. "Who's hungry? Let's all go to Mugly's. My treat."

"Yes," Caleb hissed under his breath. "Let's."

We all got up and piled into Caleb's truck. I sat in a Jacobson man-sandwich of him and Peter. Caleb snorted at my thought and shook his head at me. With Caleb's hand stuck between my thighs and Mutemath on the radio for his mom, we rode the short distance to town and parked in the lot.

He helped me down from the massive cab and I looked around. You could see the benches and the lake from there. I felt my lips lift in a smile as I remembered our first date. My first motorcycle ride. My first time eating at Mugly's. My first time with jealousy. The first time Caleb showed me a vision. I sighed. It felt forever ago. I felt Caleb's arms go around me from behind. He rested his chin on my shoulder. "The first time I fell in love with you," he added to my list.

I turned slightly, letting my cheek rub his. "Really?"

"Really. When you took off down the boardwalk and dared me to chase you? I was a goner."

I chuckled under my breath. "Well, I was on the track team."

"Which was why I couldn't catch you. But you came back to me, like a moth to a flame."

"Because you tricked me!" I said playfully.

"Admit it. You just couldn't stand to be away from me," he said huskily and nipped my chin. "Admit it."

"I will not."

"Hey!" Bish called from the restaurant door. "You two coming?"

"Coming!" I called. "You just got lucky. I was about to challenge you to a rematch."

He laughed. "*Please!* I may not be as fast as you, but my reflexes are like lightning."

I reached for the door handle and he jerked forward so quickly that I didn't even see him move, and took it from me. "Let me," he said and smirked as I laughed at him.

I let him lead me to the table where our family was sitting. We laughed and ate, and let Bish try all the Bar-b-que dishes. And try he did. The guy could win an eating contest easily. Then I heard a sound I never thought I'd hear ever again. And for good reason. It was like nails on a chalkboard.

Ashley.

"Caleb," she purred. "Hi."

Caleb and I weren't facing her so we all turned to look at her. She soaked up the sudden attention, poking her chest out just a smidge and tilting her head. I swallowed to keep from saying anything.

"Ashley," he said and everyone but her could tell that he wasn't happy to see her. She smiled and put her hand on his shoulder. I saw Peter's eyes bug at that. He glanced to me and then back to Caleb. He must've thought I was going to take her head off. And when I looked back at her and saw her lean in a bit, I realized I was about to. I went to stand, but felt Jen's hand on my arm.

Just wait.

I looked at Caleb, waiting. Last time he'd sent her packing, but only after she insulted me. Would he really just let her touch him like that in front of his-

He pushed her hand off and stood, glaring at her. "Go home, Ashley."

She scoffed. "I'm here with my family."

"Then go back to them." When she just stood there as if she were waiting for the punch line, he went on. "You can see Maggie right here. You know we're together. I've told you more than once that there is no chance for you and me. Absolutely none. Maggie and I are getting married this weekend."

"You're marrying her?" she screeched. She thought and then smiled. "Oh, my gosh. Look, Caleb, when you knock a girl up these days, you don't have to marry her anymore."

I heard Rachel and Peter's gasps. I could take it no more. My body was about to explode with the need to hurt this girl. I took a deep breath when the lights flickered a little. I saw her look at me with disdain before looking back to Caleb. He shook his head and waited a beat. He was trying to calm himself. She was a girl after all. "Ashley, Maggie's not pregnant. I'm just in love with her."

She wrinkled her nose like something stunk.

Caleb forged on. "I love her with all that's in me, so stop being childish and move on already."

"Fine!" she pouted. "Marry preschool, I don't care. I'm so over you. You can just forget all about me because we are so through!"

"We're not through." He waited a dramatic beat as she stared. "We never started."

She marched off with a flip of her Barbie blonde hair. He turned and immediately started to apologize. I put my thumb over his lips. "Don't," I whispered. I closed my eyes and took a deep breath. When I opened them, I saw her pouting across the restaurant with her family. The significant in me said, *Go ahead. Just rip one handful of her hair out. You'll feel better,* but I took another breath to calm myself. "Just don't. It's fine."

He was all mine after all.

He touched my neck, letting his knuckles rub over the Visionary mark. I moaned a little as his calm finally hit me. His lips held the smallest of smirks at my reaction to him. "Don't be so smug, Jacobson."

"What?" He leaned forward a bit. "I told you how hot it is when you're jealous. And then those noises you make when I touch you…" he whispered the last part into my cheek. "God, help me."

I let a little half annoyed, half amused sigh escape. "Oh, boy. So this is what I have a lifetime to look forward to?"

"You bet your pretty tush. And so much more."

I finally let my grin take over. "Good."

He kissed me quickly and then sat back, popping a corn nugget in his mouth. I sat back, too, and could feel eyes on me. I peeked over at Rachel. She was giving me the weirdest look. She pointed to her ear, meaning for me to listen.

I can't believe you didn't cold-cock that girl.

I jerked at her remark. She continued.

There was this woman who used to work in Peter's first office and she was so in lust with him. I saw Peter smile and shake his head, but she kept going, leaning forward to look at me from across his chest. *It seemed like every time I went to bring him lunch or drop by for...a visit, she was there. Touching his arm, leaning on his desk, calling his office when I was in there with some emergency. Ugh. Anyway, the very first time I got her alone in the elevator I cornered that hussy and told her she had better keep her paws off. That I was watching her and that hunk of a man was taken.* I covered my mouth to keep from bursting out laughing. *So I admire your restraint. Significants usually don't have much when it comes to our mates. I would have given Bimbo a black eye at the very least.* Then she winked. Winked!

I nodded and smiled. "Thanks."

She reached across the table over Peter and grabbed my hand. "Anytime, honey."

It was such a mother-thing to say. I smiled again and returned to my food. I felt strangely like crying as I took a bite of garlic bread. The taste was something not of this world. It danced on my tongue. I looked at the waitresses in their cute boots and skirts and wondered how they kept their figures working there. I would have problems with the garlic bread.

After we drove back to Peter's, we parted, going our separate ways. Bish pulled me aside and asked about the wedding. Jen had told him I wanted to share the day and he wondered why. I said it just made sense for us all to be together. All three of the members of my family had imprinted. That was miraculous in itself. What better way to feel good about all three of us being split up than to be present for each other and watch as we devoted ourselves completely to the one we loved? It made complete sense in my mind.

"I know, I'm not saying I don't want to, it's just…with you rushing the wedding, it's not giving me much time to come up with everything that I need to."

"For your apartment," I guessed and understood.

"Yeah," he sighed.

"I'm sorry. Look, Bish, I know this is hard for you, but honestly, this family is just happy to have you in it. The way they know you're going to make Jen happy is worth it. And don't ask me how I know." I smirked. "I can read minds, remember?"

"I know," he said, not taking my bait. "I just always feel like I'm a step behind somehow. And with school…I mean I took art classes. What the heck am I going to do in Tennessee with Art classes?"

"I think I can help you there," Peter interrupted with hands raised. "I'm sorry. Didn't mean to pry, I just overheard you as I was walking inside. Listen, Bish, we have lots of uses for an Art major at the firm. An architecture firm," he said meaningfully. "We pride ourselves in bold designs and things others haven't come up with yet. I think you'd make a great addition if you're interested. And Jen already works there, of course. So it wouldn't be hard on you the first couple years to be apart."

Bish looked at Peter's shoes. "No offense, sir, but you're only offering me this job because I'm about to be your son-in-law."

"You're daggum right I am," Peter said and laughed. It reminded me of Caleb and I couldn't help but smile. "But I'm also offering you this job because you're my daughter's significant. Not only will it make it easier on you and her, but we like to keep this a family affair. Almost all of my family works in the business in some form or fashion. So I'm not being biased by offering you the job, technically, I'd be biased by *not* offering you one."

His lips held the Jacobson smirk as he realized he'd just put Bish in a corner. He waited and I listened to Bish work it out in his mind and finally relented. "You'll never know how grateful I am to you, sir."

"Son," Peter said, putting a hand on his shoulder. His lips twitched with what I thought was a smile, but I realized it wasn't. Peter was fighting tears. "My daughter has been through more than any woman ever should. Our women are precious to us, the center of our universes. For me to think that after all that she wasn't even going to bond with anyone, that she wasn't going to know what it felt like to literally feel someone's heart in your chest…it tortured me as a father. But then you…come along," he growled. I bit my lip as I watched him fight his emotion. "And you make her happier than she's ever been save the day Maria was born, and you really have to wonder why I'd want you around?" He laughed a little. "In my eyes, you are my son now, and I want nothing more than to be your family. My daughter finally has someone to look at her the way I look at Ray and you'll never know how grateful I am to you…sir," he spouted Bish's words back at him and chuckled with emotion. Then he pulled him into a manly hug.

Bish patted his back and mumbled his own emotional thank you before letting go. I heard Jen's thoughts before Bish did. She was waiting at the door and wondering what was going on. Bish looked over at her and smiled. Then he nodded to Peter, hugged me hard, and then made his way to her. He picked her up off the ground in a bear hug and carried her inside that way, giggling.

"Thanks," I said to Peter, because Bish had been through a lot, too, and the poor guy needed a few breaks.

"My pleasure, and I meant every word." He pulled me to him and kissed my forehead. "I think your chariot awaits."

I looked confused at him until he nodded to the garage. Caleb was sitting on the bike, my helmet under his arm. I squealed, actually squealed, and ran to him. I heard Peter laughing behind me, but I didn't care.

Caleb got off just as I reached him and slipped the helmet on my head for me. "I take it you missed Lolita."

I laughed. "Shut up and drive, Jacobson."

"Yes, ma'am," I heard his laughed words through the mic before we climbed on and he eased us down the driveway. As soon as he reached the end of his road, I waited, knowing what was next.

"Hang on, gorgeous."

I giggled and gripped him tightly as he sped away laughing. We leaned forward on the bike a little as he zoomed and gripped the road tightly with each turn. It didn't matter that my heartbeat sped, it didn't matter how fast we were going.

I was with Caleb. And there was no safer place on the planet.

Twelve

Caleb

I RAN across the beach…it was so hot and humid though it was nighttime…she ran faster than me, daggum Track team…I tried to catch her…Bish and Jen were huddled, oblivious…Maggie reached then just in time…to stop the bullet…blood was everywhere…my Maggie…I tried to save her, but couldn't…she was drifting…drifting…she looked in my eyes and silently told me it was all right…it wasn't…

I felt her hand on my cheek and jolted awake in bed. I was sweating and Maggie attempted to help me calm my breaths by pressing her lips to my neck. She didn't kiss me, just pressed them there.

My Maggie…

I jerked her as easily as I could into my lap. I wrapped my arms around her small frame and held every piece of her against me. I breathed in the smell of her hair to reassure myself she was there. She was and she was just as shaken as I was. My brain switched gears then and I instead leaned back and cupped her cheek, letting my fingers caress her lightly. "I'm sorry," I told her, but I had no idea what I was apologizing for.

"It was a nightmare, Caleb," she lied badly.

"It wasn't, and you know it, sweetheart." I sighed. "I think I must've borrowed your ability in my sleep. That was almost the same vision you had, but this one…" I choked and swallowed, "was so, so, so much worse."

I pulled her to me, letting our foreheads rest together. Now it wasn't just about Bish and Jen anymore. It was about Maggie. We had to figure out a way to stop the vision.

"We will," she assured me. "I'm not going to stop until I do. After the wedding, it's my mission. Along with finding Marcus." It was her turn to sigh. "Both seem kinda impossible," she mumbled in defeat.

"I won't stop either. None of us will."

"Let's just…go back to bed. We both have a long day tomorrow."

"I'm not sure I can," I said truthfully. I had just watched my significant die.

She watched me, and then said. "Let's go somewhere."

I looked at the clock. 3:34 a.m. "We've got lots to do tomorrow, baby," I reminded her. Our last day as single folk.

"Tomorrow will still be there. Right now, come with me."

I nodded. Anything she wanted, it was hers.

We got dressed and she grabbed her cell and my iPod from the dresser. We took the bike again and she told me to drive to her town. So I did. When we got closer, I heard where she wanted to go and smiled a little as I took the necessary streets to get there. I parked the bike on the side of the road, took Maggie's hand as we crossed the abandoned street, and we stood there under the crosswalk sign.

The place that started it all.

She pulled the hoodie of my jacket that she was wearing up and towed me by my arm down to sit on the sidewalk with her, our feet and legs touching as they outstretched into the street. She took my iPod out and gave me one of the buds, put her head on her shoulder, and played *Right Before My Eyes* by Cage The Elephant as she tapped her foot. The song I was listening to when she saved my life.

We leaned our heads together and listened as he crooned his words to a nameless girl. *Right before my eyes I saw the whole world lose control.*

God, I was so thankful that I wasn't paying attention that day.

We sat there, believe it or not, until daybreak. I turned to her and let my fingers sweep across her cheek. "It's tomorrow. Only one more day. I can't wait to have you in my space," I told her. "To hear you in the shower, or walk in on you changing clothes." She laughed a little. "Or smell your perfume in every room. Or hear you humming while you make coffee."

"Don't worry," she said softly and kissed my palm. "I'm not going anywhere."

When the sun peeked over the houses, she sat up straight and smiled. "Ready to go?"

"I'll go wherever you want me to, gorgeous."

"Then let's go see Dad, get all this last-day stuff out of the way, and then let's go home. We can tuck in early. Get ready for our big day tomorrow."

"Nothing sounds better."

"You're very agreeable today, Jacobson," she joked.

"I want your last day as a single lady to be a good one."

She laughed and wrinkled her nose cutely. "You don't have to put a ring on it," she said. "A house will do just fine."

"You got it."

"Come on. Let's go wake up Dad and Fiona with some breakfast."

I quirked a brow at her, knowing exactly what she had in mind. "Are you seriously going to make me face Big John the day before our wedding?"

"I've got to keep you honest, don't I?" she said laughing and tugged me to the bike.

We pushed our way through the revolving door of the 25 Hour Skillet and the smell and music brought me back to the very first time I'd been in there. I looked around for John and his meat cleaver. They were nowhere to be seen. I sighed in relief just as I felt a strong, large, overly warm hand on my shoulder.

"Bike boy."

"Hello, sir." I swallowed and turned, looking up to his steely eyes. I could appreciate his protectiveness of my girl. I understood it more than anyone, but...dude was bigger than any man I personally knew.

"BJ!" Maggie said excitedly and let the man lift her feet off the floor. I searched for weapons on the man, but found none. "You look like you've lost weight."

"I have, but don't tell anymore," he said gruffly and cleared his throat as he set her on the floor. "Smarty's been on me about my health."

"Well..." she said carefully. "You have owned the place for a while and all this fried food can't be good for anybody."

"Oh, not you, too," he complained.

"I'd miss you if you weren't here anymore."

He sighed and then perked up. "Speaking of not here anymore," he said and shot me a little glare before turning his glare on her. "Where have you been?"

She thought, her mind running through the scenarios she could give him that he'd believe. "Just...trying to get my life together. You know, college, housing, making sure Dad's taken care of...getting engaged."

He stopped all movement and I sighed, knowing what was coming. "Where's your ring if you're getting engaged?"

"Well," Maggie started, "I don't have one yet."

He turned a deep crimson before yelling over his shoulder. "Smarty! Get my meat dicer!" Every customer is the joint turned to stare at us, the ones causing the commotion.

Maggie tried damage control. "Big John, it's fine. I didn't want one. Caleb's family is very...traditional. He has other things planned for me instead of a ring."

"Like what?" he boomed and got closer to look down at me. "What kind of dolt doesn't get his girl a ring?"

"The kind that buys her a house instead," I said quietly. He looked confused. "It's a family tradition. Besides, the only jewelry Maggie really wears is that bracelet you gave her. She's not really the big ring type, as I'm sure you know."

He pursed his lips. "Course I know that! It's just weird, that's all."

"And Dad got engaged, too," Maggie intervened.

Big John stopped and looked at her, his face softening. "He did?" She nodded. Smarty came from a back table and eyed the situation carefully.

When she saw his face, she put her arm around him and he pulled her into his side. "Well that's something else, Sweat Pea."

"It is," Maggie agreed. She scooted closer to me to move out of a customer's way and stayed close. She gripped my hand and I welcomed it. "Fiona. She's really sweet."

"That was kind of fast, wasn't it? For both of you."

"When you know, you know, right?"

He tried to stay mad. He scowled, but it quickly melted away with Smarty rubbing her hand over his large stomach. "Yeah," he agreed. "Yeah."

They took our order and Big John went back to pretending I didn't exist. That was OK. I knew he thought that I had taken her away, and I pretty much had. If I were in his shoes, I probably wouldn't have liked me either.

When we left, they all blubbered and kissed and fawned all over her. I couldn't help but smile at the display. She promised to come back and visit. Her dad still lived here after all. Smarty smiled and patted my back, saying her congratulations. Mena said I better take care of Maggie and then winked at me as we left.

Maggie wasn't regretful though as we decided to leave the bike and walk the few blocks to her dad's house. That gave me some comfort about being the bad guy in the scenario.

Almost as soon as we knocked, Fiona answered. She was wearing a bright purple robe and her hair was in a messy bun on the top of her head. She gawked as Maggie said good morning and pushed her aside. "We brought breakfast."

"I see that." She shut the door and followed us into the kitchen.

"Honey, you didn't have to. I would have made breakfast if I'd known you were coming."

"It was spur of the moment," Maggie said as she pulled out the take-out pan of sausage. Her moments slowed and she stopped, biting her lip.

Oh...I don't live here anymore, do I? I guess I should have called or... something.

Fiona noticed Maggie's sudden mood change and went to her side. "Listen, I'm not telling you that you can't come over whenever you want-"

"No, it's fine." She started to pack up the sausage again, mumbling in her mind about being stupid for thinking things could be the same. "I shouldn't have just come over like this."

"Maggie, stop." She did, but didn't look at her. I did though. I was surprised that Fiona had said that. It hadn't taken her long to get over the Visionary thing. "Honey, I'm not saying you're stepping on my toes. Your father will always be your father, and this will always be your house. Me coming here doesn't change that. What I meant was that if I had known you were coming...I wouldn't be standing here in my purple silk robe with nothing on underneath and my hair a crow's nest!" She laughed and Maggie reluctantly joined in.

"I wasn't thinking about intruding. I just thought since we were here anyway we'd bring breakfast," Maggie tried to apologize again.

"It's all right." She smiled and turned to me with a wry smile. "I think I'll go get dressed now."

"OK," I said and tried not to look at her. She quickly scooted out of the room and Maggie turned to me to complain about her being an idiot when her dad came in. He was wearing jeans and a t-shirt, which was...

weird.

"Mags. Hey, baby girl," he crooned softly and happily. Fiona may not have been the happiest to see her, but her dad sure was. "Mmm, is that sausage and gravy?"

"And biscuits," Maggie supplied. "I'm sorry I barged in on Fiona."

"You didn't," he insisted and looked at her full on. "This was your house first and you can come anytime you like. Fiona understands that."

"But I wouldn't want someone to barge into Caleb's apartment in the morning," she said and sneaked a quick look at me. Her dad may have missed her blush, but I didn't. "Lynne and Kyle did that the other day and I hated it. I just wasn't thinking."

"No worries, baby." He turned to me then and I was surprised to see a smile there. He usually just seemed to tolerate me. "Hey, Caleb. How are you, son?"

Son?

I felt my scowl, but tried to hide it. "Good, sir. Maggie also got you coffee." I handed it to him and then took a sip of my own.

He sipped his, too, and made a noise of contentment. "Well, as soon as Fiona gets dressed, we'll eat and then-"

My phone went off with a buzz. "Sorry," I muttered and peeked at the screen. Vic. I smiled and answered as I excused myself into the den. "Vic, what's up?"

"What's up, brother!"

I laughed. "Not much, man."

"Not much? You registering for classes today or what?"

I almost slapped my forehead. "Ah, crap. I forgot that was today."

"And coach set try-outs for today, too."

I groaned. "You've got to be kidding me."

"Afraid not. So get your rich butt up to the school."

"All right. I'll be there in a couple of hours."

"Later."

"Later." I could've punched something. Maggie had to register for classes today, too.

I relayed the news and we ate quickly. Maggie changed into something other than my hoodie and when she came down from the stairs, I felt my grin take off. "Those jeans are nice, too."

"Thanks. Sorry I don't have any clothes for you to change into."

"Nah, I'm fine. It's just school."

"Just school..." she muttered. "Right."

"It's not a big deal," I soothed and we waved to Jim and Fiona in the kitchen as we left. "I'll be there to tell you what classes suck and what professors will rip your heart out for being late."

She giggled. "That does sound pretty good. My own personal tour guide who's already been through this."

"Yep."

We walked to the bike and made it to the school in record time. I parked in my usual spot on the side lot under the trees and helped Maggie de-bike. I smoothed her hair back and she let me with a smile.

I took her to freshman registration. She was a little shocked when she said her name and they had her packet all ready to go. She gave me a kind of wild look before taking it and thanking her. Then we went to my own registration. After we got our packets and everything turned in and filled out, ran through the ringer and got our student IDs, we made our way to gym.

As soon as we walked in, the catcalls began.

"Oh, so *that's* where Caleb's been all summer," Mark said.

"Shut it, Barker!" I said laughing and pointed to Vic across the pool. "There's Vic, babe. Why don't you go wait by him while I get changed so the uncaged animals don't eat you alive."

"Hardy, har," Mark yelled and dove in splashlessly.

"OK," she agreed. "And you're going to be wearing that when you come out?" She pointed to Vic's Speedos with the VOLS 'T' on the front.

I heard myself make a throaty noise. "It's the uniform, babe."

She grinned and walked backwards slowly. "I can't wait to see that." She then turned and looked at me over her shoulder. I groaned.

Holy hell, Maggie.

I heard her giggle in my mind before she greeted Vic. He recognized her immediately and hugged her to him before waving to me, telling me he had her.

I sprinted to the double doors leading to the locker room and hurried. Several people tried to talk to me, but they didn't understand. It was the day before my wedding. I couldn't tell them that, of course. They'd want to know why they weren't invited. They wouldn't understand. So I'd tell them later that Maggie and I had eloped, but until then, I just needed to get this practice over with and get everything that needed to be done, done.

I emerged from the locker room to find Maggie right where I left her, and Vic was charming the smile right out of her. I shook my head and somehow snuck up on her. She must've been listening pretty intently. I wrapped my arms around her and she didn't even jolt. She just sighed and leaned back further into me. I stopped that right then, pulling her under my arm.

She gave me a once over, and then repeated it. Her eyes held mine for a couple beats too long.

Stop that right now.

What? she said innocently.

You know what.

Your underwear are cute.

Speedos. Uniform. Required.

Call them whatever you want, Jacobson. They're hot.

Will you go bench yourself before I have to drag you outta here?

She giggled. Giggled at me.

Gorgeous, you're torturing me.

She rolled her eyes good-naturedly and made her way to the benches behind the pool. I took a deep breath and swung my arms to warm up. Vic flanked me and grinned like an idiot. I could hear every thought in his brain with Maggie's ability there to borrow. "Shut up," I muttered before he could say anything.

He laughed. "She's the cutest little thing I've ever seen. You're gonna be fighting the boys off with a stick. You gotta know this."

"I know this," I told him and felt a growl rise in my throat.

"Did you just growl?" he asked through his belly shaking laughter. "My man's got it bad!"

"I'm not the only one, am I?" I nodded my head to his girlfriend sitting in the stands. She was sitting next to Ashley. I didn't look that way again.

"Oh, Vic ain't whipped!" he said loudly and sniffed as he rolled his shoulders. "Vic ain't whipped."

"Who's whipped?" Mark asked.

I ignored him and went on. "Talking about yourself in the third person doesn't make it less true, Vic."

Mark laughed along with me while Vic mumbled, "Laugh it up, yuppies. Laugh it up."

Coach called the meet to a start and we got in starting position. I could hear Maggie silently cheering me on in her head. I smiled as I took my stance. She had never seen me swim before. I actually missed it. A lot. Swimming was something that came naturally for me. I was fast, clean, and efficient.

When the buzzer sounded, I leapt into the water. I felt calm though my arms and heart beat with exertion. I swam and pushed myself. I didn't look at the other swimmers. I didn't want or need that kind of motivation. I wanted to swim for me.

When I finally made it back to the platform, I didn't even look to see what order we had come in at. I just got out and grabbed a towel. She sat there on the bench, her lip between her teeth, contemplating if she was in the way of me being with my friends. I smiled and shook my head.

Come here, gorgeous.

She made her way down the bleachers carefully and stood in front of me. "You did awesome," she said kind of breathlessly.

"Did I?" I glanced back at the board. I came in second. Daggum Vic. He was egging me on, shooting me the rock-first. I turned my back on him and heard his laugh echo across the pool. "I guess."

"I had no idea you could swim that fast."

"I love it," I admitted.

"I know. But in your head it's just fun for you. You don't see yourself as being awesome at it. I had no idea that you…"

I gulped at the look of reverence on her face. "That I what?"

"That you were this amazing at everything," she whispered.

With my towel wrapped around my shoulders, she leaned in and kissed me, sucking on my bottom lip. I could taste the pool water through Maggie's mind.

"Holy. Mother." We turned to find Vic watching us curiously.

I cleared my throat and started to dry off. "So we've got to get going, Vic."

"You can't! You just got here," he complained and threw his towel at a freshman who muttered a 'Hey', but went no further. "Dude, you can't leave!"

"We've got to. Sorry. So much stuff to do."

He scoffed and turned to Maggie. "When can we see your pretty face around here again?"

"Day one, I'll be here."

"Awesome. Later, dude." He bumped my fist as I waved to the rest of the team and snuck Maggie into the locker room. Big no-no. The things I did for this girl.

She sat on the bench in front of my locker and I jumped into the quickest shower I'd ever taken. I heard Maggie's thoughts as she checked her phone once more. She'd texted Beck four times already today and this was the third text she'd gotten from Chad.

Chad…

Apparently he heard about the wedding from her dad when he stopped by his house today and was hell bent on seeing her tonight to talk sense into her. I threw my clothes back on and came around the corner to find her guilty face resting her chin on her knees drawn up to her chest.

"How can I make him see that I'm fine and this isn't a mistake?" she asked.

"Why do you have to justify anything to him?" I said softly and squatted in front of her, pulling her legs down.

"Because he was my friend my whole life and this isn't just about getting me back. He really thinks you've tricked me or something. He's really worried, I can tell."

I sighed. It wasn't that I didn't trust her. It wasn't that I was jealous. It was just the fact that I knew he was going to be looking at her like he wanted to take her away and my body was going to want to pummel him for it. "Tell him we'll meet him at your dad's."

"Really?" she asked and smiled small.

"Yeah." I leaned up and kissed her forehead. "Whatever keeps my girl happy."

"I just don't want him to worry." She stood and looked up at me. That reverence was there again. "I want him to know that I'm fine. That I'm safe and happy with you."

"OK. You've still got lots to do though. I have a couple of pre-wedding things that I have to do, too."

She nodded. "I need to get something from Dad's anyway. I'll meet him there, be quick, get what I need, and then be all ready to go."

"Sounds good."

So we drove to her father's house once more. This time to let Maggie and her ex have a pow-wow about the wedding...the wedding that no one was supposed to know about until afterward. I sighed and rubbed her jean-clad knee as I drove us through the city. We just had to get through this day. Tomorrow we'd be married and not just significants. It would be real for everyone to see.

And she'd be all mine. Screw anyone else who wanted her time. She would be mine until we decided to come back to reality.

Thirteen

Maggie

CHAD WAS on the steps just like he'd been the last time we'd pulled up this way. His scowl was more contained this time. More accepting, but ready to fight anyway. I put on my boxing gloves and got off the bike. Before Caleb could even suggest that he leave, I asked him to come with me. I did love Chad. He had been one of my best friends for all my life. I didn't want him to hurt or worry. And if he saw us together, maybe he'd understand that I wasn't jumping into a tank of sharks.

"Mags," he sighed. "My g…you look really great."

"Thanks." I looked at him. Really looked. He looked the same as always. He was still thin and seemingly ready for anything. His favorite position when we all hung out at my house was laying on the couch with my feet in his lap. He was what I needed at the time, but now I just felt sad for him. I needed him to move on with the surety that I was going to be just fine. "You remember Caleb," I spouted hurriedly.

"Of course." I thought they'd shake hands. They didn't. "He's the guy you're getting married to…after only a few weeks."

"Maggie wanted to come because you're her friend," Caleb said solidly, but easily. "I'm not going to interfere or play along with your jabs to provoke me, but you better not lay a finger on her and you need to listen to what she has to say."

"Lay a finger on her?" Chad said, ruffled, and stepped forward. "What the-"

Caleb stayed put. "I know all about your hail-mary kiss," he told him and I was proud of his control. I could tell how much he wanted to do more.

Chad looked at me like I had betrayed him. "You told him about that?"

"Why wouldn't I? He was my boyfriend, Chad. And he's my fiancé now."

"I don't understand why you're so-"

"Hey, there!" Dad called from the porch. He came outside and I gasped at seeing Haddock by his side. "Look who came to pay you a visit."

"Haddock?" I asked stupidly, like I wasn't sure.

"Maggie," he said with a smile, unconcerned with my shock at seeing him. "It's really good to see you."

"What are you doing here?" I asked carefully, and he answered back just as carefully.

"I'm coming to visit, like I told you I would." He grinned handsomely and bowed a little before catching himself.

I tucked my hair behind my ear and looked at them. My two dads. Ugh…

"Who's this joker?" Chad mumbled under his breath.

I gave him a look that said to shut it, and cleared my throat. "How long are you here for?"

"Well…I had a house here, and since I won't be needed in London, I'm moving back. I came over to see if you wanted to go to lunch."

"How do you know this guy?" Chad asked, his lips touching my ear. I shivered, not in a good way.

"Back. Off," Caleb told him as he pulled me closer. "You don't follow directions very well."

"I know everything there is to know about her!" Chad challenged. "Don't I, Mr. Masters?"

"Chad," Dad warned.

"So I don't think you get to sit here and tell me that I can't whisper to the girl who was mine for over three years! She can make up her own mind. That's why I came here. To talk some sense into her and let her make up her own mind. Because there's no way that she chose you like this. You…tricked her somehow. She's gullible sometimes."

I scoffed. "Chad, stop. I'm not a child! I don't need you to help me make my decisions."

"Someone has to!"

"I'm happy, Chad. Why is that so hard to believe?"

He scowled. "You were happy with me, too, and yeah, I know I ruined things, but we could have been fine and gotten back together. You were just too stubborn to even give us a chance. And now you're being stubborn about him." He thought. "Is this because your mom left and you think you can't do any better?"

Caleb broke in and I could hear the grating anger in his tone. "You're right, she can make up her own mind. So stop trying to tell her what she does and doesn't want."

Chad took a deep breath for his rebuttal, but a car screeched to a stop on the curb and someone stumbled out ungracefully, her heels clacking on the pavement, and then disappeared into the grass as she came to us. My mother. I opened my mouth to ask her what she was doing there, but Dad beat me to it. "What are you doing back here?" He moved forward a little and gritted his teeth when she stayed silent. "Didn't we say all there was to say?"

"I couldn't leave," she declared spitefully. "I couldn't just leave town even if you don't want me here. I belong here more than anyone! I'm her mother and you don't get to tell me to leave."

The car threw a suitcase out and yelled something before taking off. She glanced at the suitcase and back to me, but then her eyes drifted to my Dad. Then widened to impossible lemons. "Haddock?" she whispered, but we all heard.

"Sarah," he said angrily. I swung my gaze to look at him. What was he angry for? He saw me looking and took a calming breath.

She took you from me, Maggie. It wasn't right for us to have the affair, I know that and you'll never know how sorry I am, but she took you from me.

I closed my eyes, trying to keep my feelings from getting the best of me. Caleb's hand wrapped around my wrist, his thumb rubbing the pulse beating rapidly there as my parents went on.

"How do you know Haddock?" Dad asked suspiciously. He looked between the two.

Mom looked at me to see if I was going to spill the beans or not. I turned away, letting my forehead rest on Caleb's chin. If she was waiting for my help, she could just forget that. She eventually said, "He used to own the flower shop in town."

"Still do," he said and crossed his arms.

"Ok, you didn't answer my question," Dad continued. "What are you doing here?"

"I don't care that you've moved on so quickly," she said snidely. I rolled my eyes though they were closed. The woman was unbelievable. "Some of us are just trying their best here! Some of us can't move on so quickly."

Dad chuckled without a trace of humor. "You moved on plenty fast enough for all of us."

"Besides," she said as if he hadn't spoken. "I have nowhere to go. All the money's gone and-"

"Where's the bracelet I gave you?" I said softly. It wasn't because I wasn't angry, it was because I was about to explode. "Where's the family heirloom you just had to have back?"

She pursed her lips. "A girl's got to eat, Maggie. No matter how small her figure. And have somewhere to sleep since her family just kicks her into the street like a dog."

Before I could say a word, Dad boomed, "Don't. Don't, Sarah. You don't get to treat people this way without any remorse and then come crying back when you've run out of gumption on your journey for self-discovery."

"Uh..." Chad muttered beside me in a low voice. "You want to go somewhere with me, Mags, and talk? Let them get out all of their fighting while we're gone?" I looked at him and he smiled in a placating manner. "Just you and me."

I felt overwhelmed and looked away angrily. For the first time in a while, I felt like it was too much. Their thoughts, my feelings, their anger, Caleb's feelings...and then my mother and Haddock began to go back and forth. She called him all sorts of names, asking what business he had at her home. He in turn took the insults and tried to calm her, but it was clear that he was angry as well. My father was just confused and kept asking what was going on. My world felt like it was crumbling right in front of my feet, but there was no way to take a step back and save it.

When my mother asked in an insinuating tone what Haddock was there to see me for, Haddock's disgusted face was enough to wipe away any notion of that. His angry boiled over. "Don't you ever-"

"She's my daughter. Look at her. She looks just like me. And she does have good taste in men," she sneered in our direction.

My dad cut her off, his voice dangerous. "Don't ever talk about my daughter that way. She may look like you, Sarah, but she's nothing like you."

She walked right up to him and slapped him across the face. The stunned silence of the yard was suffocating my senses. He didn't fight back, just stood there in containment of his anger.

"Mom!" I yelled at her.

She turned and glared. "Shut up, Maggie!"

My dad's sudden burst of anger at what she'd done was the last straw in my mind as I overloaded and went down. I wasn't worried. I knew Caleb would catch me, and he did. I welcomed the reprieve from their minds, from their thoughts; all angry and ready to lay some claim to me. Right then, I didn't want anything but darkness.

I was in my room. I knew because it smelled the same as it always did. Caleb had taken me there after my inability to control my emotions and the effect they have on my head. I sighed. Even after everything we'd been through, I still felt so helpless sometimes.

I felt his lips press to my forehead. I opened my eyes to find him watching me as he held my head on his lap. "Sorry," I muttered lamely.

"It's all OK," he assured and smiled down at me with a smirk. The lamp beside my bed was the only light in the room. "It got them all to shut up, that's for sure."

I heard their thoughts downstairs. "They're still here?"

He nodded. "Yeah. No one would leave."

I exhaled in a huff. I didn't want to deal with them. Any of them. It was the day before my wedding! I may have pouted, full on. His lips tilted to the side in a lopsided smile.

"Man, that's cute." All of a sudden, he completely switched gears, looking guilty as he played with the front pocket of my jeans. He let his finger slide along the pocket seam before saying, "I'm sorry. I shouldn't have egged Chad on. I just made it worse."

"No you didn't. I understand."

"You can take care of yourself." He pictured me in his mind when I stood up to the council in London. "You don't need me to be all beating my chest and claiming you, though that's what I want to do. You don't need me to fight your battles for you."

"I don't think you went too far. It's OK for you to protect me. Besides, Chad was the one getting all up in your face."

"I'm just trying to figure out the balance between being the tyrant and letting you be you."

"Babe." He lifted his head. "I don't think you're being protective because you're trying to control me. I think you're being protective because you love me."

He shook his head, his mouth slightly open. "I thought you'd be angry with me about what I said to Chad."

"No, I'm glad you said it. He was the one who wasn't even trying to understand." I lifted a little on my elbows. My head ached a little and Caleb pressed his lips to my forehead once more to draw it off. I sat up fully and licked my lips. "I wanted our last day to be peaceful and happy. Instead it's been chaotic and emotional."

"I know," he sighed. "I'm sorry. Those people down there…they may not show it well, but they care about you, even if it's in their own small, selfish way."

"What are they waiting for?" I asked.

"You to wake up. They said they wanted to make sure you were OK first, before they left. Jim practically tackled Chad to keep him from following us upstairs." He chuckled.

"He just doesn't understand," I said and wished there was some way to make him. "He'll never understand that you didn't steal me away from my life."

"I know," he whispered against my skin. He leaned down and kissed my cheek. "I'm sorry."

"It's not your fault that Chad's being a jackhole."

He cracked a beautiful smile. "Jackhole?"

"Yep." I ran my thumb over the scruff on his chin. I noticed how wound up he was. It was about more than my passing out again. "What's up?"

"Nothing," he said too quickly and began the math again. "Let's just get this over with and then we can blow this joint."

"Gladly," I accepted his subject change. As we made our way down the hall, Caleb asked me to text Bish and tell him to meet us. So I did. He replied back immediately, and Caleb made me add on not to bring Jen. I gave him a quizzical look, but made the request anyway. The response wasn't as fast. I could almost hear the pout in his voice when he texted back.

OK...Be there soon

While I had my phone out, I decided to go ahead and text Beck again. She had to speak to me sometime, right?

Where are u? I'm worried. U don't have to tell me where u r or come home, just let me know that ur ok

I stuck the phone back in my pocket and forgot all about it once we entered the hall. There they were. All sitting like ducks in a row in my living room. My mother, who carried the scowl of a scorned woman instead of the one who did the scorning. My ex-boyfriend, who glared at Caleb's hand in mine as if he'd never laid eyes on such a scene before. My new step-mother, whose eyes danced around the room in her uncomfortableness. My father and then my...father...

I blinked hard and leaned into Caleb to steel myself before looking back at the motley crew. "Are you all right?" Dad asked and came to wrap me in his arms comfortingly. Haddock looked like he was in actual pain not to be able to do the same. Caleb and I looked at each other and he gave me a sympathetic smile as Dad let go and gave my mother a warning glare as she started to lift from the couch. She sat back down with a huff. Chad just watched the whole thing. "I'm fine," I spouted.

"What happened?" Chad asked and lifted his eyebrows waiting for the answer.

"I just don't feel well. And you yelling at Caleb, and then you showing up," I told my mother, "I just couldn't handle it. I can't deal with all of this right now, OK?"

I turned and paced the room. No one moved but Haddock. He came up behind me and I turned to find him with a sad look on his face. "I'm sorry if my coming here upset you."

"It didn't, I promise. We just have so much going on right now." I whispered, "The wedding is tomorrow, too."

His eyes lit. "Oh, really?" He looked over his shoulder just a bit. "Would you mind if I came?" he asked softly.

I thought. "Is that even allowed? You're not of this clan."

"I think since you're the ones making the rules now, you can make an exception." He smiled. When I didn't smile back, he recanted. "It's all right though. I understand. I'll be staying at my house about twenty minutes from here. If you were to need anything, let me know."

"Haddock," I stopped him. He looked back at me hopefully. I hoped I was making the right decision. "It would be great if you could be there tomorrow."

He looked a mixture of relief and devastatingly happy. "You're sure?"

"I'm sure." Then it came to me. He may be the key to finding Marcus.

"In fact, I have something I want you to help me with."

"Anything," he said without hesitation.

"Have you heard from Marcus?"

"No. I've heard from no one. Why?"

"Because I have."

He blanched. "Maggie..."

"We'll talk later," I promised. "I'll call you tonight and tell you all about it."

He didn't look happy about leaving it at that, but he did. "OK. Please, please, call me. I'll be waiting."

"I will."

He nodded and then waved to my father. "Thank you for letting me wait for Maggie here. I'll...see you soon."

"Not a problem," Dad answered and pulled Fiona up from the couch, placed his arm around her, and sighed. "Well..." he said awkwardly. "I guess it's time for everyone to scoot. Lots to do tonight, unfortunately."

"You're kicking us out?" Mom yelled, but Chad stood. He gave me the sulkiest and most annoyed look I think I've ever gotten from him.

"Can we talk outside for just a minute?"

I took a deep breath through my nose. I glanced up at Caleb, who bit into his bottom lip, but nodded his head toward the door, telling me he wouldn't hurt him if I went with him. "All right," I agreed. "Let's go."

He smiled like he'd won. Like I was going to hop into his Honda Accord with him and ride off into the Gainesville, Florida sunset. I rolled my eyes as we reached the front porch. "You've got three minutes, Chad."

He huffed. "Why? Any more than that and you know I'll talk some sense into you, Masters?"

"Two minutes, forty six seconds."

He sighed. "All right. I've already said my peace. You know how I feel. I just wanted to get you alone for a second without that meat-head with you."

"You can leave if that's all you have to say."

"I want you to reconsider. If you don't want to be with me, OK, fine. I'll get over it eventually, but this? You getting married just because you think that's what you've got to do? That's so stupid, Mags."

"That's not why I'm getting married. I love him. That's why."

"Careful," he taunted. "Your low GPA is showing."

I gritted my teeth. "You can be a real jerk, you know that?"

"And you were never this dumb when we dated!" he yelled. "I can only account it to the company you're keeping."

"And that's your cue." I turned to leave and he grabbed my arm.

Then he yelped and glared at me. "How do you keep doing that?"

"Doesn't matter," I muttered sadly. I felt Caleb's anger as he heard what was going on through me. I assured him it was OK. I was sending Chad home anyway. "Go home, Chad. I'm sorry that you think that I'm ruining my life, but it's the opposite. One day you'll meet a great-"

"Oh, really?" He turned in an angry circle. "The old *You'll meet a great girl and forget all about me* bit?"

"I was going to say you'll meet someone and know what it's like to want to be with them, no matter what."

"Ah... I guess this is it. I tried. At least I can say that I tried."

"I guess so." I swallowed. "I really do hope you have a great life. I hope school is great and you do well with football...meet someone one day."

He nodded, deflated. "I'm sorry. I shouldn't have said that stuff. I just love you, Maggie. And I hate to think that your life took a turn for the worse because of a stupid thing I did last year."

"You don't get to take credit for my decisions, Chad," I said softly. "I didn't take a turn for the worse. I would never have met Caleb and his family, and Dad would have never woken up from his funk if everything hadn't happened that way. You can't…outrun your destiny."

He gave me a strange look, but eventually just nodded once. "Bye, Mags. See you around maybe."

"Probably not," I said, not unkindly. It was just facts.

He nodded with his back turned as he strode to his car. I felt a heavy relief tainted with a hint of disappointment. I needed a minute before going back inside. I went to the side of the porch and stood, watching the cars as they zoomed and crawled through my neighborhood. My older neighbor lady was shelling peas or something on her porch swing. She waved and I waved back just as the front door opened. I stayed put. I heard Mom's thoughts as she pulled her phone out and dialed a number. She was angry.

"Haddock's here!" she hissed. "Maggie's real father. How the hell did Haddock find out about Maggie? How the hell did Maggie find out about Haddock?"

The person on the line, a male, said, "Sweet thing, just keep focus. I just need you to come back to California and forget all about those hillbillies."

"Oh, I will," she said with surety. "I just need to do a couple more things and then I'll be on my way."

"Did you get the bracelet?"

"Yep. And I stole a couple rings and things from that twit that lives with him now." She laughed. "That'll fetch a pretty penny for when I get back. And I talked to Jim about Maggie coming back with me. He refused to hear a word of it, of course. She's fallen in love with some boy here."

The man laughed and I wondered why he would be happy to have me come back with her to California. "Well, they could both come and work in our restaurant if they want."

"He's loaded. Hiring Maggie for cheap, live-in labor is out now. Besides, she's really too pretty for manual labor."

"If she looks anything like you, she's as pretty as a peach."

I swallowed vomit.

"She looks just like me," she said proudly. "Anyway. I got most of the things I came for. All of which should set us up for a little while. Maggie won't be able to help us like I thought, but it's fine. She can stay in this po-dunk town all she wants." She examined her nails.

"What about life insurance. She got any?"

"Jim does." She laughed. "Too bad we're divorced now or I could kill him before I leave. Then he would have at least been of some use to me."

I felt the last remaining shred of feeling for my mother drain away. As I watched her back leave, I knew there was never any real love for me from that woman. I felt an odd, dull ache. It was as if I was sad, but it was irrelevant. The hole or void she may have inflicted on me was long filled. But it didn't mean that it didn't hurt like the dickens to see with your own eyes that your mother could give two craps about you.

I heard Caleb come onto the porch and I waited, knowing he would find me within seconds. He did. The hard set of his mouth told me he already knew everything. He pulled me by my elbows and rubbed my back.

"Don't spend another second thinking about that woman," he commanded softly.

My phone buzzed with a text. I assumed it was Bish telling us he was almost there, but it wasn't.

It was Beck.

I jumped and scrolled to read it.

We're fine. We holed up somewhere Ralph knows out of the way. Stop texting me. I don't want to see u. I don't want to know u anymore. When the coast is clear, let me know. Otherwise, we'll stay gone for a while.

I stared at it sadly. I had saved her life and she didn't want to know me anymore?

I slammed my phone shut and looked up at Caleb. "Wow. What an ungrateful cow."

Fourteen

Caleb

Yikes.

Maggie was livid. With good reason, mostly. Beck was being childish. Yes, humans didn't understand us, but this was a little ridiculous. Or maybe I was just being biased because she was hurting my Maggie.

"Baby, don't worry about her. She's just…"

"I just don't understand how she can be that way. And my mom? And Chad? Is everybody out to make me feel like crap today? I shouldn't be having doubts the day before our wedding."

"What kind of doubts?"

"Not wedding doubts, just…doubts. Why is all of this happening?" She sniffed and the first – of what I figured – of many tears slid down her cheek, effectively breaking my heart. "You don't have any doubt?"

I took her face – her gorgeous, tear-streaked face – in my hands and looked her straight in the eye. "Doubt? No, not ever. Not about you, not about us, and not about what we're meant to be doing right now."

"But all of these things keep popping up," she argued, but the fight was just gone right out of her. She sniffled, her fists wrapped in my shirt front, whether she knew it or not. "I don't doubt us either, of course not. I just don't understand why things have to be so hard-"

"It's worth it because it's hard, baby. Your dad, your mom, Bish, Haddock, me...Chad," I growled his name, disgruntled, "every one of us has been pulled to you for a reason. We just need to see how we can make it all work...where hopefully, they don't kill each other." I smirked for good measure.

The desired effect was a smile and she complied with a sigh. "Yeah, I know. You're right." She slipped closer, her hands going around my waist. "You're really amazing, you know that?"

"I am looking forward to an eternity of you stealing my lines, sweetheart." I pulled her closer, loving the way she bit her lip sideways, her heartbeat hitching a slight bit, in anticipation of my kiss. "An eternity."

Then I worked hard to keep in a groan when her lips wrapped around my bottom one and tugged. Bish had the worst timing a guy could have when he pulled into the driveway at that moment. She licked her lips as she pulled back. She smirked at my expression.

Smirked!

"Thank you."

"Don't thank me yet," I said in a foretelling manner.

She cocked her head to the side. "Am I about to find out what all the sudden math problems have been about?"

"Yep." I took her hand and we met Bish halfway.

"What's up?" he said easily.

"Something," I said. "Something that is breaking all the rules. Something that I hope you'll accept and understand." I turned to Maggie. "And something I hope you'll forgive me for."

Her lips fell open. "What..."

I nodded for Bish to follow me and pulled Maggie with me to the smaller, but nice three bedroom, Victorian house next door to Maggie's father's. She got a little excited, thinking the obvious conclusion, so I hurried, hoping to stop her disappointment. "This isn't the house I bought for you, baby."

"It's not?" she asked softly.

"No." I turned to Bish. "It's the house I bought for you."

"What's that now?" he said in utter confusion.

I started with a breath. "The groom is supposed to buy his bride a house and present it to her on their wedding day. Please don't be embarrassed or anything. I understand how hard it's been for you. I know without a doubt that given enough time, you could have bought my sister this house yourself, but there isn't any time left. I want you to have it."

He sputtered. "But what about Maggie's house?"

I gulped a little and peeked at her. "I...have other plans for us. Don't worry. I'll take care of her."

"But..." he tried and stopped. "No. No, I can't take this. It's too-"

"It's not too much. You gave my sister the one thing she's always wanted, and to know that she and Maria will be safe and sound with you there to protect them and make sure they're happy, and I have no doubt that you will, is worth so much more than any stupid house." I looked him straight in the eye. "We've had our differences, but this house is my gift to you as a thank you for taking care of Maggie all of those years, and now moving on to taking care of my sister. She's been through… so much." I felt my throat betray me with a choke. I cleared it. "Take it. Take the keys and start your life with her knowing that every bad thing, every sacrifice you both have made, wasn't in vain. It wasn't for nothing." I reached into my pocket and held out the keys for him to take. "Take them."

I heard his prideful thoughts through Maggie, but they swiftly drifted away as his need to make my sister happy replaced them. He still had to protest though. "Caleb, come on…"

"You don't need to thank me or do anything," I told him. "Taking care of my sister is thanks enough. You promise to take care of my sister, and I promise to take care of yours."

He looked like he wanted to tackle-hug me. Luckily, he just shook my hand and nodded. "Yeah. Promise. Thank you, Caleb. Gah, just… thank you. This was all that I wanted…to give Jen and Maria a home." He scoffed at the house with a smile. "And the house beside Dad's just happened to be on the market?"

I smiled and shrugged. "I plead the fifth."

"Thanks. If there's ever anything…"

I nodded and looked down at my Maggie. "So…"

"So this is what you've been hiding?" I nodded. "And you really thought I'd be upset with you about this?"

"I just want you to understand that I didn't buy you a house. I know I was supposed to, but I have other plans for us that I'll spring on you later. A house isn't one of them."

She took my face in her hands as Bish went inside. "You are the sweetest man that ever walked this earth. You know that?" She was crying again, but happily this time.

I just shook my head. "The guy almost pummeled me daily trying to protect you. How could I not appreciate that?"

"I love you a million times more than I did two minutes ago. I didn't think that was possible." She sniffed and I wiped the tears under her eyes with my thumbs.

"Me either," I told her and moved one of her hands to my heart. "Feel that? A million times a minute for you." I smiled and enjoyed the way her heart sped up in happiness. "Your family is my family. And if there's ever anything that I can do for them for taking care of you until I found you, I'll do it."

She let her nose rub mine once. Then she leaned back and took a shuddering breath. "Give me the tour?"

"Sure." We met Bish inside as he looked around the empty rooms just waiting to be filled with their things. Maggie ran her fingers along the windowsills and followed him. She listened to him as he pictured bringing Jen there tomorrow after the wedding and what she'd think of it.

He turned to us once we reached the kitchen. "Wow, it's a gorgeous house."

"Yes," Maggie agreed. "And you have plenty of room for Maria…and maybe more one day."

He gave her an affectionate look. "Only you would make babies walk through the door before I've even had a chance to bring the bride."

"I'm just saying."

He laughed. "I know exactly what you're saying." He shook my hand. "I think I'll head back before Jen starts to wonder. Ought to be fun trying to keep this a secret all night."

"Math works wonders for me," I told him.

He hugged Maggie into his side. "I'll try that. Thank you. I guess... I'll see you tomorrow."

She nodded and smiled cutely. "I'll be there!" she sang.

"I can't wait," he said, seemingly to himself. "Bye, guys."

"Bye," Maggie said softly. She turned to me. Her eyes held the promise of something that would make me a very happy guy tonight. "Take me home, Mr. Jacobson," she said and bit her lip.

"Yes, ma'am," I whispered and took her hand to lead her to the bike.

I was surprised to find Kyle and Lynne gone when we got back to the apartment. I was glad, let me tell you, but surprised. It didn't matter that tomorrow was our wedding and I had major plans to run away with her for days after. It didn't matter one bit. I still wanted her every night, every minute.

She pulled the hoodie off as soon as we got in, kicking her Converses off by the front door. I smiled at the display. "I'm taking a shower, OK?" she called.

"Need any help in there?" I bellowed and held in my laugh.

I heard her giggle. "Tomorrow night, I will definitely need your help."

Backfire. Daggum... I swiped my face and looked for something to do. I went into the kitchen and saw Bella's bowl on the counter. I sighed.

That was something that was going to change as soon as we got back. I missed my girl. She stayed with Mom and Dad most of the time because I was in school, but no more. She and Maggie got along great and we were going to be our own little family. Bella was going to be included in my plan, too. I couldn't wait until tomorrow where I could tell Maggie everything and hope she was as excited as I was.

There was laundry folded on the counter, which meant that Rose had been there. I set out to put it all away to give me something to do. The obsidian box I gave Maggie was on her side of the bed. I peeked in it quickly to see if my vows were still inside. They were, still folded as I'd put them in there. I knew she hadn't written hers yet, what with all the craziness going on, but I really wanted her to read mine before tomorrow. Oh, well. They were just words, right? She knew I loved her.

As soon as I was done with the clothes, Maggie and I traded places. She came out in her towel and pawed through her clothes on the chair for something to wear. I went into the shower and hung my head, letting the scalding water beat on my neck and back.

I found myself smiling. Even after everything that happened today and yesterday and the day before that, tomorrow was what mattered more than anything.

She was almost mine.

Fifteen

Maggie

I COULD hear his thoughts in the shower. That man was so happy about tomorrow and was even wishing the minutes away so that it would get here faster. I found myself giddy as I pulled my shirt over my head to go with my gray sweatpants. It was an old cheerleading shirt of mine from camp. It said, "Yeah, that's it, that's right!"

I rolled my eyes at the girl I used to be. There was nothing wrong with cheerleading and in fact, I kinda missed it. It was a good workout and those girls were funny and so competitive. But it just wasn't me, wasn't who I was.

This was me. I looked around the room and rubbed the bedspread. This right here.

I glanced at the little obsidian jewelry box on the bedside table and noticed it was turned the opposite way. I glanced at the bathroom door and realized that I'd completely forgotten to write my vows and he'd been checking to see if I'd read his yet. I felt awful. He'd put so much thought into it and I had just forgotten all about it.

I knelt down on the floor and placed the box on the bed like the precious thing it was. The lid lifted soundlessly and I opened the crisp paper. His handwriting was totally a guy's. I smiled at it as I began to read.

Not a day has gone by for me that I haven't been waiting for you. That I haven't dreamed of a faceless you. That I haven't imagined what you would feel like under my palms. Waiting was never the problem, it was doubting. I began to doubt that you were real, that you were actually coming to me.

But I should never have doubted you.

I'm amazed when I look at your face to see the love I feel for you smiling back at me. I would do anything you asked of me to keep that smile there. You are all there is, my world...

I'm honored just to be in your presence, let alone have your heart. I adore the way you look at my world. The love you have for my family. How you can be so completely innocent and so achingly sexy all at the same time. How you're always selfless, and there, and full of love even after everything you've been through. Baby, I've said it a million times and I'll continue to say it 'til my last breath...

You're amazing.

Tomorrow you'll be mine in every way, every sense, every second, but I know that no matter how tight I hold you, it'll never be close enough. No matter how long or hard or passionately I kiss your lips, it'll never be sating.

You're my soul-mate, my reason to keep pulling air into my lungs, my gorgeous significant that fits in my arms and my life perfectly, my whole life, my love, my partner in crime, my very heart, my amazing girl.

Marry me. Take the beating heart in my chest and do with it what you wish. It's been yours since the day you saved my life. You've been saving it ever since. I love you, baby, more than will ever be understandable, but I dare you to try.

Every tomorrow is all that matters, my love.

The tears that blurred my vision pulled a good ache in my chest to the surface.

Oh…

How was I supposed to follow that? Now I had to write my vows to him and try to be as perfect and spot on as he had been? He was *my* very heart. He was *my* love, he was *my* everything… I felt so inadequate compared to him. I wiped my eyes with my palms and sucked it up. I had to do this. I took a deep breath and focused on Caleb. He had some black boxer briefs on and he stood at the sink getting ready to shave. The mirror was fogged over and he hadn't wiped it yet.

I decided not to wait and write them all out. I would just tell him how I felt right now. No worrying over pencil and paper and trying to word things just right This was me, real, alive and in love with him. I was about to hand myself to him raw on a platter.

I kept my eyes closed and took my pinky finger in the air, imaging the words as I wrote them out in the fog on the mirror in front of him, little section by little section, and then letting the steam cover it back over before starting again.

I know you think that on some level I regret the day you touched me. I don't. Not on any level, not even a little. You've changed me in the most profound ways. When I was a little girl, I always imagined that I'd grow up to be like the women I saw in town. Women like my mom, who took care of everything so effortlessly and reveled in their status and small accomplishments. But it was all fake.

Your family made me see that you should take care of your family because you love them, not because someone important is watching. And I want to take care of you. In my body, down into my veins is this itch, this need to make you absolutely happy. You don't try to keep me down, you keep me safe while also letting me be me. You said you we trying to find the balance between being the tyrant and letting me be myself? You're there, baby. You take such good care of me. And the fact that you worry about it is the best part. It shows how much you love me. And there's no doubt in my mind at all that I'll be happy with you. I only hope that I can make you as happy, too.

I love feeling your heart in my chest, knowing that mine is beating there right beside yours. I'm right where I belong. So do I regret the day you touched me? The day you made me yours? Never, Jacobson.

No matter where we go, what we do, what we see or have to deal with as the leaders of our kind... You're amazing, you're sexy and fun, protective, ambitious, and sweet.

I am so ready to live this life with you.

He emerged from the bathroom, his boxers the only thing he wore. His reverent face was ruggedly beautiful. When he bounded toward me, his bare feet padding on the tile floor, I welcomed the crash of our bodies. His hands wrapped around my thighs to lift me up and he held me to him and squeezed the life out of me as he said, "Is it tomorrow yet?"

I smiled against his mouth. "Almost. Thank you for what you wrote. To say it was beautiful is a terrible understatement."

"I meant it. And vows on the bathroom mirror? I bet I'm the only Ace who can say that that's how they got them."

I shrugged and smiled in embarrassment. "I improvised."

"I loved it. Thank you," he said in my favorite growly voice. He nipped at my chin. "You want to straddle the line with me, Mrs. Jacobson?"

"That's all I want to do right now," I said breathlessly as he took me and placed me gently on the bed before following me down. His mouth claimed small pieces of skin that seemed so miniscule in the grand scheme of things, but he also lit me on fire with every inch he moved to.

We stayed decent, dressed and technically innocent, but satisfied. The boy was a genius at knowing me, at knowing my body, and knowing just how far to go and what each sigh and gasp meant.

The blue energy ribbons that came when we melded our minds wasn't eerie any longer. It was now a part of me and I welcomed it. It felt like it belonged. And watching his face through the glow as he kissed my shoulder and neck was one of the most beautiful things I'd ever seen.

As we lay together in his warm bed, reveling in the feel of each other and trying to tell our bodies to calm down, it was the best kind of Hell.

The worst kind of Heaven. We only had a few short hours until Heaven and Hell would collide, and I wasn't scared or worried or even anxious. I was just ready.

Pull the gate and let this racehorse go. I was ready for the marathon.

I woke to the tune of *We're Not Gonna Take It.*

I sat up so quickly my head spun. I mumbled through my teeth, "Ohmygoshwhatisthat…" I looked around and saw my cell phone bumbling around on the nightstand. I grabbed it up and answered with a groggy, "Hello?"

"Maggie, Maggie, Maggie. So good to hear your voice again." I froze. Marcus. "Do you like that new ringtone I got for you?"

He had my phone? He had been…in our house….

I shook Caleb, but he was already awake, feeling my scared heart beating in my chest, and glaring up at the phone in my hand. "What do you want?"

"You. Dead. Too much to ask?"

"What do you want?" I said more forcefully. My mind immediately flitted to Beck, that he was calling to tell me he'd found her and she was dead. Caleb shook his head, took his own phone off the dresser and dialed her number.

"I just wanted to tell you that I heard about your friend's passing. Sad really. Those pesky fuel lines… Anyway, my family is back home now. The compound is all they've got left. They are so pathetic, moping around and trying to find jobs. But I just can't do that. I didn't enroll in college or anything. I was always too busy helping Sikes with his schemes, and now he's gone, and Donald is gone. My father is the most pathetic of them all. Marla was his golden child. You did me a favor, by the way." He laughed, though I could hear the slight crack telling me he was lying. "She was always the soft one, the one who flew by the seat of her pants and just wanted everyone to kiss her butt and tell her she was pretty and special." There was a pause. "Anyway, I'm going to be in the neighborhood and I thought maybe I could stop by your dad's house tonight. I figured that since I haven't seen you, you aren't interested in retaliating against me for Rebecca like I assumed you would. I assumed you wouldn't stop until you found me. So I guess I'll have to go higher in the ranking and take out dear old daddy."

My breath caught in my throat. Caleb took the phone from me then and yelled into the receiver. "Stay away from them. You're a human now. Do you really want to test Maggie right now?"

I could hear it all through Caleb and heard his gutturally grunted words.

"I want to do more than test her. I want her to die in your arms and watch as you cry like a girl for your fallen, pretty, little Visionary." He chuckled under his breath. "I guess…I'll see you soon."

The line went dead. Caleb dialed Rebecca's number as I glanced at the clock. It was only a little after seven in the morning. Caleb's hand shook with anger as he tossed my phone onto the bed. "Beck's fine. She answered and said to stop calling her and hung up. So, she's fine."

I swallowed, my throat dry. "Ok, now what?"

"Well…I had planned to-" He sighed, long and hard. "I had planned to take you to the apartment I got for us in Arizona. But Marcus is screwing all of that up."

I felt my breath catch in my throat. "Arizona?"

He nodded and gave me a wry smile. "I wanted to take you there and tell you all about the plans I have for us and my company." He slid down to the floor, kneeling at my feet as I sat on the bed, and rested his arms on my knees as he continued. "I thought long and hard about this. I knew not buying you a house for our wedding is going to upset some people, mainly my dad, but I knew that Bish didn't have the money and that you wanted to help any way that you could. So, I decided to buy the house for Bish and then rented us an apartment for your wedding gift in Arizona for us to go back and forth from here to there." He gulped slightly. "I want you to work with me. I want you to help me expand the centers to other states. It's what I've always wanted to do and I know you haven't decided what you wanted to major in or anything yet. You can do anything you want, I promise I'll stand behind you in whatever you decide, but I would be honored if you'd be my co-pilot." He grinned. "My co-CEO of my company and travel with me to get the centers started and hire the staff. I'll buy you a real house for us to settle down in whenever you're ready, but for now, I just thought this would be make more sense."

I spoke slowly. "It makes perfect sense. I love it."

"You do?" he said in relief.

"Yes. And I want to be available to the other clans as much as I can, too. This should help keep our schedule pretty open since we're not going to be on a set daily time that we have to work like we would at your dad's office."

He nodded. "Right."

"You're the sweetest. Those kids are so incredibly lucky to have you."

His cheeks may have turned a little pink. I couldn't be sure in the dark. "Yeah."

"So what are we going to do about Marcus?"

"Well instead of going to Arizona, I guess we better leave after the wedding and take your dad with us. And Bish. And Kyle, too, for that matter. I'll book us a couple of cottages at Virginia Beach or something. It won't be the honeymoon I wanted to give you, but…"

"It's perfect. We'll still get a honeymoon and knowing that everyone else is right there with us safe will be better." I took a deep breath, trying not to cry as I thought about it.

He noticed though and looked at my eyes closely. "You nervous?"

"Not even a little." He looked skeptical. "I just can't believe it's today."

He smiled and snaked his arms around my waist. "I bet Marcus was so smug thinking he'd ruined your day. He always underestimates you."

"I won't let anything ruin this day."

He kissed the end of my nose. "Today is all that matters, my love," he whispered into my hair.

"And what is today?" I asked cheekily.

"The day you pay the consequence for saying 'yes.'"

I giggled and opened my eyes to find him over me on his elbows. "I'll gladly pay that penalty."

"Good." He kissed my forehead. "I'll go drop you off at Dad's and all the girls can get ready there. Kyle said we'd get dressed at his house. Don't worry. I'll bring Bish and your dad so you don't have to worry about them. I've got 'em."

"Thank you." I kept my face straight. "Are you nervous?"

"Hell no," he said with a grin. "Let's go, gorgeous. Everything you need is at Dad's."

"OK." We got dressed and he drove me over to Peter's house. The new butler had started that day and he wasn't nearly as funny or as friendly as Randolph had been.

Caleb kissed me on the cheek and said he'd see me later. I looked over my shoulder at him as I climbed out of the truck. Bish came out and hopped in with him. He waved at me and smiled the biggest grin. It made me want to cry at seeing him that happy. I looked past him to Caleb and waved my fingers at him.

Bye.

Bye, baby.

They drove away to Kyle's, leaving me standing in the massive driveway. I turned around and half expected to find white tulle and bows everywhere, but the place looked the same.

I made my way through the garage and down the maze of halls, remembering the way to navigate it that Caleb had taught me. Bella met me first, circling me and licking at my fingers. Then Maria ran and tackle-hugged me around my middle. Rachel was next, asking how my night had been. I couldn't stop the blush that crept up. So I wasn't surprised at all when Gran gave me a scowling look.

I ignored her and tried to move on. "So…"

"So. Nervous?" Gran asked, fingering a curl near my ear.

"No. Why? Were you nervous?"

"I was so scared that I thought I'd never make it to him without passing out." She smiled, her eyes far away and clear. "But I did. How come you ain't nervous?"

"What's there to be nervous about?" I told her, but looked at the floor. "It's just Caleb. I know he loves me, so why would I be nervous about this?"

She lifted my face with a finger under my chin. "You're telling the truth," she said in revelation. I nodded. "Well, I'll be... And here I thought I was supposed to be on runaway-bride duty."

I laughed. "No need. So what's first on the agenda?"

"First?" Rachel asked and put on her apron. It said, "I'm flippin' awesome" with a picture of a spatula. I pressed my lips together so as not to laugh. "Let's get some food in the bride's bellies. Pancakes or eggs?"

"Pancakes," Jen and I said together and laughed. Lynne was absorbed in squeezing oranges for fresh-squeezed orange juice. I went and started a pot of coffee. Surely, I couldn't screw up coffee, right?

After we finished cooking and eating, she pulled me aside and handed me a leather bound book. I looked quizzically at it and she urged me with a nod to open it. She had over 100 pages of handwritten recipes, all neat and orderly, organized by types of food. I felt my mouth drop open when I saw *Gran's Honey Bun Recipe*.

"Gran was one who taught you to make those divine honey buns you made in California?"

"Mhmm. She taught me a lot. There's a lot of Gran's recipes in there, along with tons of our old family ones. I just knew that learning to cook was something that was important to you, and I wanted you to have a fresh start at it. If you ever have any questions or anything, you can call me anytime. It took me years – years, honey – to be a good cook. But I love it now."

"I think I'll love it, too."

"And we got you something else, too." I waited, knowing that she'd tell me without being prompted. "It's from Peter and me." And she handed me a small box. I opened it and produced a small locket. It looked just like… "This is Gran's locket."

"It's just like it." She lifted her hand, making the locket lift from the box. She moved her finger to tell me to turn around and she lifted the locket into the air and let it fall gently around my neck. "We got Jen one, too. Though finding a picture of Bish was challenging." She smiled in amusement.

I opened the locket and there was a picture I'd never seen before of Caleb. He was doing that half smile, half smirk thing that he was so good at. I lifted my head and said, "Wow, thank you, really."

She pulled hers from beneath her blouse. "It's a Jacobson tradition. We want to keep it going with you both."

I nodded. "Thank you. It's beautiful."

"I just can't believe this day is here," she said, her voice, cracking. She looked out at Jen and then gave me a small smile before walking to her. She embraced her, and Jen sighed and laughed at the same time.

"Mom, you've got to stop crying already."

I laughed silently at them.

We all nibbled and watched an old movie together, My Fair Lady, until the afternoon when it was time to start getting dressed. I was glad that no one seemed to be making a fuss. Your wedding day shouldn't be stressful, it should be relaxing and filled with laughter. That's exactly how it was.

I sat in between Fiona and Jen, and we all laughed and made our own Eliza Doolittle accents. Fiona was the best Eliza Doolittle.

When it was time to get dressed, that's what we did. Gran had made everyone's dresses for them, according to their likes and measurements. Lynne and I both chose a shorter dress while Jen and Fiona chose the more traditional long looking ones. But they were all blood red and as gorgeous as could be. I wore my new locket and let Rachel do my hair in big curls, and put in little diamond earring studs. Maria painted my toes for me, red of course, since this was a barefoot event.

When they said it was time to go, it seemed almost a little anti-climatic. I had been waiting for this and now it was here. I felt so calm and just ready for it.

I gave myself one more look in the mirror.

The dress was gorgeous. The red silk shimmered just a bit. The length was right above my knee, but the part that was hard to take your eyes off of was the neckline. It was an off-the-shoulder, but the sleeves were longer and flowy. It looked like something out of a magazine, not something a cranky old woman had whipped up at the last minute. The necklace could be seen perfectly with the low neckline and my shoulder was exposed in the most elegant way.

I was ready. This was it. The next time Caleb called me Mrs. Jacobson, it would be the truth.

So I didn't stall, or shake or worry. Honestly, I didn't even know how all of this was going to play out. There had been no dress rehearsal or anything, but it was all OK.

I padded down the hall with my bare feet and made it to the backyard double glass doors that Gran had said to meet her at. She was there, bare feet and a red shirt with black slacks. She held her arm out to tell me to wait. Soon I was met by Lynne, Jen, and Fiona. They all made their way out, Fiona first, me last. When it was my turn, Gran swept her arm for me to come. I walked to her and she put a red Malva flower behind my ear. I remembered the one Rachel had in the vision she showed me of her wedding. It was a tradition.

"Some people eat Malva flowers," she informed softly, rubbing the ends of my hair sweetly. "They think it helps with maintaining weight. Some eat them as vegetables or in herbal teas. Some say they can cure stings on the skin. But though it's delicate and pretty, it needs help from no one to grow. They spread their own seeds with no help from anybody. You're just like a flower, pretty girl. You're beautiful, but strong. Useful, but fun and wonderful. And you don't need help from anybody to do what you need to do. But it never hurts to have a handsome guy around." She winked, causing me to laugh. "Caleb is the perfect guy. He's sweet and caring, very much like a flower himself with that pretty face. And though he would be fine all on his own, it wouldn't hurt for him to have someone that he belonged to. You two, though beautiful and strong separately, are like this Malva flower when you're together. I'll know how good you'll be for and to each other. I'm glad that my Caleb can finally say he's found you."

I nodded my head and wanted to scold her for making me want to cry before we'd barely even started the ceremony. Just the Jacobson family was there, no one that I didn't already know, and they all smiled and parted a path for me to go through. The more people I made it through, the louder a guitar rhythm got. I recognized it as *Beautiful Love* by The Afters.

Uncle Max was the one playing guitar. He grinned and nodded as I passed him. Everyone was so close as I made my way through that we rubbed elbows and I could smell the perfume of several mixed together.

Haddock, I realized, was the only person there from another clan other than Fiona. He smiled at me and touched my hand as I passed him.

Then I saw Peter. I realized that I hadn't seen him all day.

Then Caleb was there as the last people parted the way to reveal him. They circled and enclosed around me, almost pressing in to suffocate me, but none of that mattered. My mouth fell open and a small gasp fell from my lips. I looked him up and down, lingering on his bare feet before moving back up to his clean shaven chin, his lips that were slightly parted, and his button-up red shirt with the top two buttons undone.

God…thank you, for he was beautiful.

He moved the small inches that were between us and licked his lips before wiping under my eye with his thumb. I hadn't realized I was crying, and being without him all day made me sigh when he touched me. His calm, his love, his touch was just what I needed. He moved forward and kissed my cheekbone where the tear was and I practically melted right there in front of his whole family.

He leaned back and looked me over, letting his fingers fall to my shoulder.

That dress is…

Gran made it. I stated what he already knew.

That's not what I meant. At all. His fingers moved along my skin and I got his meaning exactly. I shivered and he smiled in satisfaction.

All right, you, I scolded.

He grinned and put his arm around my back, pulling me into his chest. We both turned to face Peter. I saw Dad and Fiona on the opposite side of us, Bish and Jen were next to us, and Kyle and Lynne on Caleb's side. We all faced Peter as he stood in the middle of the vortex, we circled him as a rim and the family circled us as the outer crust. It was like our own little world. Nothing mattered except this.

Peter began to speak, facing us and being a little biased, I think. Caleb was his son after all. "Imprinting isn't a life sentence. Our people thrive with our significant by our side. We all know the importance of what has happened since Maggie came into our lives. The proof of how destiny works and moves is right here in this circle, in these four couples that will be joined today. But more than destiny and purpose is love. The love one feels for his significant is bigger than any ocean, deeper than any well, more powerful than any storm. When we join these significants today, they are telling us that they want no one else, will always be there for each other and will never part from their mate. Not that I have to tell them that."

The chuckles resounded around us as Peter turned to Kyle and Lynne. "Do you dedicate yourself to your significant?"

Kyle spoke first. "I do, with all that I am."

Lynne said, too loudly, "I do, too, with all I am."

Peter smiled, but didn't join in the laughter with the others. He turned to my dad and I felt my eyes crinkle as I watched him say that he accepted Fiona as his significant. He met my eyes across Peter's shoulder and smiled, showing full on teeth and everything. Then it was Bish and Jen's turn. Peter choked up asking Jen if she would take Bish. And then Dad choked up when Bish said he would take Jen. Bish locked eyes with me and winked. I smiled and looked up at Caleb and it was so cliché. So predictable. So...everything I always imagined it would be. I was breathless and stuck in the trance of watching Caleb as he watched me.

When I heard my name loudly, I pulled my gaze from his and looked at Peter. He looked at me expectantly. "Oh," I realized he'd asked me already. Even Gran's cackle didn't distract me from saying, "I do…with all that I am." I whispered it and didn't wipe the tears that fell. I wore them like a badge that said how happy I was. I was so full that it was spilling over.

When Caleb said his words, they were low and filled with emotion. He brought his hand up, placing his thumb under my chin and his fingers on my cheek "I do, take you, Maggie, with all that I am."

I tried hard to keep it together and not crumble.

Peter cleared his throat several times and when I looked at him, he was fighting his own tears. "Now, as your first act as a married, mated couple, kiss her and claim her for all to see as your true heart and only love."

Caleb pulled me to him, and claim me he did.

Sixteen

Caleb

HER MOUTH had never tasted better.

She let me control her and I just couldn't stop. The feel of her lips, the smell of her cherry blossom perfume, the grip of her fingers in my shirt. Gah... I forced my lips to let go and looked at her as I barely pulled back. "I didn't say it yet, but...hell...you are so beautiful. And that dress is possibly the sexiest thing I've ever seen."

"I'm glad you like it. I wore it for you," she said and smirked up at me. "You're welcome."

I laughed and pressed my nose to hers. I breathed her in.

"All right, you two," Gran spouted from behind us. "Make out later. Especially since we're all just standing here waiting for you to finish smooching. I'm ready for some cake."

We burst out laughing. I nodded to Gran. "Thanks, Gran. Way to stay on top of things."

"Don't sass me, boy." She grinned and pushed past my uncle to reach us as everyone dispersed. She cupped my cheeks. "You're married," she mused. Her eyes took on that sheen that said tears were next. I balked in shock. Gran was crying for me?

"Ah, Gran." I hugged her to me. She fit under my chin like Maggie. "Don't cry, come on."

"You're just so grown up." She leaned back. "A man now, with his own wife and house and life. Pretty soon, you'll be giving me great grandkids and -"

"Hold your horses, Gran," I said laughing, stopping that train right there. Maggie was smiling, but her blush was a clear indicator. "Let's just worry about cake for now, OK?"

"Good idea." She patted my cheek and strutted away toward Kyle, to give him the same speech I assumed, her bare feet small in the grass.

I turned back to Maggie. "First it's having the "No sex" talk and now it's the "Grandkids" talk. The woman switches gears quicker than a five speed."

Maggie giggled. "She's just happy. So am I."

"So am I," I repeated in a growl. I pulled her up to meet my lips and kissed her good. When we finally moved into the garden where the food was, I saw that all the married couples had lingered and were currently making good use of the dark garden corner. Especially Jim. Way to go, Mr. Masters....

Maggie slapped my arm and rolled her eyes. "Eew."

"What?" I laughed.

"Come on, Mr. Jacobson." She tugged my arm as she walked

backward. "Dance with me."

"No," I said.

She looked startled before hearing my thoughts about my wanting to give her a present. "What kind of present?"

"This kind." I took the guitar from Uncle Max and sat in the chair he vacated. The yard was filled with white lights in the trees, looking like stars right above us, but other than that no other decorations. I thought it was kind of hilarious how Maggie hated that sort of thing. It wasn't my family's thing either. She fit right in.

She knelt down on the grass at my feet and looked at me like I was a rock star. I played the song that I wrote, a slow, steady, strumming rhythm and sang the words in my mind just for Maggie to hear. My vows that I made a song with.

You're amazing.
Today you'll be mine in every way,
every sense, every second,
but I know that no matter how tight I hold you,
it'll never be close enough.
No matter how long or hard or passionately I kiss your lips,
it'll never be sating.
You're my soul-mate,
my reason to keep pulling air into my lungs,
my gorgeous significant that fits in my arms
and my life perfectly,
my whole life, my love, my partner in crime,
my very heart, my amazing girl.

She had cried a lot already today and I hated to be the reason she was doing it again. But she reached up and put her arms around my neck, the guitar between us. "Thank you."

"Don't thank me." I sat back and set the guitar aside as I stood and pulled her elbows to help her stand, too. "I love you."

"I love you," she replied in a whisper.

I took her and put her hand on my shoulder, while taking the other in mine. My palm pushed against her lower back and I pressed her to me. My body hummed and told me to touch every piece of skin that I could see. I tried not to let it consume my thoughts, I tried to keep my hands to myself, but I'd find them wandering along her back, caressing down her bare, tan shoulder, linking and lacing our fingers as the skin I touched buzzed with eagerness.

When she started to shiver in the warm night air, I knew I had to stop. She wasn't cold and if I didn't watch it, I was about to embarrass myself. So I focused on the surroundings and let Maggie's thoughts guide mine as she watched her Dad and Fiona. She bit her lip and tried not to cry again. Kyle bumped my shoulder. He had Lynne wrapped up in his arms like a cocoon. He glanced between us and gave me a knowing look.

Things always work out, his look seemed to say.

He and Maggie shared this look, too, that spoke volumes of their past. Of the way Kyle chased her when she wasn't his. About how life finally got right when he decided to let Maggie go. I wasn't surprised when she let me go to hug him. He gripped her tight and I heard his thoughts that he was thankful for unanswered prayers. He loved Maggie, that never changed, but it was the *way* that he loved Maggie that had made the transition. I used to be envious of their past, how he knew so many things about her, but not anymore. Maggie deserved to have a friend like Kyle. He was a good guy and he was going to make a great husband.

When they let go, he hugged me next, patting my back in a brotherly way. He whispered in my ear, "If only Rodney were here with us."

I felt my chest jerk. God help me, it hurt to know that he wasn't here and he should have been. I nodded and he gave me knowing look. "Yeah," I muttered. "That cowboy knew how to party."

Kyle laughed and nodded once. "Yeah."

It was a lame attempt to make it all OK, but it was all we could do.

We danced, and everyone else danced, and Bish and Maggie danced, and Maggie and her Dad danced, Maggie danced with Haddock, and I danced with Jen. I could tell from using Maggie's gift that Jen still had no idea about the house. I grinned and had to give Bish props for doing a good job with keeping it secret. I knew how hard it was.

I looked around at the chaos. The next time a wedding happened in this back yard, I'd be officiating, because I was the Champion now. I was glad that Dad got to perform a service though. He deserved to.

So, then we did the traditional cake eating\feeding thing for Maggie, Lynne and Jim's sake, but that wasn't something we usually did at our weddings. Next, we did our Virtuoso traditional dance. It starts with the bride in the middle, or brides in this case, and the men circle her, link arms and 'protect' her as we do our footwork of leg over right and then back again before kicking your foot right and back again. It was an old folk dance our ancestors started. It was a mix between all sorts of cultures. While each of the men took turns going to the center and dancing with the bride in a circle once before going back to his spot and letting the next man have a turn. Once again, I thought these dances were stupid. Just like at the Reunification where they swap wives for dances for the night, I just got married and I didn't freaking want to share her. But as I watched her dance with all of my uncles and cousins, my annoyance melted away and my laughter replaced it. Especially when Uncle Mike made an ivy vine crawl up and wrap itself around Maggie's arm before attaching it to his, effectively handcuffing her to him. She laughed so hard and giggled it carried over the music.

All I could do was stand there and watch her.

When it was Dad's turn with Maggie, he took all the salt shakers from the picnic tables and dumped them over the girls' heads high enough so that the grains floated down. It fell around us all like sand or snow. It was so cheesy, but I could tell that Maggie and the rest of the girls were mesmerized by it.

After we ate dinner and more cake, and everybody was thinking about heading out, I sprung the news on them that we'd gotten a call from Marcus. I told them I had made reservations at the cottages for us like I told Maggie I would. I instructed them all to get the bags that I knew they had already packed for their honeymoons and meet us there in an hour. Kyle was the only one who grumbled, but he did as we asked. Bish was disappointed. He was looking forward to springing the house on Jen tonight, but understood that everyone's safety was first priority. The rest of the Jacobson clan was on lockdown at Dad's, per my order.

I had to make sure everyone would be safe while we were gone and Dad's house was the safest and biggest place. No one grumbled about my order either. Those Jacobsons were all about a party. Mom was ecstatic to have people to cook for.

We waved and said our goodbyes. Mom cried and fussed over me and then cried and fussed over Maggie. There was no throwing rice, no party favors, no changing of outfits, though we did put some shoes on.

Bish and Jen, and Jim and Fiona rode together while Kyle and Lynne rode with Maggie and me.

I had to turn on the radio pretty loud to cover up the smacking noises of Kyle and Lynne making out in the backseat. Maggie thought it was hilarious and giggled into my arm half the way. I thought she'd sleep, but her fingers kept moving along my arm and fingers. She was absolutely calm. She was calmer than I was.

It made me pause, made me wonder what the reason was for her calm. Instead of making me feel better, it made me worry.

I stopped at the light before the cottages and I felt her palm on my cheek, making me look at her. She didn't say anything, but she didn't need to. The small, honest smile that sat on her lips told me she was just happy…and ready.

I checked us in, gave them their keys, and tried not to be awkward when I gave Jim his. He wouldn't look me in the eye and it took a lot not to groan at the elephant in the room as we all stood around and pretended that we weren't all about to be on our honeymoons.

"So what now?" Bish asked as we stood between our cars in the parking sand.

Jim gasped under his breath and Kyle laughed at the insinuation.

"I meant…what now like tomorrow. Not…right now…" he mumbled, embarrassed. But really, all you could do was laugh. Bish started and the rest of us followed. Once we stopped laughing I answered him, my hand wrapped around Maggie's.

"We're going to hide out here. I used an emergency credit card that Dad has that's not traceable to us. We just need to stay low for a while until we figure out what to do about Marcus."

"So we could be here for like a week?" Lynne asked.

I nodded. "Maybe more."

"Sweet!"

"Well, I think we should check in with each other regularly just to make sure everything's fine. So…tomorrow, let's meet up at lunch?" I suggested. I tried to act totally cool and casual, but everyone saw right through it.

"Yeah. Lunch," Kyle agreed in a snicker. "That ought to be *plenty* of time."

"Shut up, Kyle."

The silence stretched. The awkwardness was so thick I was choking on it. I tried to think of something, anything, but I felt like anything I said would translate to Maggie's dad and brother as, 'Can't wait to bone, Maggie.' So I kept my mouth shut. The thick silence was better than the latter.

Leave it to Kyle not to give two craps about any of that. "Well, goodnight! Sleep tight," he said brightly and practically dragged a giggling Lynne away.

That was my cue.

"We'll see you tomorrow, Dad," Maggie said softly. She hugged him around his middle. "I'm really happy for you," she whispered.

"Me, too," he said. He looked at Fiona over Maggie's head. He smiled at her and she smiled back. She stood there in her red dress, purse in hand, and she didn't look very nervous either.

I took a deep breath. It wasn't a steadying breath, 'cause I didn't need that. It was just a breath. Dad had sat me down earlier today, pulling me away from Jim, Bish and Kyle and all of my uncles. He wanted to speak to me about Maggie…and the wedding night.

"Son, I just want you to be prepared. I know it's awkward to have this talk with me."

"Awkward," I mused. "Yeah, that pretty much covers it."

He smirked. "Look. I know that you know that your imprinted body will know what…to do. And I know that you know the basics and what happens. What I want to talk to you about is the other stuff."

"Other stuff?" I asked.

"Things like the fact that our bodies don't allow us to hurt our mate." He gave me a knowing look. "Ever think about that? We aren't allowed to hurt our mate in *any* way. Not even on our wedding night."

Oh, yikes. That had never even crossed my mind. "Oh…well then what happens? What am I supposed to do?"

"Well, your body will take care of her. She won't actually feel but a split-hair second of pain, if that, before your body is already healing hers. I just wanted you to understand that the birds and bees discussions we had, they are still true of course, but things are a little different for Aces."

I pondered that. It was actually a relief now that we were having this discussion. I would have probably freaked later on tonight and screwed up everything. "Is there anything else?"

"Well, I know that you've mutualized already," he looked at the floor for a few seconds, "but things are also a little different when you add… things to it."

And so the conversation went. By the time we were done, over an hour had passed. I was so grateful for it now. I was grateful in general. In relative terms, Maggie and I were pretty lucky. Our families were great. No matter what happened, even when Dad didn't agree with my decisions, he still was my father and helped me in any way he could. I hoped to be half the man that my father was some day.

Maggie released Jim and he nodded to me before taking Fiona's hand. They were the laid-back couple of us all. They walked leisurely away and Bish and Jen followed a few seconds later after saying their goodbyes to Maggie. She turned with a small smile to me. Her star bracelet jingled as she rubbed her arm. The wind off the ocean was warm, but steady and lots of it.

I held my hand out to her and she took it willingly. I grabbed our bag from the back of the truck and went to the door of the cottage I'd rented. It was a gated condo community with a few cottages right on the beach. It seemed safe for our situation, but still romantic and secluded enough for a honeymoon. It was pretty perfect for last minute.

The door opened with a click and Maggie flicked the lights on with a flip of her hand to the small living room. I put the bag down in the foyer. There was only one bedroom and the door was wide open in invitation. I shut the front door and wondered how long we were going to dance around the obvious before starting the awkward advance toward that room.

But I underestimated her once again. She surprised the heck out of me by not even taking in the room, not even looking around. She kicked her shoes off by the door. Her Converses. I smiled at them before looking at her face again. She was right up against my chest and took my hand, putting it on her cheek. I leaned down and kissed her slowly and sweetly. I thought about my strategy. I should take things really slow and, even though she was calm, I wanted to keep her that way. If she started to freak out…I'd freak out. Just thinking about her freaking out was making me crazy. The imprint in my chest started to hum. It was telling me I had to take care of her, that I needed to make sure she was perfectly comfortable and-

She cupped my face and looked at me closely. "Stop."

Then she lifted up on her toes to kiss my mouth and I chuckled under my breath. I was completely being the girl in this scenario. She smiled against my mouth and I leaned back just an inch to see her.

"I love you," I told her with her hands still on my face. My hands rested on her hips, claiming their first piece of her for the night. "I don't have to tell you this, I know, but if there's anything you need to say or do, including telling me to stop, at any time, say it."

She nodded and I swooped down to claim her lips once more. Her hands were cool on my cheeks. When she opened her mouth to me, that effectively ended everything but resolve.

I pushed her gently to walk backward as I guided her to the one bedroom in the house. The light remained off and we didn't even know what color the walls or bed was, but it didn't matter. When we reached the end of the bed, I debated on how I wanted to take that dress off. I leaned down and kissed her bare shoulder. My hands made the decision for me and bunched the hem of the dress in their fingers. I paused just a beat to make sure Maggie was on the same page with me. When she lifted her arms, a little growl escaped my throat. I couldn't see her, but I knew she was smiling.

I lifted it gently over her head and tossed it behind me. I reached

for her sides and found them as I found her mouth again. She was unbuttoning my shirt before I could even think to do so. I let her and didn't help her. I reached into my pants pocket, pulling the cog family object out that I always kept with me, and set it on the bedside table. When she reached for the button of my black slacks, I couldn't stop my breath from catching. She let them drop and I stepped out of them as I moved closer to her.

I stopped thinking. I let the way my body wanted and knew her guide me. Her heart in my chest beside mine beat steadily, and her happiness and contentment coated my tongue. It was everywhere. I was drowning in her, a dying man, content to asphyxiate as long as I could keep my lips on her.

My hands ran the path from the front of her belly to her back while my lips moved in to kiss the side of her neck. She leaned her head back, giving me an all-access pass to her skin, and her fingers dug into my shoulders. I moved my lips lower to her throat, and then the lowest I'd ever been, and kissed the spot right above her bra. If the little noise she made was any indication, I'd say she was enjoying it.

We'd barely even started and it was already the best freaking day of my life.

Her fingers hooked into the waistband of my boxers as my mouth moved back to her mouth like a magnet. I swept in deep and long. I'd never get tired of this. When I felt her fingers slide my boxers down in slow inches, one side an inch and then the other, I felt a slice of ego go through that she wanted me just as badly as I wanted her.

I hugged her to me to tackle the bra and found no clasp in the back. "Front," she whispered. I gulped in thanks to whoever had put her in that daggum bra. For some reason a 'front' clasp sounded a hundred times more sexy.

I could just make out her face and silhouette now that my eyes had adjusted to the dark room. I could hear the waves outside and there were no streetlights, but the moon was bright. I kissed her nose and all the freckles there. Though I couldn't see them, I knew they were there.

I kept my eyes on hers as I let my nimble fingers find the clasp that was about to change my world. Her eyes bore into mine and when the clasp clicked, she didn't flinch. The kissing took on new meaning after that, the touching took on new levels, the tingling and humming on my skin from my body finally getting what it needed took on new heights. I knew she was right there with me, on the same page, feeling the same things and understanding them for what they were.

"I love you...with all that I am," I heard myself whisper before gently laying her down and then following her.

"I love you, Caleb," she sighed my name. "Oh, my..." She gasped when my tongue touched her collarbone.

"I once told you not to say my name like that because it was too distracting," I mused and chuckled. "But now I'm asking...say my name again."

She pulled me down to her, pressing her lips to my ear. "Caleb," she whispered it and then bit into my earlobe, causing me to groan.

"Yeah," I praised. "Ah, hell yeah." I hadn't felt her try to press into my mind yet, but I knew exactly what I wanted. "Baby, listen. I want the first time to just be us." I felt her confusion. "I mean, let's save the mutualizing for another time. I just... this time, I just want to feel you and only you."

I felt her nod. "I love you," she told me. "I love you so much."

"Gah, do I love you, baby," I growled. Then I stopped talking.

Seventeen

Maggie

His HEART worked its way into my chest to beat with mine and I'd never been more focused on anyone's every move and every thought before. His sole purpose, his only motivation, was me. His heart pounded in his chest and I clung to him as he did everything he could to put me at ease, while simultaneously driving me insane.

His lips proved to be their own entity. They were alive, and as they worked over my throat, I was lost. "Caleb," I found myself saying once again. I couldn't seem to stop saying his name.

He stopped and lifted his head. He didn't say anything, but this was his way of silently asking me if I was ready. There was nothing left between us and straddling the line was a thing of the past now. And yes, I was ready.

I pulled him down to me, giving my answer as I kissed him. He moved his lips to kiss my forehead, my cheek, my nose. He stopped there, letting his forehead rest to mine. "You're mine," he said softly. "And I'm yours."

"I'm yours," I repeated to him and he smiled as he kissed me.

"I won't hurt you, Maggie," he promised gruffly.

"I know," I said with certainty. "I'm ready, Caleb," I whispered.

His breathing was rough. "I love you."

Before I could say it back, I was lost in him. I welcomed it. His hands possessed me. His mouth owned me. I was his.

The morning light swept over me. I was warm and comfortable in a big, white bed. I moved just an inch to get comfortable and heard Caleb's grunt as he pulled me closer back into the cocoon of blankets and his chest. I felt my lips smile as I remembered everything from last night.

Everything.

The trail of clothes was just one reminder of the night I'd had. If that wasn't reminder enough, I was naked, too.

I giggled into my pillow. I couldn't believe it! I was married. I was Caleb's wife. I was a woman and I felt like one. I turned a bit to see his face over my shoulder. The man could pull off the tussled look better than anyone. I rolled over to snuggle into him and let my fingers run the length of his jaw and chin. He had one arm under his head like a pillow and the other arm was thrown over my waist.

He already had a little scruff going on. But last night...it had been smooth and soft as he nuzzled my neck. I let my fingers run through his hair. I enjoyed, very much, the groans and little movements he made as

I did it. I leaned forward and kissed his nose. Then I kissed his cheek and he moved his face to find my lips. I laughed silently. He wasn't even awake yet. So I kissed his other cheek and covered my mouth to stop the laugh when he moved his face again to find my lips. So I gave in and gave the poor guy what he was looking for.

I kissed his lips and he immediately tightened his grip and kissed me back. When his eyes started to flutter, I knew he was waking up. He looked at me like he was expecting me there, like it was natural and the most comfortable thing in the world. "Hey, baby," he muttered sleepily and huskily. "Good morning."

"Good morning."

"Did you sleep all right?"

I paused for dramatic effect. "I slept great," I whispered.

His eyes opened wider, completely awake. "Oh, really?" I nodded slowly. He grinned. It was one of those completely all-male, smug, sexy grins. "Well, that's great. That you slept well." He was still grinning.

I laughed and burrowed further under him. He was leaning over me barely on his one elbow. "And how do you feel this morning, Mrs. Jacobson?"

I smiled and bit my lip. "Perfect."

He put one hand on the other side of me on the bed and leaned down to kiss my lips softly. With not an inch between his mouth and mine he said, "The words for what I want to say right now don't exist. Everything sounds…so cliché."

"You don't have to say anything, Jacobson." I smoothed his chest over his heart. "I know exactly what you want to say."

"Well, *right now*," he started and then leaned in to nibble my throat,

"I don't really want to talk anyway."

I sighed as I felt my skin start to tingle. "OK," I agreed.

He chuckled. "Oh, you're *really* putting up a fight."

"Shut up and kiss me," I said before pulling him to me.

His hand found my leg and moved up to my thigh as his lips stopped talking.

And he claimed me once more.

"We should probably get going," he said, but made no advances to move. "We need to meet up with everyone soon."

I was almost back asleep again as his fingers traced little star patterns on my back. "Boo."

He laughed, his warm breath stirring my hair. "Come on, gorgeous. Don't make this harder than it already is."

Then we heard a knock. "See?" he said laughing and jumped up to get dressed. "Now you've done it." He could have been speaking Chinese for all I knew. Because last night had been dark, and now it was daytime. I wasn't closing my eyes this time. I watched eagerly as he slipped his black pants back on without his boxers. "Your pops is here to scold me for not letting his daughter outta bed."

I smirked. "I'm going to say it's all your fault, too."

He smiled devilishly as he turned and called over his shoulder. "Don't play with fire, baby."

I giggled into the covers before throwing them aside and running to the bathroom. I put a thick robe on and went out to greet whoever had come to pay us a visit, but Caleb was alone. He carried a tray to the bed that held juice and two huge plates of pancakes with clear covers over the top. "You ordered room service?"

"No, he said that someone else had. Probably someone at the office knew it was our honeymoon. That was nice of them."

"Yeah," I agreed and sat on his lap. I lifted the lid. "Now we don't even have to leave the room to eat."

He pulled the robe off of my shoulder and kissed my skin as I bit into the bacon. "Oh, my...I've created a monster, haven't I?" he mocked.

"Well, then I can get dressed and-"

He grabbed me to keep me there when I started to get up. "Don't." He pushed my hair aside and kissed my neck. "Let me rephrase that. *You've* created a monster."

"That's right," I joked and turned to straddle his lap. I fed him a bite of bacon. "This feels so normal. For once, I feel like we're just a normal couple with normal things going on. I like all the supernatural stuff, too," I assured him. He smiled and nodded like he understood. "But being normal is underrated."

"Yeah..." He sighed. "I wish I could just run away with you somewhere. Never look back."

I tilted my head to the side. "No, you don't." He smiled at being caught in his lie. "You'd miss Maria and Bella like crazy."

"I would," he agreed. "I miss Bella right now. She'd be stealing my bacon."

I laughed. "Is she going to live with us or stay with your parents?"

"Us. She likes you too much."

"I like her, too." I took a deep breath. I couldn't believe how happy and just...calm I felt. "I'm so happy," I heard myself say.

He did this half sigh, half laugh thing. "You have no idea how happy that makes me."

He kissed me, wrapping his arms around my waist, and pulled me to him sweetly.

When we finally managed to finish our breakfast, and juice, and get dressed, it was almost lunch. We moseyed through the back door across the sand to the veranda. This place looked like it was made for honeymoons. The white sheer curtains matched the ones in our room. They flowed in the wind and blocked the sand from blowing on us as we sat down on the lounger. The rest of them joined us shortly and I closed my mind to them all, not wanting to hear their thoughts about their nights, and not wanting to hear their questions or...whatever...about my own.

Dad wouldn't even look at me. Neither would Bish. Kyle and Lynne were the only ones who were normal, asking the waiter for sweat tea for everyone, and laughing and joking with each other. Caleb watched the fabric on the chair beside us like it was made of gold.

I started to giggle. I couldn't help it. It was so funny to me that we all knew what we'd all done last night and now everyone was acting so weird about it, like it wasn't normal or something. Caleb started to laugh under his breath with me.

Dad looked at me curiously, but Bish must've caught on, because he and Jen both leaned into each other laughing. I guess he finally understood the discomfort everyone was putting out was the cause of our outbursts. He chuckled a little and shook his head. "So anyway," I said with a smile. "Now that that's out of the way, we need to just figure out how long we're going to be here. What we need to do as far as Marcus goes."

Caleb answered me so everyone could hear, but so that it didn't carry out to the other people on the beach. "Dad's having the family look. He hasn't shown up at the Watson compound or any of the family houses. He ditched his cell. We have no idea where he is."

I grumbled, "If I only had something of his, I could touch it and find him."

He rubbed my arm, "It's OK, baby. We'll make sure we find him."

"Have you heard from Beck?" Kyle asked.

I nodded. "She's fine. They're safe somewhere, but she said to stop calling, so…"

"Aw, Mags. That sucks. Rebecca was always pretty stubborn."

"Not to me she wasn't," I said softly. Caleb's arm came around me and he pulled me to his side, kissing my temple.

"She'll come around," he soothed, but his calm didn't come. I was just about to panic, when I finally felt it seep into my skin. I looked at him and he had been feeling the same thing. His browed scrunched.

You must be too worked up. I didn't realize you were that upset about it.

Neither did I.

I shook my head and went on. "We'll call Peter later and see what's up with the search."

"In the meantime," Kyle said playfully and pulled Lynne into his lap, "we'll have to be miserable at the beach." He nipped her shoulder. "With a room all to ourselves. How will we ever survive?"

"Shut it, Kyle," Caleb joked.

Everyone laughed. Then Dad pulled Fiona to him and leaned back in his chair with her leaning on his chest. It was very sweet and it was good to see Dad being normal again. He was so sweet to Fiona in the way that Virtuoso men were to their significants. It made me happy to know that not only would Dad have a good life because of their finding each other, but so would Fiona. He said, "So we just wait here until we hear back from Peter about Marcus? That's it?"

"I'm going to start calling and texting the other clans to see if anyone knows anything, or may have heard something even if they didn't understand what it was they were hearing. They might not think it was anything. But we're going to keep looking." I looked to Bish, who was already looking at me. "We have to."

He gulped visibly and gripped Jen's hand tighter in his as he pleaded with his eyes to please find a way to stop the vision.

I nodded a little. I was going to stop that vision. No matter what had to happen, I was going to make sure I stopped it.

Once we sat around and ate some lunch, we all decided to go to the beach for a swim. We rented surfboards and Caleb, Kyle, Lynne, and I surfed while Bish and Dad sat with Jen and Fiona on the lounges in the sun. I forgot almost all he'd taught me, or my body had, because it was practically impossible to stay on the board. I fell every single time I tried to glide, and may have pouted a little.

Caleb and I went to lie on the beach towels while Kyle and Lynne kept surfing. I traced the star tattoo on Caleb's shoulder with my finger as he dozed beside me when we heard Lynne's scream. He jolted awake and we both ran over to where Kyle was carrying her and putting her down in the sand. He held her foot in his lap as he tried to heal the cut from the shell she stepped on. It had sliced her foot from toe to heal. I cringed as the blood stained the sand under them.

The others ran over, too, and watched Kyle concentrate. He looked up at her and huffed. "Why isn't it working?"

I watched her cut and it wasn't healing. And then it was. He sighed loudly and rubbed her leg to soothe her. "Must've been too worked up, I guess," he said out loud, but his mind said, *What the hell! Thought I was about to have another situation like her cheek.*

Lynne sat up and gave him a scolding look. "Stop. I'm fine."

He rubbed his thumb over the scar on her cheek and sighed. "You're beautiful. Even with this."

"Kyle, stop beating yourself up."

He shrugged like he was appeasing her, but had no real plans to do so. I broke in.

"Why don't we all go take a nap? I'm pretty tired actually."

"Yeah right," Kyle said and grinned deviously. "We all know why you want to drag my cousin back to that room, Maggie Jacobson."

I glared and Caleb punched his shoulder. "Shut up," he hissed and glanced at Dad.

"Mr. Masters knows why you want to, too," Kyle joked and dodged Caleb's swing.

"Kyle," Dad complained and rolled his eyes. "That's a good idea. I am actually pretty tired. Want to meet back up for dinner?"

Caleb held up his hand. "There's this great little seafood place right around the corner the guy I booked the cottages through told me about. We can try it if you want."

"Yes!" Jen said and smiled pleadingly at Bish. "Aw, I've been dying for some real crab cakes!"

He quirked his mouth to the side in a half smile. I knew that smile. He used to use it on me when I was a kid and he thought I was being adorable. I'd seen him use it on Maria when she asked him to dance at the Reunification, too. Now he was using it on Jen because even I had to admit she was adorable. She was so happy and almost silly. That just wasn't Jen, and it was good to see her kick back and be able to be young again.

"Yeah, let's," he agreed. She squealed a little. Squealed...and jumped up to hug him around his neck. He held her to him easily and looked at me over her shoulder. He smiled the biggest smile. It was amazing.

So that's what we did, and that night at the restaurant, Dad gave us some big news. I must've been too focused on Caleb to pay attention to anyone else's thoughts because I was a little shocked. "So..." he started and made this noise like he knew we weren't going to like it, "I've decided to go and live with Fiona's family...clan...for a while."

Bish was the first to respond. "But why? We're going to be..."

He stopped his thought of saying he was going to live right next door and immediately started using Caleb's trick to keep Jen from seeing about the house. His thoughts of an art project he was working on flitted through his, Jen's and my minds. He was thinking about finishing off the trees on his canvas with a light stream from the sun. What brush stroke to use.

Jen looked at him with a curiously raised brow. He just smiled and turned back to Dad and frowned. "Why are you leaving?"

"Well…for one, I don't think it's right for her to have to leave her family like that."

Fiona butted in. "I told you, it's tradition. It's just…the way we've always done things. I'll still see them, just not all the time."

He took her hand in his. "I understand, but Bish and Maggie are getting on with their lives. I'm ready to get on with mine. We can travel, see your family and stay with them for a bit, and then we'll come back in a few months. I just really would like to get to know your family, learn where you come from."

She blushed with pleasure. "And I really love you for that."

He smiled. "So, we're going to leave," he announced. "I figure that Marcus or whoever else is trying to get to us can't do that if we're with her family. He won't even know that we're there. And you," he said to me, "well, you're very capable of kicking anyone's butt, so I don't think I have to worry."

I laughed. As much as I hated that he was leaving, he had a point about not being here. And it was really sweet that he wanted to get to know her family. In his mind, he was thinking that he didn't want her to lose touch with her mother like I had mine.

Eighteen

Caleb

"Well...call me and let me know that you made it there, OK?" Maggie sniffled a little and it kinda made me want to tell ol' Jim off for making her cry. But the guy was just trying to make his own significant happy so I couldn't blame him too much.

He hugged her hard. She hugged him back just as hard. He leaned back and put his hand on her cheek. "Love ya, baby girl."

"I love you, too, Daddy," she whispered. He smiled tightly, trying to hold in his emotions. He moved on to Bish, and Fiona moved on to Maggie.

She smiled with chagrin. "Well, Maggie, I'm sorry that it seems like I'm stealing him away."

"It's all right. I understand why he's doing it. It's really sweet. I'm glad that he actually wants to do something like that. It was just kind of sudden, that's all."

Maggie hugged her, which surprised Fiona, who made a little, "Oh," sound.

"Take care of him, OK?"

Fiona nodded quickly. "Of course. I promise, Maggie. Thank you." She touched Maggie's shoulder. "Don't worry about him, OK?"

She hopped in the cab and Jim came to me. Of course, I was last. "Well, son, I don't think that I have to convey how much I'll hurt you if anything happens to Maggie, right?"

"No, sir," I said and stuffed my hands into my pockets. "I'll take care of her even before myself."

"Good." Then he hugged me. I gulped, waiting for the pun, for the shoe to drop. There was none. He leaned away and gave me a crooked smile. "Take care of yourself, son. I couldn't have handled Maggie ending up with anyone else."

Did he really just say that? "Thank you, sir."

"Jim," he corrected.

"Jim."

"Bye, Caleb. We'll see you soon!" Jim called before getting in the cab.

Then they were gone to the airport and Bish turned to Maggie. "Well, little sister, we're all alone with no parents to watch us. What mischief can we get into?"

She smiled along with his joke. "We could bake every pack of sugar cookies in the cabinets again. That went over well when they got home last time."

He slung his arm over her shoulder and chuckled. "Boy, I've never seen a woman so worked up over cookies before."

They began to walk back to the rooms. Jen came to my side and we watched.

"Yeah," Maggie said laughing, "well, it was over a hundred cookies."

"They totally overreacted."

Jen laughed. "They're happy," she mused, like it was amazing.

"And you're happy." I mirrored Bish's pose and threw my arm over her shoulder. "It's about time."

"I was happy," she rebutted. "Maria makes me happy."

"Yeah, but not like that." I nodded down to her tattoo that had Bish's name on the outside. There was an infinity symbol in the middle. She blushed like I've never seen her blush. "When did y'all ascend?"

"Last night." She sighed like I was being dramatic. "It's not a big deal. We didn't say anything because-"

"You didn't want the spotlight on you. I get it." I waited as we walked. She folded her arms over her chest as we swayed with each step. I stared. Finally, I saw her mouth crack a smile.

"Stop staring, weirdo." I kept staring until she finally caved. "What is your deal?"

"What's your ability? You know what I'm asking. Don't withhold just to be mean."

She smiled at me like I was a child. "Whatever. It's, uh…I can kind of blend into my surroundings."

I felt my eyebrows rise. "Blend in?"

"Mmhmm."

I grinned. "Say it."

"I will not say it," she laughed.

"Come on, say it."

She fought it for a few seconds before she smiled. "Fine," she groaned. "I'm the invisible woman."

"Sweet."

We laughed as she lightly punched my gut and caught up to them.

That night we ate steak, homemade bread, and honey butter on the veranda. I had to hand it to the place, as Maggie moaned and licked it off her fingers, the food was killer.

Then we turned in, and went back to our own cottages and…man, I just couldn't believe how much pure elation I got when it was time to go back to our room at night. I chewed and sucked on my bottom lip as we made our way through the sand. I looked back to see where Kyle and Bish were. They were almost to their rooms, too. When I turned back, my arm swung right into a cactus. I hissed and cursed.

I felt her heart skid as she turned with inhuman speed and came to me to see what was up. "What happened?"

"Freaking cactus. Who plants cactuses at the beach?"

She smiled and kissed my finger. That got my blood boiling. She pulled me up the step to the porch and then swung open the bay doors. I pushed her with my hands on her waist to the big white bed and went down with her. The wind blew warm and salty air through the sheer white curtains. I kissed her mouth, her neck. We traded places as we rolled and then I was back on top.

Then I saw in my mind, the vision. This was one of Maggie's visions from when we imprinted. We walked through the sand, came through the bay doors and I kissed her 'til she couldn't breathe in a big white bed. Maggie broke the kiss and gasped as she realized, too. "That's two. Only one left to go," she mused.

I thought for a second. I wondered if it was too soon to show her the one I had. I looked up at her wide, expectant eyes, and decided she was ready for anything I could give her. "Want to see?" I whispered.

She didn't hesitate. "Always."

I took a deep breath and got ready for the vision, the one that made me want to burst into tears every single time I remembered it. Maggie snuggled in and pressed her forehead to mine. I let it flow through me to her and heard her intake of breath when it started to play. Maggie was sleeping. She heard a noise and rolled over, her hand reaching across the bed until it reached the alarm clock. She stretched and then got up, going into the yellow room down the hall. I was there, rocking the little boy in my arms and smiled when I saw her. She came in and kissed me full on the mouth over the baby, and then laughed when the boy complained and reached for her. She took him. He was very little still and she kissed his forehead, making my heart melt like an ice cube. "He's hungry, Mommy."

"He's always hungry, aren't you, Rodney?" she cooed and smiled at him.

"Daddy!" we heard down the hall. Our girl that looked like Maggie's mini-me ran in and the vision faded. Maggie shook beside me and I hugged her to me tightly, understanding.

I pressed my lips to her head and whispered into her hair. "See, baby? We're going to have it all."

She leaned back, her face wet. "I want it all. Caleb...Rodney..."

I shook my head. "I know. I never really understood why we named him that until he died. Now it makes perfect sense."

"I can't wait," she said in awe. "I know we're young and barely even getting started, but I can't wait to hold that little girl in my hands."

"You will," I promised. "And everything will be perfect one day."

She pulled me down to kiss her lips. "I love you. Thank you."

"I love-" She cut me off with a kiss and I chuckled against her lips. I surrendered. The girl was good at persuasion. We melted into the white sheets and comforter. I had been the one to control the bedroom so far for the most part, but tonight, Maggie was on fire from the inside out. She drove me to new heights in record time and I just held her and tried not to combust into flames. Man, she was hot, and so freaking sexy.

We had yet to add mutualizing to the mix. That was OK. Maggie was a beautiful force all her own and I was plenty occupied. I pulled her shirt over her head and 'oomphed' when she pushed me back down to the bed. I laughed at her enthusiasm. She grinned sexily with her hair across her face.

Soon I was lost in my beautiful girl. And I wasn't ready to be found.

In the morning, I knew something was wrong. Even though neither of us had clothes on, and almost every inch of our skin was touching, I was in withdrawals. I groaned and swallowed the pain down in my throat. Maggie jolted awake and threaded her fingers through my hair to bring me closer. Finally, after long seconds of panic, I began to feel her touch seep into me. She sighed and I pulled her closer. "What the hell..." I groaned.

"I'm starting to worry now," she said. "Yesterday was weird, too, right?"

I nodded barely. "I wonder if it was just us."

I rolled over and took her with me. She lay on my chest and breathed deeply. It was almost as if we were scared to stop touching each other. "It's OK, baby. Let's go and see if the others-"

Our room's door swung open. Kyle and Lynne stood there with angry and scared faces.

"Dude, freaking knock," I yelled and pulled the blanket up to Maggie's chin.

"We have a problem," Kyle barked back.

Maggie sat up a little, taking the blanket with her, pulled tight. "We know. We were in withdrawals, too."

The blanket around her wasn't enough for me. "Get out so we can get dressed."

Kyle huffed. "You are such a-"

"Out!" I yelled. "Sorry, Lynne."

"It's all right," she assured and tugged his arm. "Come on, babe. Just let them get some clothes on."

"So stupid," he complained and pushed through the doors to the sand.

"Babe," Maggie complained, "he's just freaked out."

"And you're just naked," I grumbled.

"Yeah," she agreed. She pushed the covers off and went to the suitcase to pick through and get some clothes. I stared, even with everything going on, I stared. I saw her grin and shake her head in her peripheral. She threw a t-shirt at me. "Get dressed, you," she laughed her words.

So I did, and then we met Lynne and Kyle on the back porch where they were sitting at the umbrella table. "Nice threads," Kyle sneered, "now can we get back to the fact that my significant was in withdrawals this morning even though I was right there beside her?"

"So was mine," I growled.

"OK," Maggie interceded and took my hand. "OK. Let's just sit and figure this out. Something happened. It must've just been us. Surely we would have heard from Peter and the rest if anyone else had this problem, right?"

I sat in the chair and pulled Maggie to sit in my lap. I didn't want to be away from her touch right now. "Yes." I sighed. "Dad would have called."

"Maybe we should go check on Bish and Jen," Maggie suggested, but we saw them walking up the beach. Maggie could hear the confusion in Bish's mind. "Oh, no…"

They came up and plopped down on the patio sofa. He leaned forward, his elbows on his knees, and held Jen's hand tightly. "So, I guess it wasn't just us this morning?"

"No," Maggie said sadly. "We're trying to figure out what happened."

"It doesn't make any sense," Kyle said angrily and touched Lynne's arm. "I can feel her right now. It's just like it always is. And we were touching all night, so why are we in withdrawals one minute and just fine the next?"

"We don't know," I said back. "That's what we need to figure out. Just let me think."

"Call Uncle Peter," Kyle barked and glared at me. "When he was Champion, he didn't just sit there with Aunt Rachel on his lap, he got to work to see what needed to be done."

I felt anger roll through me.

"Kyle!" Maggie scolded and turned sideways to put her hand on my arm. "We'll figure this out. There has to be a clear-cut reason. Something happened. We just need to figure out what."

"You do that," Kyle muttered under his breath.

Maggie rolled her eyes and stared at me.

He's being a jackass because he's scared for Lynne. Don't sweat him.

I breathed deep and let her calm me. I could feel it seep into me. Kyle was right. It didn't make sense why it only worked half the time.

He's right.

But he's not right about you. You made sure all of your family was safe before we left.

I shrugged. Now I was failing at keeping the most important person to me safe. It felt like everything was coming to a head. That vision\ dream I had of Maggie dying… I just felt like this had something to do with it.

"Don't," she said harshly.

Bish and Jen said they wanted to go back and lie down. I agreed. I needed to go and make some calls, think, try to see what we could find out. Jen knocked over one of the tea glasses left on the porch. It shattered on the wood deck. She bent over to pick up the pieces, even though Maggie said she'd get it, and cut her finger on a shard. It was like time just stopped. We all stared at her cut, barely breathing, as Bish gulped and took her hand in his, trying to heal her.

It wasn't even thinking about healing. Maggie breathed out a sigh. "Oh, no," she whispered.

"What?" I asked and stood. "What, babe?"

"Your calm didn't come to me earlier yesterday either, remember?

Then this morning, and now this." She knelt down to Jen and put her hands on her face.

I wanted to scream when the vision hit Maggie and me both. I heard her gasp as we saw Marcus…and he was here.

The vision started with room service. They were getting the breakfast carts ready to bring to our rooms. Marcus was off to the side, speaking with the concierge. "And the juice, too, for all of them. I want them to have everything they need."

"And would you like to address a card to them, sir? So they'll know who to thank?"

"No," Marcus said quickly. "I want it to be a surprise. I don't want them to know I'm here." He smiled. "They've just always been kind to me. I want to return the favor."

The man smiled. "Very well, sir. I'll get the glasses and then have this delivered."

"Great." Marcus watched as the man went to the cabinet behind him. Then he took a vial from his pocket and poured a little bit into each pitcher of juice. It was a light liquid and didn't change the color of the contents. He stuck the vial back into his pocket as the man turned and put the glasses on the trays.

"Thanks for doing this."

"No problem, sir. I'm sure the newlyweds will be very grateful."

Marcus grinned. "I can't wait to see their faces when they find out it was me."

The man winked. "It'll be our secret."

The vision faded and I wanted to punch something. Jen's breathing was ragged as Bish pulled her up and to him. He touched her cheek and they stared at each other. We all knew it. This was it. This was Marcus' big move, his plan, the visions we'd seen before all led up to this. And he was ahead if we were keeping score. He'd managed to scare us into secluding ourselves, then getting us where our abilities and healing touch stopped working on each other. We were vulnerable and he knew it. He was just playing with us, waiting for the right time.

I wondered if we should leave. Pack up and head home, but if we did that he'd follow us and we'd be putting the whole clan in jeopardy, not just us.

So I was basically choosing the clan over Maggie, my sister and cousin. I gulped at the ache in my chest at that thought. But what was I supposed to do? I was the Champion.

"You're right," Maggie invaded my thoughts. "We need to deal with this here, once and for all, and be done with that bastard."

I opened my arms for her to come into and she reeled toward me. Everyone's thoughts that I could hear through Maggie were solemn and thoughtful. We all wanted to come up with a plan, but we didn't even know what game we were playing. Was Marcus here alone? When did he plan to attack? Was he just going to watch us for days and then kill us in our sleep? We knew nothing at this point.

Bish's sigh drew all our attention. We watched as Jen's cut on her hand began to heal slowly. So slowly that I wondered if my eyes were playing tricks on me. But eventually, it sealed itself. I shut my mind to them all. I needed to think and be in my own head for a minute. So I didn't hear their internal conversation, I just heard Jen's whisper.

"Bish…no."

His thumb rubbed over her cheek. "I pushed you. You told me this would happen and I made you feel guilty about not touching me. You'd be safe. The vision Maggie had wouldn't be about to come true."

"It won't," Jen begged, breaths shuddering. "Bish, don't say that."

"It's true," he said a bit harshly, getting more worked up by the second, and shook his head. "This is all my fault. I just wanted you."

Maggie turned, tears on her eyelashes as she remembered us having a similar conversation. Bish was being an idiot, just like I had been. I wrapped my hand around Maggie's wrist to calm her and was so happy when it worked. But Bish was a part of my clan now whether he wanted to be or not, and I wasn't about to stand here and let him say something he'd regret. Jen was my sister.

"Bish, come on, man," I told him. He looked over at me. "Why don't we take a walk?"

He laughed without humor. "So now that I'm in your clan, Champion, you're my boss?"

"I am your Champion," I made sure to say, "but you're married to my sister." I looked at her and she pleaded with me not to say anything, but I had to. "And you're making her cry."

His face fell. I saw his throat work through a gulp as he turned back to her. She was trying so hard to hold it together for him. He sighed. "How can you even forgive me for doing this to you? To Maria?"

"It won't come true. It won't. We'll make sure of it."

"We're on the beach," he told her. "This is where it happened."

"No. Stop it!" she shrieked and he yanked her to him. She cried into his shoulder as he shook from his own emotion.

"God, help me," he whispered, "please."

Don't let this happen. She's mine to protect. Mine. Please don't take her from that little girl because I was selfish. Please.

Maggie had graduated to full-on sobs in my arms as we listened to Bish's plea. Kyle and Lynne stood stupefied on the steps. Kyle's anger at me was long gone. It was sinking into everyone what our honeymoon had become.

A trap.

Maggie was solemn as she made calls to the other clan members later that afternoon. I was on the phone with Dad behind her. We sat on the bed against the headboard and she sat between my legs on her cell. I could hear their enthusiasm when they realized it was Maggie calling them, but soon sobered when she started asking about them seeing or hearing from Marcus or the other Watsons. No one knew anything, but a couple more clans had members that had imprinted. They were waiting for us to get back from our honeymoon before telling us.

Maggie's emotions were all over the place. She was so happy for them and glad. She felt like we had to be doing something right and on the right track or things wouldn't be moving so smoothly for our people. But even though Maggie had seen the vision of her and me when we were older, it was hard to put all your faith into a vision when we'd seen with our own eyes how they could change.

In fact, we were hoping the one with Marcus would change. So we were *hoping* for one and *damning* the other. It made no logical sense, but it was all we had.

And we were clinging to it.

Nineteen

Maggie

We went to Bish and Jen's room that night for dinner. We had no luck with the other clans as to any plans they'd heard of. We alerted the staff and concierge of the villas to the presence of a stalker. He apologized and said, after being shown a picture, that he had seen the man, but he had pretended to be our friend. They set up extra night guards, but we knew it didn't matter. If Marcus was here, he wasn't going to be stopped by a guy with a taser.

So we ate our divine clam chowder, and I didn't even taste it. Bish was just…sick with the knowledge that a madman was out to hurt them. We debated once more about going home, but upon calling Peter, Caleb learned that the alarms had been going off on the outskirts of the property.

It didn't make any sense. We were just sitting here. What was he waiting for? We were all starting to feel the withdrawals from our significant. Caleb and I sat with our hands linked and we'd finally start to feel a little seep in, but it couldn't replace what was lost before it was already draining us back down. Still, I clung to that hand because he was all I had.

Caleb started to prowl and I knew things really were bad.

He paced back and forth, his face angry and set as he tried to think of a trap or a set-up for Marcus. A way to lure him to us so that we could end this on our terms instead of waiting for him to catch us off guard.

"Wait!" I shouted as I had an idea. "What about Gran? Why can't she heal us?"

Kyle deflated and answered. "She can only heal supernatural things, injuries caused by someone's ability. This...this is alchemy."

"Oh..." I deflated, too.

"Let's just go to bed here. All of you," Bish suggested. "I'd feel better if we were all together."

"Ah, you do care for me, you big lug," Kyle said in a girly voice.

"Not you, hair-brain. Maggie."

I saw Caleb stiffen with his back to me. "Not that you think Caleb can't take care of me or anything, it's just safer for us *all* to be together."

"Right," he agreed distractedly as he looked around. "There are blankets around here somewhere, I'm sure."

"I'm not staying here," Lynne said, her lip trembling. "I'm on my honeymoon! Don't I deserve to have a few days to just-"

"Lynne," Kyle said and scoffed. "Our abilities don't work anyway. No mutualizing tonight, babe."

"That's not what I meant!" she shrieked.

He scowled with chagrin. "I'm sorry. That wasn't funny." He swiped at his hair with his fingers. "I get weird when I'm freaking out."

I used that as my chance to maybe get everyone to calm down. "Like the time you caused a mini-riot at school and all the teacher's cars got egged at the pep rally?"

He laughed in surprise. "You remember that?"

"Are you kidding?" I grabbed Caleb's arm to make him sit on the sofa in Bish's den with me. He would never stop pacing and worrying if I didn't. "You're an infamous troublemaker, Kyle. Everyone remembers that."

He grinned in amusement. "That *was* a good prank. Those teachers needed to learn to lighten up."

"What was the prank?" Lynne asked. I leaned my head on Caleb's shoulder and felt him sigh. It wasn't because my calm was hitting him, it was just because. My back began to ache, but I tried not to notice as Caleb stuck a hand between my thighs and listened.

"Well," Kyle said and rubbed his chin, "they were taking the candy machines out of the school."

"You guys had candy machines?" she asked.

"Focus, babe," he said grinning. "So, they had this assembly saying they were taking them all out, so we retaliated, saying that if they were going to do that, then they should take them out of the teacher's lounge, too. They were so mad!"

"So what did they do?"

"They cancelled our pep rally, stating it was academic probation for misconduct. So we said we were having one anyway, and when the teachers showed up to close it down, because we knew they would, we egged their cars."

"Wow. So you were like some kinda...rock star in high school or something?"

Kyle laughed so hard.

"Don't feed that ego, Lynne! Come on!" I played along.

I felt Caleb shake with a little chuckle beside me. Bish and Jen were shaking their heads as they lay on the bed.

Then it hit me.

"Ah! Dad!" I whipped out my cell, even as Bish tried to find out what I was talking about. He answered groggily. "Yeah?"

"Sorry. I know you were sleeping, but...how are you?"

"I'm fine, Maggie. Is something wrong?"

"You're not in withdrawals?"

A long pause. "Noooooo." A few whispers. "What's this about?"

"But..." that didn't make sense, "didn't you eat the breakfast that room service brought you the other day?"

"No, we had already ordered something earlier. We sent it back. What's this about, Maggie?"

I sighed. "Nothing. We're fine. I just wanted to make sure you got there all right."

"We did. We're just tired. It was a long flight. You're sure you're OK?"

"Yeah. I'm fine," I lied. I looked at Bish. "Everyone's fine."

"All right...well, I'm going back to bed then." He laughed a little. "Good night. Love ya."

"Love you, Dad."

He hung up and I was relieved. At least Dad was safe.

The last thing I remembered before dozing off was Caleb laying me down and getting a blanket from Bish before coming and scooting in beside me on the small sofa. Then morning broke through the window and I remembered with perfect clarity what being in serious withdrawal felt like. I shook and pressed my face into his neck, begging my body to accept his touch.

It didn't.

His fingers gripped my shirt and pulled me closer before he opened his eyes and realized what was going on. His breath rushed out and he groaned. "Hell…holy hell."

He sat up and helped me sit up, too. He pressed me to him out of desperation and whispered. "Maybe I should have mutualized with you last night. Now it looks like I may never get the chance and that's a travesty."

"Don't," I scolded softly. "We're going to do everything together," I promised. "Everything." A little boy in my arms named Rodney came to mind and I closed my eyes to keep the memory safe. Caleb joined me and we just sat, thinking about all the things that we wanted one day, all the things that visions had promised us. Kyle had once told me that Destiny was a meddlesome wench. In this case, I prayed he was wrong.

We sat like that pretty much all day. We couldn't eat, we couldn't sleep, we could barely even walk. Bish and Jen hadn't moved from their spot on the bed and Kyle and Lynne's pallet on the floor had been occupied since then, too. We all tried not to be annoying with the moaning and groaning, but it was kinda hard to concentrate on anything but that.

The worst part was that there was no end in sight. And there was no Marcus either. We still had no idea what he was doing or waiting for. Later that afternoon, almost at dusk, it began to all be too much. Bish and Jen got into an argument about this being his fault again. There was no calming touch to make her feel better so she got up on shaky legs and basically waddled out the back door. He followed after her slowly, feeling sorry for himself.

I tried not to think about any of that. I had to focus. I had to figure out the game Marcus was playing.

Caleb went out to check on Jen when they didn't come back after about twenty minutes. I heard Caleb's thought of panic right before I heard nothing. It was like his brain just turned off. I stood and held onto the chair arm to keep me steady before making my way out the back door to find him.

The sun was beautiful as it sank into the water and left the sand in an orange glow. "Caleb?" I called and heard nothing. The wind whipped. My back hurt so badly, I debated just hunching down right where I was, but Caleb wasn't answering my call or my heartbeat, which was going crazy. Something was wrong.

"Caleb!" I called more frantically, and heard the dark laugh as I turned. I gasped in utter horror as I saw Marcus up the beach, standing over Caleb with a baseball bat. Even from this far away, I could see his evil smile. He waved for me to come.

What could I do but go? So, that's what I did.

Caleb was alive, I knew, but seeing him like that on the sand hurt my heart. I wanted him to stand up and break all of Marcus' teeth. That's what he would have done if he was conscious. I hated the fact that whatever was about to happen, Caleb would blame himself.

I got closer and Marcus practically danced with anticipation. Once I got close enough to see the color of his eyes, he started his rant. "Hey there, human. Oh, wait. That's me."

I gulped and stared at Caleb on the sand. I wanted to run to him so badly, but I held off, hoping for my one shot to end this.

"What do you want, Marcus?"

Before he answered, I made myself get angry. I got white hot angry and tried to use my ability to lift the bat and beat him senseless with it. But it barely lifted itself in his hand. I felt drained and a failure.

He tsked me. "Your abilities not up to par? That's what happens when you can't get your significant's touch. Sucks, doesn't it?"

"What do you want?" I yelled.

He leaned his head down and looked at me right in the eye. "I want him," he kicked Caleb's shoe, "to watch you die. Slowly."

"I know," I said, "we saw the vision."

He stepped toward me. "Then you must know that I was going to do this."

The bat swung hard and even though I put my arm up to shield myself, it was like using a feather to stop a bullet. I felt my arm crack before I was out cold.

When I came to, I was off to the side behind some bushes in the sand and I could hear Marcus' voice. He was talking to another man. I looked around and barely suppressed my gasp at seeing Caleb at the new man's feet. I recognized him as one of the ones who had helped them at the compound when they kidnapped me.

My hands were tied as I lay in the sand, and I spit out dirt and sand, but it was hopeless. They turned to find me awake and Marcus grinned. "Showtime, little Maggie." He bent down on his haunches. "We…took care of the concierge and the guard that was outside your room. And this nice, private beach is completely empty of anyone to hear you scream."

He picked me up by my arm and didn't grunt or hiss. My body didn't burn him anymore because he was human. I could barely hold myself up as he pushed me hard and hissed for me to stand on my own. I saw Caleb jerk, too. His eyes opened and he looked around. When he saw Marcus behind me, his face contorted with pure rage. "You are a dead man."

"The Jacobson prince awakens!" Marcus taunted. "Glad you decided to join our party. It's just getting started. If I'm right…" He looked across the beach and smiled. "There they are! The lovebirds have returned. I knew they'd be heading back soon."

I looked over, dreading, but knowing what I'd see. There Bish and Jen were. They were making up on the beach…just like the vision, holding each other and completely oblivious. I closed my eyes to stop the tears, though I deserved every ounce of pain I felt. I had failed them. I had failed us all.

"No," he barked and glared at me. "You look. You watch them as they die all because you had to have your precious Caleb."

He gripped my shirt front and turned me toward them. The one helping Marcus stomped his boot on Caleb's chest to hold him down. I whimpered and tried to shake free of his grasp, but he was stronger than me when I was this weak.

Marcus grinned and got right in my face. "It's your fault, ya know. Not just this whole thing, 'cause that is, too, but this. The way your bodies have turned against you and you can't figure out how I did it. Well, I'll tell you." He got as close to my ear as he could without touching it. "It's your blood." He laughed. "And mine. It's amazing, isn't it? Something that seems so small and insignificant is what keeps us alive, is what feeds our bodies and makes up our very core. It's powerful and can be used in ways people never imagine. And now your blood is the very thing that will be your demise. It's the very thing I used against you to make it so very easy to kill you."

Even in my weak state, I managed to spit in his face. "Just kill me and get it over with."

He wiped his face with his palm and sneered, "No, this way is much more fun." He looked over at Caleb. "Later after we've killed your brother, Caleb will get to watch as you're tortured, and he won't be able to do anything about it."

I shivered at the thought and couldn't look at Caleb. I'd lose it if I saw his face right now. I tried to keep it together and think. It started to sprinkle. I shivered for more than one reason as I tried to keep my sanity.

"And on with the show!" he bellowed gleefully and bowed dramatically to his friend. The man smiled as he pointed his gun. I yanked at Marcus' grip, but it was hopeless. Caleb bucked and punched at the man's leg just as he aimed for his first shot, but he couldn't aim right with Caleb's movements. He reached back to kick Caleb's head and it was as if time stood still as my mind took over. I swung around, roundhouse kicking Marcus in the neck and then circling once more to do the same to his friend. Caleb was already ahead of the game and punched the guy in the only place guaranteed to make a man fall to his knees.

Marcus stood and just as he barreled toward me, out of nowhere it seemed, from the shadows of the bushes and darkness…was Haddock.

He ran and swung Marcus around, landing a solid blow to his jaw. He went down.

The first thought I had was his accomplice and when I looked, he was gone. I knew right where he was going and swung around. I saw him make a swift ascent to Bish and Jen. He was determined to finish the job. I heard Caleb's argumentative, "No, Maggie," a split second before I took off. This was it. This was Caleb's vision that he'd had the nightmare about. I *was* going to get shot and I *was* going to die on this beach. Because I *was* going to stop him from taking out two people who just wanted to be happy, who just wanted to live their lives and had been caught in the crossfire because of my collateral damage. Bish and Jen deserved every happiness. I just hoped that Caleb could forgive me and understand that I had to save his sister and my brother. They couldn't die just because Marcus hated me. I would never be able to live with myself.

So I pushed harder, forgetting about the pain and aches my body complained about. Forgetting about the searing burn of the arm I suspected was broken. None of it mattered now. Caleb ran behind me, but we both knew he wouldn't catch me. I was faster. I hated the agonizing pleas as he begged me not to, he couldn't live without me, please stop, please stop, stop.

I couldn't.

It all happened so fast, but the world seemed to slow to a crawl at the same time. I saw as he raised his arm, Bish and Jen so absorbed in each other that they still hadn't even seen him. I yelled, but the wind was so loud, they didn't hear. He raised his arm, gun in hand, and pointed it at my brother and his significant. Though I knew I'd never get to see the children that I'd seen in the vision, never get to see Caleb graduate college and keep his dream of opening his centers, never get to intimately mutualize with him like we'd talked about, about how it was so mind-blowing, and I'd never get to see Caleb's face again when he looked at me like I was his everything…

I leapt.

As the bang entered my ear, the bullet seared through my ribs. I closed my eyes, relief filling me. I stopped it. I stopped the vision. Bish and Jen were safe. I saw Caleb tackle the man and toss the gun into the waves before Bish ran and took the man's collar in his grip. One swing of Bish's fist, even when he was weakened, and he was down.

Caleb sprinted to me, skidding in the sand as he reached me. "God, no. No, no, no, no." He picked my head up as he looked into my eyes.

"I stopped it," I said proudly.

"I can't heal you, baby." His eyes glazed over. "The bullet…" He looked at it and then back to my face. "My touch won't heal you, remember?"

"I know. I'm sorry," I said sincerely, my voice cracking.

"But you still did it," he growled. "Knowing that I couldn't heal you, you still did it."

"I had to." I sniffed. "I had to."

His face contorted and he pulled me up to kiss my forehead. I felt a tear fall to my skin. "I know."

He tried anyway, he poured every ounce of his healing touch and calm into me, but it just wasn't enough. He leaned back, his face wild and hysterical. He looked where we had just run from and I saw in his mind that Marcus was just getting up.

"Bish, take her to the truck. Hospital. I'll be there in just a second."

"What are you-"

"Just do it!" he roared. "There's something I have to do. It won't take long. If I'm not there in two minutes, leave without me."

He kissed my lips sweetly. "I'm no good to you anyway, so there's something I have to do. I just…have to," he told me in a low voice.

Marcus. That was what he had to do.

"I love you," I said, because I knew I wouldn't make it to the hospital. I knew.

"I love you with all that I am," he promised in a growl before kissing my forehead and jumping up. He took off and yelled over his shoulder. "Take her now!"

I was lifted into Bish's warm arms and the last thing I saw before darkness sweeping in and claiming me, was Caleb's running form and him silently promising me that this ended here. This ended tonight. He would avenge me and no one else would ever suffer at the hands of Marcus Watson.

I thanked him and closed my eyes for the last time.

Twenty

Caleb

I shook with a rage that I'd never felt before. I'd always heard rumors and stories about a man that was avenging his mate was something not to be trifled with. That it consumed you, and gave you this strength in your bones that you didn't have before. There was something in me telling me that I couldn't function, couldn't eat, breathe or sleep again until Marcus was six feet under.

I'd never been one for retaliation. My family and most clans practiced a more peaceful way, but this was almost supernatural. This was... ingrained in my very core. I wasn't allowed to do anything but kill that bastard.

I started to run. He was getting up, rubbing his head, and looking around. He saw me coming and the coward in him took over as he scrambled up, slipping in the sand, and then making a break for it through the bushes. I jumped and landed on his back with my knee, my hands wrapped in his shirt. I drove his face down in to the dirt and immediately turned him to see his face, to look at him as I choked the life out of him.

I gripped his throat tightly and ignored the scratches and marks he made as he tried to fight me off. I couldn't even take pleasure in it. It was just something I had to do. Maggie was all I could think about as I sat there on autopilot and drained the life out of him. I prayed they made it to the hospital on time. That was the only thing that could save her now since this spineless worm had made sure that I couldn't heal her.

I squeezed harder.

A bang resounded behind me and I jerked to the side. Just in time, it seemed, as Marcus' cousin took a shot at me. Marcus wheezed and coughed as his cousin took aim on me again. I rolled to miss the next shot and it shot sand up in a blast beside me. I stood, hands raised.

Marcus stood, too, and bent in his disorientation, holding his throat. I grabbed him just as his cousin shot again and placed him to my chest. Marcus' eyes were wide with shock and betrayal. It made me a terrible person, I knew that, but I watched as his eyes fluttered to a close and he fought to catch his breath. He wheezed one last time before going limp in my arms. I peeked over his shoulder before letting him fall to the ground and saw Haddock with the bat in his hand and Marcus' cousin on the ground.

With the amount of blood coating the dirt under him, I didn't imagine he'd be getting back up. Haddock tossed the bat aside and looked to the house as we heard the sirens. He tossed me his keys. "Go. I'll take care of this."

I ran as fast as I could manage. My truck was just leaving the parking lot and I pushed myself faster to run in front of it. Bish slammed on the breaks and I threw the back door open and was surprised to see Maggie's eyes open. "She just gasped and woke up a minute ago," Jen explained.

Maggie reached for me and I obliged wholeheartedly. I pulled her gently into my lap and was slammed with a hit of her calm. Jen looked stunned, and she and Bish both reached for each other at the same time. They clasped hands and both groaned as they were filled with each other's touch.

That meant…

I lifted Maggie's shirt and watched as the bullet pushed itself out from between her ribs. She winced and breathed raggedly. It hurt me to watch it. I pulled her closer and kissed her forehead, leaving my lips there to give her as much of me as I could. "Wow, that hurts," she breathed.

"I know," I said wryly.

"I knew it," she said in awe. "It hit me after you left…something Marcus said about my blood and his blood." She gulped. "He's dead, isn't he?"

I knew what he'd done to Maggie over and over again, how he'd tortured us all, but having just watched him die in my hands made me feel kind of raw. "Yeah," I whispered.

She wrapped her arm around my neck and pulled me closer. She spoke against my lips. "I love you and I understand why you had to do that. I understand. He would have never stopped." I nodded. "Look at me," she said harder.

I opened my eyes and met her gaze, so close. "Don't you dare take blame for sticking up for me. Marcus did this to himself. Now it's finally over, because of you." She broke down. "Thank you. I'm sorry you had to do that, but thank you for putting my mind at ease. We can finally live without looking over our shoulders." Her voice broke with her tears and I just held on to her. I pulled her to my chest and squeezed, probably too hard, but it was just what I needed to do.

I heard someone walking in the gravel behind us and whipped around. Haddock was there with a policeman. "Caleb, they need a statement."

I looked at Maggie's face and gritted my teeth. I did not want to move away from her for a second. "I'll be right back," I told her.

She nodded and I walked over to the cop and told him as much as I could tell him. And I didn't lie. I told him how his friend had tried to shoot me and I used Marcus as a shield out of self-defense from both of them. "I'm sorry. I know you've been through a lot tonight, but with the staff dead, too, self-defense or not, we have to take you both in for questioning," he told Haddock and me. I groaned and ran my fingers through my hair. There were sounds of sirens and doors opening and closing behind us

"Fine," I said, because there was nothing else I could say.

When Maggie realized that they were about to take me, she jumped from the back of the truck. "No," she begged him. She hugged me around my middle and I felt like I was leaving her once *again* when she needed me most.

She looked up at me. "You don't understand at all, do you?"

I scowled in question.

If Marcus was still alive, we would still be in withdrawal. Don't you see? He poisoned us with my blood and his. One of us had to die for the

blood bond that he put on us all to break. It was either him...or me.

I did see then. That was why the thing, the need, the ache in my chest made me go after him. Killing him saved us all.

Yes, she agreed.

I gulped and nodded. "I understand."

"All right," the officer said. "Come on. Let's go."

They turned me, pulled my arms behind my back, and handcuffed me. Bish hugged Maggie to his side and I gave him a grateful look. Kyle and Lynne were running across the lot, but it was too late. He ducked my head and slid me in the back seat, along with Haddock.

I watched Maggie, my eyes never leaving hers, as they drove us away.

"So, no offense, man, but what are you doing here?" I asked. We'd been in there for hours now. They questioned us for what seemed like forever. They separated us, hoping to catch us in a lie. I explained everything to them. That Marcus held a grudge, had followed us here while I was on my honeymoon, and had murdered the guard and the concierge in an effort to ambush us. Eventually they told us to wait in the cell, and they'd come later and let us know something. That had been over five hours ago.

"Jim called me," he said. He rubbed his head and sighed. "He called and said he knew I was in town and that the Jacobsons were on lockdown. He said that Maggie sounded weird on the phone and was there any way that I could go down there and make sure everyone was OK. So I jumped right in the truck and here I am. Just in time, too, it seemed."

"Yeah," I agreed with a humorless chuckle, "the timing couldn't have been better. Thanks, man. I…" I didn't know what to say. The guy had killed someone for me.

"It was for Maggie," he corrected as if he could hear my thoughts. "I wasn't about to watch her live without you. That kind of agony…I just couldn't do it."

"Thank you, regardless of why you did it."

"I'm so sorry about Marcus. I distanced myself from the family." He leaned back harshly. "If I hadn't done that I might have known what he was up to."

"Don't apologize for trying to make things right. That bastard made his own decisions."

He nodded. "Yeah, he did. So, tomorrow is Maggie's birthday." I didn't say anything. He knew that I knew that. "She'll be eighteen. Eighteen years that I missed."

"Can I ask you something?"

"Shoot."

I spoke slowly. "What did you see in Maggie's mom? You and Jim both…I've met her and I just don't see the appeal. I mean Jim practically went catatonic when she left. I don't see what was so hard to stay away from."

He seemed surprised. "Well, she used to come into the shop and order flowers once a week. Every week she talked more than the week before. She was so sweet and then when she started telling me about how mean and horrible her husband was…honestly, it was as if I was trying to stick it to the guy. I took her word for it, but she was a great actress. I thought I was in love with her, and with the imprints gone, I thought maybe I could still be happy even without it. So I planned to take Sarah away from him, run away with her one day and never look back. But the one time I brought it up, she told me she had no intentions of leaving him. That she was just looking for some fun on the side. By then, I was in too deep and honestly thought that she'd eventually come around to love me the way I loved her. But she didn't. Then she just dumped me one day out of the blue and told me she never wanted to see me again. I know now that it was because she was pregnant."

I thought on that. "I guess I can see that. She puts on a good show."

"I hated Jim. But I see now that everything she told me was a lie. He was…a great father to Maggie. That girl is just…amazing."

Before I could reply, the big, heavy white door opened with a creak and the police officer unlocked the door. "You're free to go now."

"What took so long?" I asked. "We didn't do anything wrong."

"Well, some things didn't add up in your story, like why you never called 911, and the fact that your girlfriend was covered in blood."

"Wife," I corrected and glared at him.

He shrugged. "Anyway. Everything checked out. Let's go."

They opened several doors that were blocked off in sections before finally reaching the last door. Bish and Jen were asleep in the chair and my Maggie was worrying like a professional. She stopped as soon as she saw me and then sprinted to me. I caught her as she crashed into me.

"She's been here all night," the man said and lifted a disapproving brow, "even after she was told to go home."

"He is my home," she said.

The officer rolled his eyes and left.

I held her tight, loving the feel of her calm and warmth seeping into my skin. So, everything really was back to normal.

"Yes," she whispered in my ear and kissed my neck under my ear. "Yes."

I pulled back and took her lips. Those lips that I thought I'd never kiss again. She growled – growled – causing me to laugh into our kiss. She smiled in embarrassment. "Sorry."

"Don't ever be sorry for that." I licked my lips. They tasted like her. "What are those knuckleheads doing here?" I nodded my head toward Bish and Jen.

"They drove me here, but wouldn't leave me. Bish said you'd kill him if he left me here alone."

"He was right." I'd forgotten all about Haddock. I looked back at him. He smiled wryly.

Maggie walked quickly to him and he enveloped her in his arms. "What are you doing here?" she asked and then laughed. "Not that I'm complaining."

"Jim called me," he said and explained the same thing to her as he had to me. "So here I am."

"I should have known he'd know something was wrong," she mused.

"I'm just thankful that I made it in time," Haddock said, emotion evident in his voice and on his face.

She gazed at him in a new way. In her mind, she was finally starting to see why he wanted to get to know her. Why he was so interested and invested in her. He cared for her, that was easy to see, but it was more than that.

"Me, too," she said softly. She reached up on her tiptoes to kiss his cheek. "Thank you."

He looked stunned in the best way. "Of course."

We signed our release papers and Bish took us back to our cottage to pack our things. Haddock stuck around, still not comfortable with us being so far away from everyone after what just happened. That was OK. I understood.

Kyle and Lynne had slept through the whole Marcus ordeal. They had just run up the beach when they woke to the last gunshots. I was thankful. That had been two less people to worry about when everything went down.

We got home to Dad's and everyone was in an uproar about why we hadn't called them sooner on the way home, why hadn't we come home even though it would have put everyone else in danger. Why, why, why? I explained that I was the Champion. That I handled things the way that I saw fit to best protect my family in the best way for the situation. Mom cried, Gran smirked, and Dad patted my back and told me he was proud of me.

I couldn't believe it.

So we called everyone. Maggie called Beck and told her the coast was clear. She still wouldn't speak to her and hung up right after. So Maggie called her dad and told him everything that had happened. He was pretty pissed and said he was hopping the first flight home.

That night, we all watched the news as Beck and her parents were reunited on national television. Beck said they had gotten lost and were just now able to get back home. There was some speculation that they ran away to elope and chickened out, but nonetheless, it was all over the news since they'd had such a large search party for them.

The council called a meeting, saying Maggie and I were exposing ourselves to humans too often and easily, and we needed to understand the ramifications of our actions. They threatened to revoke my status as Champion, too. They had heard of Beck through the Ace gossip vines and weren't too happy that we had not only shown our abilities to a human, but then hid that human from Marcus. They set a date of two months away and said, Visionary or no Visionary, we all had to be held accountable for our actions. They were even thinking of reinstating the rule about the council members living at the palace again. They said it gave everyone a sense of order that couldn't be achieved when there was no uniform government.

So…things hadn't changed as much as we had previously thought. The vision Maggie had of us fighting when we were older, the one where we stood together against the masses; it looked like that was something we still had to look forward to. But that was OK. As long as we were together, we'd fight for the changes that our race needed.

The next morning, Jen and Maggie said they needed to go shopping for a few personal things, so I bit my tongue as they left, along with Mom, and I stayed and packed up the rest of my room. I was married and this room wasn't mine anymore, though Mom had something to say about that. She wasn't thrilled that I was taking all my stuff, but said she'd fix it up as a guest room and we were welcome to it anytime.

Later that afternoon, Bish finally got to take Jen to their new home. We didn't go with them. I wanted them to experience that all by themselves, even though he invited us to come. It was Maggie's birthday and all I wanted to do was take her home. She wasn't interested in some party, so my parents and family gave her little gifts before we left, and then we left with our things packed and Bella in the passenger seat next to Maggie, for my apartment.

That little place held a different meaning for me now. I was taking *my wife* there.

I got out and ran to her side. Bella hopped out and Maggie giggled as I took her in my arms, carried her all the way up the stairs, and worked with the key to get the door opened. Maggie eventually just turned the lock from the inside with her mind and we went in. Maggie must not have been paying attention, because when I carried her over the threshold, we were greeted by a chorus of, "Surprise!"

We both jumped, Maggie gripping my neck tighter as if I'd drop her, and then I chuckled as I saw Vic on the forefront.

"Surprise, my man!" he said laughing. "And since when do you get married and not tell me?"

"Since we eloped," I told him and put Maggie to her feet. "Who told you?"

He smirked. "Did you really think Ashley was going to keep that little tidbit to herself?"

"Oh…right. Well, how did you know when we were coming?"

"Kyle," he said and laughed at my face. "He said he'd text me once you were on your way."

I shook my head and looked around. There were five watermelons and three gallons of sweet tea lined up on my counter. I rolled my eyes, but went with it. They gave us tons of gifts and we ordered about twenty pizzas to feed everyone. They had strung streamers and balloons from the ceiling fan to the lamps. It was kind of hilarious. Maggie got to know all the people that I wound up hanging out with during the school year. The entire swim team was there, and the rest were just sprinkles of random people that I knew.

Before we knew it, they had pulled up YouTube and were showing her swim meets. I groaned and moaned as the girls giggled and oohed at the 'uniform'. Then Vic started going on about how I always come in second. They all just whooped and laughed at my misery. A few hours had passed and I sent everyone home. Vic was the last to leave, and he pulled me out the door, told me he thought I was completely nuts for getting married, asked if she was pregnant. I said no, and it took some convincing, but he thought Maggie was adorable and sweet. He was happy for me and that was all that mattered to me at the end of the day.

When I went back inside, Maggie was cleaning up. Bella was eating someone's pizza that had been left on the stool. She looked up guiltily before slowly lowering her head back down to finish it. I laughed at her. Then I took Maggie's arm and pulled her away from the trash bag. "What are you-"

"That can wait," I told her, my voice low and dangerous. I tried to breathe, but I was going to go crazy if I didn't get Maggie alone. And we were definitely alone now.

She smiled as I took her to the bathroom and pulled my shirt off over my head before helping her with hers. I turned the water hot, to soothe and relax her. She'd been through so much, knocking on death's door just yesterday. When I ran my hands over her sides, I felt the raised scar where the bullet had tried to take her from me. I fell to my knees and kissed it. She put her hand on my head and waited. When I was satisfied that I was awake and this wasn't a dream, I stood and kissed her mouth like there was nothing else in the world I wanted to do.

She ran her thumb over the scar on my own stomach and closed her eyes tighter to the memories attached to it. I kneaded my knuckles into the flesh of her back and shoulders, hoping she'd see that even weapons and death couldn't keep her from me. She made a little noise as she turned to putty, relaxed, and leaned on me, but then she groaned into my mouth and completely changed the game.

Her back hit the tile of the shower and I moved my eager fingers to knead into her hips and backside as well. I felt her nudge inside my mind. I allowed her, in fact, I rolled out the welcome mat. When the shower door started to rattle, I opened my eyes to find us surrounded by ribbons and my bathroom was about to explode like the one in California had. She bit her lip guiltily, but I just laughed.

"Come on." I pulled her from the shower and wrapped a towel around her as I whispered, "We'll work on that."

She smiled and giggled when I picked her up, threw her over my shoulder, and took her to the bed. For the first time, I didn't press her arms to the comforter above her head as I entered her mind. I let her touch me and probably even begged her to at some point. She plundered my mind happily as we were joined together in every way. The rumors were right; making love and mutualizing together was a magic all its own. It was unlike anything else, indescribable, but the best thing was how free and calm we were. The place could have gone up in flames, we'd never have known. Consumed, happy, married, and together. This was it, what it was like to be real significants.

Finally.

Forever.

Mine.

Twenty-One

Maggie

"Hey, Fiona. Sorry you had to cut your trip short. And sorry we're late." We came inside and Caleb shut the door behind us, letting Bella run in first. I'd spent all morning getting ready and Caleb had spent all morning at his desk with his Grandpa Ray's feather pen, scribing all the imprints and ascensions into the record book.

"It's quite all right," she insisted. "Your dad was worried sick. We'll go back in a while."

Dad came around the corner and barreled toward me. His hug was so crushing I thought Caleb might protest. "We're OK, Dad."

"I know. I know." He sighed. "I'm so glad that I called Haddock."

I nodded slowly. "Me, too."

He turned to Caleb. "So, you bought Bish a house, huh?"

Caleb turned red in embarrassment. "Yeah, it was nothing."

"I'd call a house *something*." He went to him and hugged Caleb, whose eyes bugged. "Thank you, son. Thank you."

"You're welcome." Dad leaned back and Caleb continued. "He's a good guy and he loves my sister." He shrugged.

"That he does." He rubbed his hands together. "Well, who wants to eat before you head off on your secret trip?" He bent and rubbed Bella's head. "I bet you do, don't you, girl?"

I smiled at him. We had never owned a dog. Mom hated them and their pet hair, but Dad seemed to be eating up Bella's attention. He stood and swiped a piece of hair back from his head and I saw it. I couldn't stop my eyes from bulging.

He took his hand and put it behind his back like that would make me forget what I'd seen. I held my hand out and waited. He sighed, even tacked on a little growl with it, and forked his arm over. I looked at his mark. Fiona's name was written delicately around the small leaf-looking tattoo. Her family crest was beautiful. She offered her arm to me as if she knew I was about to ask her for it. I felt Caleb's head beside me over my shoulder as he peeked to look at them, too. Hers had my dad's name around it with the infinity symbol in the middle.

Dad was mortified because he knew that *I knew* he'd mutualized. I smirked at him. "It's really beautiful, Fiona. I love your family's crest."

"Thank you," she said softly, her cheeks pink.

Dad huffed. "Ok. That's enough." He took his arm back.

"Dad, it's perfectly natural for Aces."

He glared. "Are you seriously having this talk with me right now?"

"An eye for an eye, Dad." I grinned.

He reluctantly laughed, shook his head and then nodded. "An eye for an eye," he agreed. "Why don't we eat before it gets cold."

So we ate and then popped over to Bish and Jen's to see them before we left for Arizona. We weren't flying. We decided to just make a road trip of it. Just us and Bella for the rest of the summer until school started.

Bish met us on the porch and let us in. Maria squealed and ran in, jumping into Caleb's arms. "Hey, squirt."

"Hey, sport!" she played back sarcastically. He laughed. Jen was in serious love with the house. It was still empty since they had no time to move anything in yet, but they were talking paint samples. That was pretty great in her book. And Maria had already decided that her room was going to be pastel green, because pink and red were 'so stereotypical' of girls. I bit my lip not to laugh at her.

When we said our goodbyes and went outside, I noticed Ralph's car in the driveway behind ours. Beck was walking up the walkway to my dad's door. She stopped and we stared at each other. She crossed her arms and moved a tad closer. "I just wanted to say thanks for saving us. Or trying to keep us safe and all. I don't know what happened with that guy...but...whatever. Thanks."

Caleb put his hands on the tops of my arms and rubbed his thumb across my neck. "OK, Beck," I said. "You're welcome."

She started to walk back to the car. "That's it? That's what you came here for?"

She looked back at me. She looked like she was about to cry. "Are you still a freak?" she asked softly.

I sighed. "Beck."

"Look, I want to move past this, I just need some time, OK? I need some space."

"Well, you're going to get it. We're going to Arizona for the summer."

"You are?" she asked, intrigued. "What for?"

"Technically…our honeymoon, I guess. Our other one was kind of interrupted-"

"Your honeymoon!" she shrieked and charged across the yard at me. "Let me see the rock."

"I don't have it yet."

"You got married…without me?"

"You weren't speaking to me!" I said, though they would never have let her come to the clan wedding anyway.

"Doesn't matter. You don't get married without your best friend, Mags."

"Oh, so I'm your best friend now?"

She fought her smile. And then hugged me. "Oh, Mags! I can't believe you got married before me! I was the one who was supposed to pave the way and be the rebel by getting married too quickly." She showed me her hand. There was a ring on her finger.

"He asked you?" I asked and peeked back at Ralph leaning on his car. He waved and made his way across the yard.

"Yes," she said and looked at the ring like it was the sun, moon and stars all wrapped into one. "And you've got to be my maid of honor. Though…I apparently wasn't yours."

I decided to just let her have it. "Look, Beck, you've been so rude and horrible to me and Caleb. You left, just left, after you called me a freak and wouldn't speak to me. After I came to find you and save you and make sure you were OK. I was worried sick about you! How could you do that to me and then just come here and pretend everything is fine just because you find out that I'm married?"

Her mouth was open and she was stunned. Ralph wrapped an arm around her waist and gave me a sympathetic look. He knew how she could be. "Mags…it was just a lot to handle, OK?"

"I get that, but I was your friend and at the first sign of trouble, you bailed on me."

"I was scared."

"Of me? What have I ever done to make you scared of me?" I almost yelled. I felt Caleb's fingers rub across my pulse on my wrist, trying to calm me.

"I wasn't scared *of* you."

"Then what?"

"I was scared that you were moving on without me!" she said and the first set of tears surfaced. "You met this guy," she swung her arm toward Caleb flippantly, "and everything just changed about you. You looked different, you acted different. I just thought you were going to leave me. And when all that stuff happened…you were just so beautiful and powerful, and I just felt so small and insignificant next to you. I knew you'd be breaking up with me sooner or later, so I saw an opportunity and decided to do it first."

I felt awful. That was how she saw me? As some person who flaunted over her?

She scoffed. "I can see on your face that you're making this out to be different than it is." She smiled. "Look, I'm only going to say this once. I was…jealous, OK? You and college boy were just so darn happy and you never fight or…whatever. And Maggie, you're so gorgeous. You don't even have to try! And I just assumed that you would eventually think I was beyond you, beneath you, something."

"Beck," I chastised.

"And I couldn't handle that, Maggie." She sniffed and wouldn't look at me. "I couldn't handle you finally realizing how much better than me you are."

I left Caleb's grasp and hugged her to me. She resisted for about eight point nine seconds. "Maggie," she whispered. "I'm sorry. I was being stupid. Ralph even told me I was being stupid, didn't you, Ralph?"

He smiled and shrugged. "The important thing is that you're here now, right?"

"I don't know..." she mused. "Is that the important thing?" she asked me. That was Beck's way of asking for forgiveness. Her mind was practically screaming it at me. Though Beck had been wrong, people make mistakes, and my whole new supernatural world was pretty hard to swallow.

"Yes, Beck, that's the important thing."

"I love you, Maggie Waggie."

I smiled, my own eyes filling with tears. "I love you Becky Wecky."

Her hug turned hard and relentless, and we stood there and squeezed each other for a long time. Caleb and Ralph bumped fists and stood off to the side and talked, giving us space and time. Once we were through, we decided to postpone leaving for our trip until later that night. We went to dinner with Beck and Ralph, and where else could we go but the 25 Hour Skillet.

When we came back and dropped them off at the car, they left just as Dad ran outside to meet us. "You left this!" he called and sprinted across the yard with my purse.

"Oh, I didn't even realize."

"I thought I was going to have to mail it to you." He smiled. "I hope you have a good trip. We'll probably wait until fall when you go to school before we go back to Fiona's clan. I want to see you one more time before we go."

"That's sounds good, Dad." Dad was thinking about everything that had happened. Even Haddock. "Something on your mind?"

"No," he insisted. "I'm just glad that you're safe." He hugged me to him. "Have a good, safe trip, all right?"

I nodded. "Yep. Plan to." He started to walk away. "Dad?" He turned almost reluctantly, like he knew what was coming. "Why did you call Haddock to check on us?"

"The Jacobsons were on lockdown," he reasoned, looking from me to Caleb and back.

"That's not why. You know if you called Peter, he would have come." Dad was staring as he tried really hard not to think about something. I felt a sense of dread come over me. "Dad?"

"I knew, baby. I knew," he said in defeat.

I knew exactly what he meant, but I needed him to say it. "You knew what?"

He sat down on the curb and sighed. "I knew that I wasn't your real father."

I felt like a ton of bricks had been dumped on me. I stared at my father's back and tried to breathe. Caleb moved into my line of sight and held my face in his hands. "It's OK. Breathe, baby." I breathed. He kissed me once. "I'm going to wait in the truck, all right? Take all the time you need."

He left, and I sat next to Dad on the curb. I didn't waste any time because I knew that sitting and trying to wrap my head around it wouldn't work or matter. "How long have you known?"

"Since your mom got pregnant with you." I cringed. That was why... that was why he was so distant after she left us... "And that wasn't the reason that I went crazy after she left." I jerked my gaze to his. He smiled. "That's my ability. I can't hear your thoughts...but I can tell your intent."

My lips parted. "That's what Caleb's Grandpa Ray's ability was."

"I like it," he said and shook his head. "It's useful." He turned to look back at me. "I knew that you weren't mine because your mom and I were always, always careful. When she told me she was pregnant, I was worried about her. She was acting strangely, like she was wearing a mask all the time. So I came home early one day when she wouldn't answer the phone. There they were." He twisted his lips. "I never saw his face, but I knew when she stopped seeing him, which was pretty soon after that. I couldn't leave her. You would have been left without a father because your mom's pride would have never let her go and be with him. She was too consumed with her image and I was just thrilled with the fact that there was going to be a baby in the house." He chuckled. "When you were born, I thought she would love me. I thought we'd be a good family and everything would be fine. And it was for the most part, for a few years. Then, when I asked your mom to have another baby, she said no. She wasn't ready to go through that again. It wasn't long after that she came home with a packet showing us how we could adopt from the state. She said she was all for bringing another kid into the house, but she couldn't put her body through having another baby. She was so excited about getting Bish. She told everyone we saw that we were adopting. I see now what that was about, her image, but I really, honestly thought that she wanted to be a family."

I soaked that in. "How did you know that Haddock was…" I trailed off and had no intention of finishing it.

"He was strange when he was here waiting for you. He was looking at all the pictures and things in the house. He was fixated on this one photo of you when you were little. I was teaching you to ice skate. Also, when you got here, he had this look on this face. The final nail in the coffin was when he said he owned the flower shop." He smiled without any real humor. "Your mom always got fresh flowers for the house, and the days she got them were the days he came over. Thinking back, I thought they were gifts from him, and they were, but it was because that was his business. It was his job." He nodded. "That was when I knew…he was your father."

"I'm sorry I didn't tell you. I found out that day that Mom came to the house before we went to London. But it didn't matter." I looked him right in the eye. "It didn't matter, Dad. You have always been and always will be my father."

"And that was why I raised you as my own. Because it didn't matter." He cupped my cheek. "When your mom left, all I could think about was that I'd done something wrong. That I hadn't been the father and husband that I needed to be and so she left. It had nothing to do with you and I beg you to believe me."

"I do. I'm sorry."

"No, I'm sorry." He pulled me to him and hugged me. "You will always be my baby girl."

The ride out of town was quiet. Caleb was patient and waited for me. When I finally climbed into the side, he immediately pulled me to his side and kissed my forehead before we pulled away. Bella slept in the back seat and I kind of envied her. I felt drained, but in a good way. So many things had come to a head and to light the last few days. I just laid my head on his shoulder as he drove, and felt everything flow through me.

We stayed at a hotel that night, and Caleb just held me. It was the longest I'd ever not spoken a word, but felt so safe and comfortable at the same time.

The next evening, we finally arrived at Caleb's dream state. I smiled as we crossed the Arizona state line and enjoyed Caleb's grin. Not too long later, he pulled into an apartment complex. It was gorgeous with bright colors painting every surface of the place. Our building was red. I looked up at it through the window as Caleb opened my door. He helped me out of it and then turned, nodding for me to jump on his back. I laughed as he hoisted me up. I pressed my face to his cheek. He took us up the stairs to the front door, Bella following behind us. "What about our stuff?"

"I'll get it later," he said and turned to look at me over his shoulder. "Ready?"

I nodded. "More than I've ever been."

He opened the door to reveal a beautifully furnished place that was nothing like the one in Tennessee. Bella went right to her dog bed by the back glass door. The furniture was brown leather and the walls were yellows and tans. The floor was hardwood throughout the whole place. And the kitchen. I gasped at it. It was any cook's dream with its huge island counter and every appliance and contraption I could think of. A skylight was open above the dining room table, giving the area a glow that matched my mood. The cherry on top? There was a wicker basket full of honey buns on the counter.

I turned to him and ran, jumping up into his arms, kissing his mouth because I could think of no better way to show him how much I loved it. He held me to him easily and chuckled under his breath as he gripped my thighs to hold me up.

"I'm glad you like it," he could finally say.

"I love it."

"We'll be here during all of our breaks at school and the summer while we get the centers set up here. When we're finished, we'll find another state and go there."

I bit my lip. "I can't wait. One day I'll be able to say that I've lived in every state."

He laughed. "Well...hopefully. That's the plan."

"I have complete faith in you."

"I know," he said in a breath. "It's pretty awesome." He carried me to the living room and put my feet to the floor. "And there's this."

There was a picture of us in a brushed nickel frame. It was a wedding photo. I hadn't even realized that someone was taking photos. My back was to the camera and I was turned just a little bit, my head on his chest. His head was leaned to mine as he held my fingers in his hand. His other hand was on my back, big and tan and strong. There was a haze over us from the lights in the trees. It was beautiful.

"How did you do all this?" I asked.

"I have my ways," he said slyly and grinned.

He went to get our things from the car and I rubbed the object in my pocket. I was actually nervous about it. When he came back, he set our bags in our bedroom. I followed him in and was surprised again at just how perfect everything was. But I was on a mission.

I sat on the bed and patted the spot next to me. He sat, looking curious. He tried to find out in my mind what was wrong, but I blocked him out. "I've got something for you."

"OK," he said slowly.

"And I know things have been really crazy so it's all right if you haven't gotten mine yet." I slipped to the floor between his knees and pulled the ring from my pocket. I looked at the inscription inside I'd gotten yesterday morning when Jen and I had gone out, *With all that I am.* The outer rim was a plain sterling silver band with a trim of filigree swirl. I looked up at him to find him looking at me. "I..."

He leaned forward while simultaneously pulling my elbows to bring me to him and captured my lips. "I didn't know that you remembered with everything that's been going on."

"I remembered." He took the ring and held it between his fingers. He read the inscription and looked up strangely. "What?"

He pulled me up and made me sit on the bed. "Stay here."

He went to the suitcase and unzipped the front, producing a box. I felt my heart leap with excitement. He knelt down in front of me, between my knees, just as I had done him. He opened the box, took the ring out, and held it out to me. It was beautiful on a whole new level. It had little diamonds that circled the silver band.

"When did you have time to get this?" I asked.

"Maggie, I…" He smiled and sucked on his lip a little. "I bought this ring weeks ago." I felt my lips part. I took it from his fingers. On the inside, it said… *With all that I am.* I pressed my lips together to stop the happy sob. "Now you see why you're so perfect for me?" he said with a smile.

I wrapped my arms around his neck and he pulled me down into his lap. I leaned back a little and slipped the ring on my finger. He already had his on and he linked our fingers together. "So I did good?" he joked.

"I'm never taking it off."

He sighed and grinned. "Good answer."

He held my face between his hands and pulled me to him. He spoke against my mouth, in the most achingly sexy and sweet way. "Gah, I love you, baby."

I licked my lips, touching his lip in the process. "I love you. Now kiss me, Jacobson."

He grinned. "Yes, ma'am."

And so he did. For hours. For days. For weeks. Months. Years. The road ahead was paved with things that we'd have to work on. The world, even the Ace world, wasn't perfect. No matter that our lives seemed to be wrapped with a pretty bow, we understood the rough times ahead as what they were.

Life.

And we'd make it through the bad times so that the good times were that much more special and appreciated. I could only imagine what our lives would look like in five years, or ten, or fifty, but one thing was for certain…

We'd be together and I had found my significance.

The End…For Infinity.

Epilogue

Maggie

Two and a Half Years Later

"HEY, MAGGIE!" I turned to find Misty. "Hey, girl. Do you have Mr. Dean's notes from last week? I failed my final." She rolled her eyes. "He said I could do a make-up this summer and the man is a freaking Nazi about things being worded correctly, and my laptop crashed."

I smiled. "Sure. What's your email and I'll shoot them to you?"

"Ah! You're a lifesaver!" She gave me the information and I waved and said my goodbyes.

I squinted at the bright light that hit me from the sun that I hadn't seen in hours. When a large, warm arm slung around my shoulder, I knew exactly who it was. "Hey, Vic."

"My girl, Maggie! What's up this weekend?"

"We're going to a birthday party. Sorry. We won't be around."

"Who's birthday?"

"My…Haddock," I answered awkwardly. Even after all this time, and though we were really close these days, it was hard to explain to people.

"OK," he dragged out for effect. "Tell Caleb to hit me up when you get back. I want to go see the new Bond movie and everyone else has already seen it."

"OK. I will."

He kissed my cheek. "You're the best, you know that?"

"Yeah." I laughed.

"Catch ya later!"

I watched him go and walked across the quad. It was so stinking hot.

I dialed Haddock. He answered the first ring. "Maggie."

"Are we still on tomorrow for your birthday?"

"Are you still coming to stay with me this weekend?" I could tell he was smiling.

"We are," I agreed.

"Then yes, we are still on for my birthday. If you must."

"I must," I said with a laugh. "And how's Heather?"

"Ah, man, she's doing great. She's waddling around everywhere and eating up all the ice cream in the house." He laughed. "I feel way too old to be a father of a newborn."

I smiled. "You'll be great." Haddock had imprinted at the last reunification almost a year ago and they were already pregnant. Granted, she was a bit younger than him, but we'd never seen him happier. And we saw him a lot. True to his word, he moved back to Tennessee and we even hung out with Dad and Haddock together at family functions.

Haddock still didn't know that Dad knew about him, and we planned to keep it that way. He was filled with guilt about a lot of things, but he'd more than made up for it. He saved our lives.

"I can't wait to see you." His voice was quiet and thoughtful.

"Me either. It's been almost a month now. Sorry, we've been so busy."

"No, it's fine. You're getting on with your life. I'm just happy that you're happy."

"I am," I said with certainty.

"Don't let the council get to you," he said, his voice turner harder. "This reunification will be rough with everything, but they'll get over it. You're the Visionary. It doesn't hurt for them to be reminded of that every once in a while."

"I'll try. It's hard keeping the balance."

"It is, but you do a fantastic job. Caleb, too. He's a great balance for the council. Well, I'll let you go. See you tomorrow and be careful on the drive, OK?"

"We will."

"I love you, sweetheart."

"I love you, too."

I hung up and saw a text sitting there from this morning. I opened it. It was Kyle.

Make sure y'all stop by the house 2night. Lynne has some stuff for u.

I texted back. **Will do.**

I put the cell back in my purse. I couldn't help but smile as I tried to follow the path of shade to keep from being scorched by the Tennessee sun. Then I heard Caleb and looked up to find him. And there he was…

I walked toward the tree he was leaning against. He was wearing jeans, a blue button-up shirt with the sleeves rolled up, and a smirk.

"Fancy meeting you here."

"Well," he said in a formal voice, "I was supposed to be picking up my gorgeous wife. But you'll do."

I giggled and accepted his kiss, wrapping my arms around his neck. "I'm glad."

"How was your last day of classes?" His hands fit perfectly on my hips. I loved them there.

"Great. I'm glad it's over though."

"Are you ready for…" he gave me a goofy smile and sang, "dun dun dun dun! The lovely state of Idaho!"

I laughed. "Idaho? That's where you're setting up centers next?"

"Yep. My analyst worked their magic. What do you think?"

"Wherever you are, there I'll be."

He smiled. The *real* smile that told me everything I needed to know. "How was it today? You feeling OK?"

"Well," I said and put a hand on my lower back, "someone was distracting me all day. It was a miracle I got anything done."

He gave me a scowl and fell to his knees. He lifted my shirt and touched my round belly with his palm. Speaking to our little girl, he said, "Have you been giving Mommy a hard time? We talked about this." I giggled as people walking by laughed at him. I put my hand on his head and let my fingers tangle with his hair. "We said no kicking during Mommy's class, right?" He smiled and kissed my belly right by my belly button. "That's a good girl."

He stood and gave a mock proud look. "She'll behave now. She's a

Daddy's girl."

"She will be," I promised him. "Of that I have no doubt."

"Haddock's tomorrow, right?" He took my hand and started to tow me toward his truck.

"Yep. Take me home and give me a warm bath before the drive?" I tilted my head to the side for emphasis.

He stopped walking and his face changed into one of my favorite expressions. "You trying to tempt me on the school lawn, Mrs. Jacobson?"

"Maybe," I said coyly. "Maybe I'm just ready to get home with you."

He picked up the pace and I couldn't help but laugh. He opened my door, but didn't help me inside. He turned me to him and gave me his proud look. "This time when you graduate, I'll scream and yell for you. No earbuds for me."

I nodded. "I can't wait to hold that diploma."

"I can't wait to *see you* hold that diploma."

I blinked rapidly. "You're going to make me cry."

"I don't want you to cry," he said and chuckled. "I just want to make absolute sure you understand how proud of you I am."

"Thank you."

I pulled him down to kiss me. He braced himself on the door with one hand and the other found my hip again. I shivered in the heat of the day. He leaned in further until I was pressed to the truck side. When I let my hand go beneath his shirt and inched my fingers into his waistband, he groaned. "You're killing me, baby."

"Then take me home."

"Done." He helped me into the truck and practically ran to get in. I laughed. He turned on the ignition and I scooted over. "Ready?"

"I was born ready."

He smiled and pulled out of the parking lot. "Yes, you were."

Even after these years, I still couldn't get enough of him. He was still my tyrant and the Champion, and I was still the Visionary. Things were about as perfect as a life could be. We made it work for the good. Because after all…

You don't choose your life, your life chooses you.

Five Years Later

"DAD!" MARIA screamed in delight and jumped up and down holding the purse clutched to her chest. "Ohmygosh, I love it. Thank you, Dad, thank you, thank you, thank you, thank you!"

Bish grinned and accepted her into his arms as he laughed. "You're welcome, sweetheart."

Jen laughed when Maria practically tackled her and they fell back on the couch giggling. Rachel laughed at them as she rocked Maria's little sister in her arms, swaying her hips slowly back and forth with a burp cloth draped over the shoulder of her black silk blouse.

The Christmas tree at Peter's house that year was unreal. With all the grandkids running around, Rachel said she wanted nothing less than a fairytale Christmas.

"You're up next, papa bear," I said coyly and handed the package we'd gotten Peter to him. He was wearing a Santa hat and playing Santa for the day as he doled out the gifts.

"You didn't have to get me…anything…" He sucked in a quick breath as he ripped the packaging off. "Where did you find this?"

Caleb and I grinned at each other. I leaned back into his chest as

Peter opened the Johnny Cash LP. Ava came and jumped up on my lap. "I picked it out, Gramps," she told him.

I swept her hair back behind her ear and she smiled up at me, proud of her gift. Ava was four and a half...and the biggest Daddy's girl ever. She looked just like Caleb, though he said she looked just like me. He pulled her to sit more in his lap instead, and spoke softly into her ear. "Ava, remember, we've got to be careful of Mommy's belly. OK, baby?" He rubbed his hand over the top of my round stomach. She followed his movements and rubbed it, too.

"OK, I'll be careful," she whispered, like it was a secret.

Ava Winifred Jacobson. Named after Gran, who bawled hard after she was born. The uncles and grandparents called her Winnie sometimes.

"I'm fine," I assured her. "Daddy just likes to worry." He smiled and kept rubbing his hand over my belly.

"Daddy does like to worry." He grinned at Ava. "But you like it when Daddy worries about you, don't you, baby girl?"

I bit my lip. I loved it when he called her that.

The baby kicked and he pressed harder. "Feel that, Ave?" He moved her hand to find it and she squealed with delight. I beckoned Maria and she knelt down and let Ava sit on her lap as she pressed her fingers to my belly. "Whoa." Maria smiled wide. "That's amazing, Aunt Mags."

It was. I leaned into Caleb's side and closed my eyes involuntarily as he kissed my forehead. "I'm ready for my cousin to be here," Maria whispered in awe.

When I felt his kick again, stronger and harder, I agreed with her. I was huge and it was almost time.

Baby Rodney was almost here.

Playlist

The best of

Intoxicated : The Cab

Stay Close, Don't go : Secondhand Serenade

Tyrant : The Bravery

Every Night : Imagine Dragons

Run : Matt Nathanson

Ho Hey : The Lumineers

Every Gets A Star : Albert Hammond Jr.

Love is a Verb : John Mayer

Oh My Stars : Andrew Belle

Madness : Muse

Kill Your Heroes : Awolnation

Kiss Me : Ed Sheeran

You Are Too Beautiful : Hawksley Workman

Wild : Royal Teeth

Keeping Me Alive : The Afters

Maggie : Rod Stewart

Heartbeats : Royal Teeth

If (Acoustic) : House Of Heroes

Many Of Horror : Biffy Clyro

Bright Young Thing : Albert Hammon Jr.

Fader : The Temper Trap

Beautiful People : Carolina Liar

Right Before My Eyes : Cage The Elephant

Lauren's Song : Breathe Carolina

Everlasting Light : The Black Keys

Lovesick Fool : The Cab

Demons : Imagine Dragons

Heartbeat : The Fray

Acknowledgements

The amount of gratitude and love I have for you, my readers, would fill a Volkswagen. This series is my most favorite and this had been the hardest book to write to date. Caleb and Maggie's journey is over. Will there be another book in the future in the Ace world? Maybe. But for now, thank you SO much for allowing me to take you on this journey. I need to go and wipe my eyes for the millionth time. I'm glad it's a closed chapter of my life, but to end this series was like saying goodbye to a dear friend. I'll miss them. I'll miss their world.

Thank you!

About the Author

Shelly is a bestselling YA author from a small town in Georgia and loves everything about the south. She is wife to a fantastical husband and stay at home mom to two boisterous and mischievous boys who keep her on her toes. They currently reside in everywhere USA as they happily travel all over with her husband's job. She loves to spend time with her family, binge on candy corn, go out to eat at new restaurants, buy paperbacks at little bookstores, site see in the new areas they travel to, listen to music everywhere and also LOVES to read.

Her own books happen by accident and she revels in the writing and imagination process. She doesn't go anywhere without her notepad for fear of an idea creeping up and not being able to write it down immediately, even in the middle of the night, where her best ideas are born.

You can contact Shelly at the following avenues.

www.facebook.com/shellycranefanpage

www.twitter.com/authshellycrane

www.shellycrane.blogspot.com

Now please enjoy an excerpt from Shelly Crane's new YA contemporary set to release soon 2013, *WIDE AWAKE*.

SOMEONE WAS speaking. No, he was *yelling*. It sounded angry, but my body refused to cooperate with my commands to open my eyes and be nosy. I tried to move my arms and again, there was no help from my limbs. It didn't strike me as odd until then.

I heard, "All I'm saying is that you need to be on time from now on." Then a slammed door startled me. I felt my lungs suck in breath that burned and hissed unlike anything I'd ever felt before. It was as if my lungs no longer performed that function and were protesting.

Then I heard a noise, a gaspy sound, and my cheek was touched by warm fingers. "Emma?" I tried to pry my eyes and felt the glue that seemed to hold them hostage begin to let go. "Emma?"

Who was Emma? I felt the first sliver of light and tried to lift my arm to shield myself, but it wouldn't budge. Whoever was in the room with me must've seen me squint, because the light was doused almost immediately to a soft glow. My eyelids fluttered without strength. I tried to focus on the boy before me. Or maybe he was a man. He was somewhere in between. I didn't know who he was, but he seemed shocked that I was looking up at him.

"Emma, just hold on. I'm your physical therapist and you're in the hospital. Your..." he looked back toward the door, "parents aren't here right now, but we'll call them. Don't worry."

I looked quizzically at him. What was he was going on and on about? That was when I saw the tubes on my chest connecting my face to the monitors. The beeping felt like a knife through my brain. I looked at the stranger's hazel eyes and pleaded with him to explain.

He licked his lips and said softly, "Emma, you were in an accident. You've been in a coma. They weren't sure if…you'd wake up or not."

Of everything he just said, the only thing I could think was, 'Who's Emma?'

He leaned down to be more in my line of sight. "I'll be right back. I promise." Then he pressed a button on the side of the bed several times and went to the door. He was yelling again. I tried to shift my head to see him, but nothing of my body felt like mine. I started to panic, my breaths dragging from my lungs.

He came back to me and placed a hand on my arm. "Emma, stay calm, OK?"

I tried, I really did, but my body was freaking out without my permission. And then his face was suddenly surrounded by so many other's faces. He was pushed aside and I felt my panic become uncontrollable.

I thrashed as much as I could, but felt the sting in my arm as they all chattered around me. They wouldn't even look me in the eye. That man…boy was the only one who had even acknowledged me at all. The rest of them just scooted around each other like I wasn't important or wouldn't understand their purpose, like it was a job. Then I realized where I was and guessed it *was* their job.

My eyelids began to fight with me again and I cursed whoever it was that has stuck the needle into my arm. But as the confusion faded and the air become fuzzy, I welcomed the drugs that slid through my veins. It made the faces go away. It made my eyes close and I dreamed of things I knew nothing about.

My eyes felt lighter this time when they opened themselves. The fluttering felt more natural and I felt more alive. I could turn my head this time, too, and when I did I saw something disturbing.

There were strangers crying at my bedside.

The woman caught me looking her way and yelled, "Thank the Lord!" in a massive flourish that had me recoiling. She threw herself dramatically across the side of my bed and sobbed. I shifted my gaze awkwardly to the man and waited as she stood slowly, never taking his eyes from mine. "Emmie?" When I squinted he said, "Emma?"

When I went to speak this time, the tubes had been removed. I let my tongue snake out to taste my lips. They were dry. I was thirsty on a whole new level and glanced at the coffee cup stuck between his palms. He looked at it, too, and guessed what I wanted. He sprung to set the cup down quickly and fill an impossible smaller cup with water from a plastic pitcher. I tried to take it from his fingers, and he must have sensed I needed help, because he held my hands with his and I gulped it down in one swig with his help. My arms ached at the small workout they were getting and again I wondered what I was doing there.

I made him fill it three more times before I was satisfied and then leaned back to the bed. I decided to try to get some answers. I started slow and careful. "Where am I?" I said. It felt like my voice was strong, but the noise that came out was raspy and grated.

"You're in the...hospital, Emmie," the woman sobbing on my bed explained. She smiled at me, her running mascara marring her pretty, painted face. "We thought we'd never get you back."

That stopped everything for me.

"What do you mean?" I whispered.

She frowned and glanced back at the man. He frowned, too. "What do you remember about your accident, sweetheart?"

I shook my head. "I don't remember anything." I thought hard. Actually, that statement was truer than I had intended it to be. I couldn't remember…anything. I sucked in a breath. "Who are you? Do you know something about my…accident?"

The woman's devastated face told me she knew everything, but there was apparently something I was missing. She threw her face back onto my bed and sobbed so loudly that the nurse came in. She looked at the man there. He glanced to me, a little hint of some betrayal that I couldn't understand was in his eyes, before looking back to the nurse. "She must have amnesia."

The nurse ignored him and took my wrist in her hand to check my pulse. I wanted to glare at her. What the heck did my pulse have to do with anything at that moment? "Vitals are stable. How do you feel?" she asked me.

How did I feel? Was she for real? "I feel like there's something everyone isn't telling me."

She smiled sympathetically, a side of wryness there. "I'll get the doctor."

I looked up at her. She was short and petite, her blond hair in a bun and her dog and cats scrubs were crisp. I watched her go before looking to the man again.

"I don't understand what's going on. Did I…" A horrifying thought crossed my brain. "Did I kill someone? Did I hit them with my car or something? Is that why you're all being so weird?"

The man's own eyes began to fill then. I felt bad about that. I knew it was my fault, I just didn't know why. He rubbed the woman's back soothingly. He shook his head to dispel my theory and took a deep breath. A breath loaded with meaning and purpose. "Emmie…you were in an accident," he repeated once again that I was 'in an accident'. OK, I got that. I wanted him to move on to the part that explained the sobbing woman on my bed. He continued after a pause, "You were…walking home from the football game. Someone…hit you. A hit and run, they said. The person was never found. They left you there and eventually someone else came along and helped you. But you'd already lost a lot of blood and…" He shook his head vigorously. "Anyway, you've been here for six months. You were in a coma, Emmie."

I took in a lungful of air and uttered the question that I somehow knew was going to change my world. "Why do you keep calling me Emmie?"

He grimaced. "That's your name. Emma Walker. We always…called you Emmie."

"My name… Emma," I tasted the name. "I don't feel like an Emma."

He smiled sadly. "Oh, baby. I'm so sorry this happened to you."

The woman raised her head. "Emmie." She tried to smile through her tears. "Try to remember," she urged. "Remember what your favorite color is?" She nodded and answered for me, "Pastel Pink. That's what you were thinking, right?"

Pastel pink was the last color I would ever have picked. "Are you sure I'm Emma?" She started to sob again and I felt bad, I did, but I needed answers. "Who are you?"

"We're your parents," the man answered. "I'm…Rhett. And your mother is Isabella. Issie…" he drawled distractedly.

"Rhett?" I asked. "Like in Gone With The Wind?"

He smiled. "That was your favorite movie when you were little."

I closed my mouth and felt the weight bear into my chest. I wasn't me. I had no idea who I was. These people claimed to know me and be my parents, but how could I just forget them? How could I forget a whole life?

I tried really hard to remember my *real* name, my *real* life, but nothing came. So, I threw my Hail Mary, my last attempt to prove that I wasn't crazy and didn't belong to these strangers, however nice they may be. "Do you have some pictures? Of me?"

In no time, two accordion albums were in my lap. One from the man's wallet and one from the woman's. I picked up the first, trying to sit up a bit. The man pressed the button to make the bed lean up and I waited awkwardly until it reached the upright position. Then I glanced at the first photo.

It was the man, the woman, two girls and a boy. They were all standing in the sunlight in front of the Disneyland sign. The man was wearing a cheesy Mickey Mouse ears hat. I glanced at him and he smiled with hope. I hated to burst the little bubble that had formed for him, but I didn't recognize any of these people. The pictures proved nothing. "I don't know any of those people."

The woman seemed even more stunned, if possible. She stood finally and turned to go to the bathroom. She returned with a handheld mirror. She held the picture up in one hand and the mirror in the other, and I indulged her by looking. I have no idea why I was so dense to not understand what they had been implying, and what I had so blatantly missed.

I was *in* the photo.

I looked at the mirror and recognized the middle girl as the girl in the mirror. I took it from her hands and looked at myself. I turned my head side to side and squinted and grimaced. The girl was moving like I was, but I had no idea who she was. She looked as confused as I felt. I looked back at the picture and examined…myself. She was wearing a pink tank top with jean shorts. Her hair was in a messy blonde ponytail and she had one hand on her hip and the other around the girl's shoulder. One of her legs was lifted a bit to lean on the toe. Cheerleader immediately rambled through my head. I almost vomited right there. "I'm a cheerleader?"

"Why, yes," she answered gently. "You love it."

My grimaced spread. "I can't imagine myself loving that. Or pink."

It hit me then. Like really sank in. I had no idea who I was. I had forgotten a whole life that no longer belonged to me. I felt the tear slide down my cheek before the sob erupted from my throat. I pushed the pictures away, but kept the mirror. I turned to my side and buried my face in my pillow, clutching the mirror to my chest. My body did this little hiccup thing and I cried even harder because I couldn't even remember doing that before.

The man and woman continued to stand at the foot of my bed when the doctor came in. I looked at him through my wet lashes. When he spoke, his voice sounded familiar. "Emma, I'm sorry to have to tell you this, but it appears that you've developed amnesia from your accident. We'll have to run lots of tests, but the good news is that in more cases than not, the amnesia is temporary."

I jolted and wiped my chin clear of tears. "You mean I could remember one day?"

"That's right."

"Don't get her hopes up," I heard from the doorway and turned to find the man-boy. My heart leapt a little. He was the only person that I remembered. Well from when I woke up at least. He felt like some awkward lifeline I needed to latch onto. He shook his head. "Every case is different. She may never remember anything."

"Mason," the man yelled, making me jump at the volume of it, and shot daggers at him across my bed, "this doesn't concern you."

"She's been in my care for six months," he growled vehemently and then glanced at me. He did a double take when he saw me awake and looking at him. I had no idea what the expression on my face may have been, but he softened immediately and came to stand beside...my parents.

"Isabella. Rhett," he said and nodded to them as they did in turn. He was on a first name basis with my parents. He wasn't wearing scrubs like the nurse. He was in khakis and a button up shirt, the sleeves rolled almost to his elbows. His name tag said "Mason Wright - Occupational Therapy". He looked at me with affection that showed the truth behind his words. "I'm Mason, Emma. I've been doing all of your physical therapy while you've been...asleep."

"You look a little young," my mouth blurted. I covered my lips with my fingers, but he laughed like he was embarrassed.

He swiped his hand through his hair and glanced around the room. "Yeah... So anyway, I'll be continuing your care now that you're awake. You'll have some muscle atrophy and some motor skills that will need to be honed again." I nodded. "But, from what I've seen from working with you these past months, I'll think you'll be fine in that department."

"Working with me? Like moving my legs while I was asleep?"

"Mmhmm. And your arms, too. It keeps your muscles from completely forgetting what they're supposed to do." He smiled.

I wanted to smile back at him, but feared that I didn't know how with this face. Plus, my body was exhausted just from this little interaction. He must have seen that, too, because he turned to the tall man who had yelled at him before. "She needs her rest."

"I know that," he said indignantly. "However, the news crew will be here later on." He turned a bright smile on the woman that was supposed to be my mother. "She'll do an interview with them and tell everyone all about her ordeal. I'm sure you could even get a deal on a big story to the-"

My father spoke up, putting a protective hand on my foot. "You set up an interview with the press the day she wakes up…and don't even get our permission first?"

They all kept talking around me. Mason started defending me along with my parents. The man apologized half-heartedly and I assumed he was the head doctor or some hospital head from the way he was acting.

My mind buzzed and cleared in intervals. I lost all track of time and eventually just turned to let my cheek press against the grainy pillow. My throat hurt from the tubes that had been keeping me alive.

Only to wake up to a reality that was more fiction than non.

My eyes still knew how to cry though and I tried to keep myself quiet as I let the tears fall. I thought I'd definitely earned them. Eventually the room quieted and the lights were turned off, all but the small lamp beside my bed. The phone on my bedside stand had a small list of numbers, for emergencies I assumed, but the name on the top of the card was what caught my eye. 'Regal City Hospice'.

Mason had been right. I wasn't even in a real hospital. They hadn't intended for me to wake up.

I wondered if that fact had put a kink in someone's plans.

END OF PREVIEW

You can find more information on Shelly and this book at her website

http://shellycrane.blogspot.com/

Now enjoy an excerpt from

HOAX

Coming January 2013

by Lila Felix

Author of Emerge, Perchance & Love and Skate

Corinne

"I'M VERY sorry Corinne but we are going to need your key, your school I.D. and your parking pass."

I looked at Head Mistress Ingrams and tried to translate exactly what she was getting at. I had carried that exact key around this school since I was six years old. And that parking pass hung from my rearview mirror since I was sixteen. And my school I.D. swung by a lanyard that rubbed and chafed my neck on a daily basis. But to give those things up?

As much as most people hated being at a prep school, especially since it was a boarding school, I loved it. I could be who I wanted to be as long as I obeyed the rules. And I always thought of some creative ways to keep within the bounds of obedience.

"I'm—I'm sorry?" I choked out with furrowed brows.

"You do not attend Wellsley Preparatory Academy any longer. Your parents came in and signed the forms three weeks ago. Please do not act daft." She made a triangle with her fist planted on her hip and acted like I was a waste of her time.

"I'm sorry ma'am, they failed to inform me. Here," I handed her the three objects of her desire and took my time letting them go.

"Thank you Ms. Novak." She thanked me and clip clopped in her sky high heels down the marbled hall to terrorize someone else.

I turned around and took hold of my rolling suitcase and stomped to the parking lot infuriated and hurt. But mostly, I was confused.

I drove down the highway with the top down in my convertible Mustang. As I made my way from Monroe to my home in the small town of Sibley I thought maybe the whole thing was a massive error. The longest I had ever spent away from Wells, that's what we called it, was three months in the summer. But Dad and Mom always made sure that I had summer camp to attend or, of late, an internship to keep me busy. During the summer I only used our home as a place to sleep and that's the way we all liked it.

I pulled into the brick paved driveway of the massive mansion with its manicured lawn and glistening windows and instead of gardeners and groundskeepers, I saw men who wore blue coveralls with the logo 'Smooth Movers' on their backs.

What, are they a moving company or constipation experts?

My father stood directing people towards the van waggling his finger at them, presumably telling them 'be careful' or 'that's fragile'. All three garage doors were open and in place of my parents' Mercedes stood a late model truck and in the next garage, a later model sedan.

What the hell is going on around here?

I parked out of the way of the movers and got out to find some answers. My questions about school had been put on the back burner and simmering on the front was now a pot full of 'Why are we moving?'

I approached my dad who refused to make eye contact with me and before I could open my mouth he pointed towards the house and turned to reprimand a mover who hefted a box marked 'CHINA'. I walked into the open door and saw my mom sitting in a lonely chair with a blank stare marring her face.

"Mom?" She didn't even twitch. "Mom!" I repeated with a little more force.

She sat up and turned to me like I had woken her from a coma.

"Hello Corinne. Your things have been packed. We are moving to a smaller house to downsize a bit. With this economy, it was bound to happen. And your school was costing us forty thousand dollars a year. You will be fine in public school, just fine."

In all my life I had never accustomed myself to the way my mother spouted out pre-practiced speeches and computerized responses to any question I ever asked. Stepford wives had nothing on my mother. They watched videos of her to up their game.

"Ok, Mom, anything else?" I asked sarcastically not expecting a response.

"Yes," she finally looked me dead in the eye. "We have to sell your car. It's just not practical for a teenager to drive a sports car." I rolled my eyes at the automated response and went to look at the damage to my room.

I found it completely empty of furniture and as I walked through the rest of the house I found that my room wasn't alone. There was no more furniture in the house with the exception of the slatted chair that Mom sat on.

I know I should have been devastated or depressed or something. But I wasn't. I just didn't care. This wasn't really a home; it was a place where my parents lived. And I barely even drove my car since everything I needed was on campus at Wellsley. But my parents and this downsizing thing confused me. Especially since they were constantly upsizing every chance they got and showing it off to everyone who would look.

I bounced down the front stairs and re-approached my dad who stood now with his arms crossed, satisfied with the micro-management of the moving crew.

"Dad," I asked.

"Corinne, did you speak with your mother?" He still had his eyes on the last moving van.

"Yes, I did. Where are we moving to?" I flinched back at my own question.

"We are moving to a lovely house much more suitable to our needs. You will not be returning to Wellsley Academy. I'm sure your Head Mistress informed you. You can go to the local public high school for your last year. I have also arranged for you to work during the summer, house-sitting for the Stephenson family. They will be going to their home in Florida for the summer and you can use the money to buy whatever you need for school. I put some money in your account which should cover anything you need now. I texted the address to your cell phone before you arrived."

I absorbed his speech with suspicion. He spoke to me as if I was a pet whose basic needs were his responsibility to handle and beyond that I was on my own.

"When do I start," I asked.

"They leave tomorrow morning. I told them you would be by at eight o'clock sharp to get instructions and information pertinent to your job.

You will be living there, so there's no need to unpack."

I'm sure most people would take offense to their father speaking to them like an employee but it was nothing new to me. I received basic instructions and followed through. One thing that prep school makes you a pro at, obedience.

He pulled a set of keys out of his pocket and handed them to me.

"The truck is yours. I will be selling your car tomorrow for another model for myself."

"Okay. Are we sleeping at the new house tonight?"

"No, we are spending the night at the Sibley Inn tonight." He checked his watch. "It is almost noon. If you need to get some shopping done before tomorrow, you should do that now. Your room at the hotel is under your name and paid for, so make your way there after you are finished."

He was cold and emotionless as he spouted out orders in my direction. I would love to have parents like those the other girls had at school. Those who kissed them, hugged them, and cried when they left their daughters at school. I had always driven myself to school every year, unpacked my own trunk and settled in with no comfort from parents.

I got my bags out of my trunk and threw them in the back of my newish truck. I headed to the mall, first calling the automated bank teller to get my balance. The computer lady said my account had $314.33, which was more than plenty to buy a few pairs of shorts, tanks and swimsuits and the leftover would last me through the summer.

The mall was not really a mall but a strip mall of clothing stores and fast food. I found the few things I needed at the first store and then I went to eat at a Chinese food restaurant. After I ate, I took the opportunity to look around and see what had changed while I was gone and to just think.

I drove to the park and got out of my truck and sat on a bench under an enormous Cypress tree. On my left I watched some guys play football while girls on the sidelines leaned back while sitting on the ground soaking up the sun and cheering them on. I sat back and watched the more interesting toddlers as they climbed the spider web rope or came out of the end of the tunnel.

I got up after most of the mothers had decided they'd had enough and were long gone and walked to the parking lot to get to the hotel and rest before my first day at my summer job. I got into the truck and drove the semi-circle to get out of the park.

I pulled up in the driveway of a house that made our house, or old house, look like a storage building. It was a two story house and the stairs that connected the yard to the second story front porch were taller than my upstairs bedroom window. A man in his thirties stood in the driveway and instructed me to park my truck in the garage. I did and got out to introduce myself.

"Hello sir, I'm Corinne Novak, you must be Mr. Stephenson." *Take that Etiquette teacher!*

"Hi, Corinne. Call me Phillip. You can drive one of our cars while you are here. Let's go meet my wife. She stayed up all night typing and printing instructions and rules for you."

We walked into the door of the bottom floor which housed the kitchen and an enormous living room. A very frazzled woman fluttered around here and there checking lists and stuffing last minute items into suitcases.

"Angela this is Corinne. Corinne, this is my wife Angela. The kids are at my mother's house spending the night. My parents are about ten minutes away if you ever need them and their number is somewhere…" He looked to the refrigerator for a phone number.

"Ugh—Phil, it's all in her folder."

"Ok, ok, ok. Let's go already. We're going to be late getting the kids and then we're going to be late to the airport. Let's go."

She walked up to me hugging a binder to her chest as if it were her last will and testament.

"Corinne, everything you need to know is in here. Let me give you a ten minute tour and then we can go." She directed the latter sentence towards Phil more than me.

We toured the house quickly and I was given a credit card for food and anything else I might need for the house. She pointed out this and that from the back porch and said something about a boy that was also hired to paint the house, the barn and the storage building as well as keeping the yard mowed. I was thankful that I didn't have to deal with that.

After they left, I relaxed a bit and took in my surroundings. It was a beautiful house. The walls were filled with pictures and kids' art projects. I got my bags out of the truck and put them in a stark white room with a four poster bed. Angela said I could sleep in the master bedroom but—well—eeeww.

I ate a bowl of cereal, crawled up on the couch and turned the TV on. I flipped through all of the channels but nothing caught my eye. So I pulled up a barstool and opened the massive set of instructions. They were basic things like no parties, keep the house clean, make sure to lock the doors every time I leave, things like that. But every rule had a long explanation about why that was a rule. I skipped the explanations. My phone beeped and alerted me to a text message.

Dad: Did you get to work on time?

Yes, I'm fine Dad. Thank you for asking. I thought to myself.

Me: Yes

I got to a divider in the binder and it was marked "Abel". I didn't know who or what Abel was but I was ecstatic that I didn't have to sit through more of rules explaining more rules.

I got up to wash my cereal bowl and through the window above the sink, saw an antique truck pulling up in the driveway. I put the bowl down and headed to the side door to see who it was.

The first thing I saw was a navy blue ball cap covering wheat colored hair and the shoulders and profile of a guy. That was enough to make me a nervous wreck and I quickly jumped back into safety and shut the door behind me. I heaved deep breaths in and out with my back against the door. I finally relaxed and hit the back of my head against it.

Way to act like a spaz Corinne.

Let's face it. I had been in a boarding school for girls since I was six years old. I hadn't had very much contact with the opposite sex.

I opened the door again and was suddenly face to face with a six feet tall guy with eyes that nearly identically matched his hair. His eyelashes were so long I swear I felt a breeze when he blinked. A breeze blew in from behind him and wafted a smell towards me of pine trees and smoke, like a campfire. What I wouldn't give to camp in that. He looked as surprised as I did.

"Hey, um, I'm Abel Collins. I'm taking care of the painting this summer. I just wanted to say 'Hi' so I didn't scare you being around."

I hesitated, still entranced by his eyelashes.

"Hi, I'm Corinne. If you need any help, let me know. There's not much to do around here."

He chuckled at me. I didn't know what he thought was funny but the sound of him chuckling brought nerve endings to life in me that I didn't know existed.

He descended the steps and I stood in the entrance for way too long watching him. He reached into the back of his truck and pulled out what looked like scrapers and sand paper. He stilled and then looked back to me. I'd been caught.

Busted!

I smiled and looked down at the ground bashfully before walking back into the house. When Angela said there'd be a boy working here for the summer, I'd pictured a boy whose mom dropped him off in the morning and who sat on the porch eating peanut butter and jelly sandwiches out of a Spiderman lunchbox and drinking Juicy Juice. She lied. No—this was no boy.

END OF PREVIEW
You can find Lila at her website
http://www.authorlilafelix.blogspot.com/

And now, an excerpt from Airicka Phoenix's YA novel, Touching Smoke, available now.

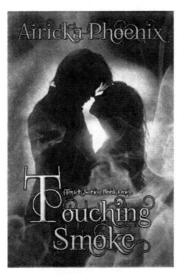

Chapter 1

"WHAT'S THE matter?" Mom honed in on my mood before I even realized I was chewing anxiously on my thumbnail.

"Nothing." I quickly wiped the spit off on my jeans and stuffed my hands into my lap. My torn and bloody thumbnail glared up at me, a sick mockery of my lie.

"Fallon…" The warning tone was in effect.

"Nothing."

It was a risk telling Mom when something was wrong. Her tendency to overreact was legendary. I spent a great deal of time and effort practicing to lie convincingly.

"Don't lie to me." But even practice didn't help sometimes.

I gave my head a shake, fixing my attention out the passenger side window in clear avoidance. Pale sunlight splashed over blooming treetops. The golden rays spilled through the knotted branches in splinters that lay broken across the forest floor. Birds flittered from tree to tree; I could hear their elated chirping over the Rust-Bucket's roaring engine.

"Fallon!" My mom seemed to think that the more she said my name in that I'm-your-mother-and-you'll-answer-when-I-ask-you-something tone, I'd cave.

Usually, it worked. I may have been sixteen, but I feared my mother's wrath like nothing else. She was downright sadistic when she wanted to be.

"It's nothing!" I insisted, already knowing even before the words were out that she wouldn't believe me.

"Okay." Her sigh resounded of feigned remorse, as if she really didn't want to have to do it and it hurt her more than it would hurt me — as if I believed that. Her hand wandered off the steering wheel and inched towards the radio.

I caved faster than a house of poorly placed cards in the wind. There was nothing worse than country music, and not just any country music, the old western kind that only played when you're in the middle of nowhere and only two stations worked on the radio: ancient western and some guy ranting about the end of the world and demons.

Give me the crazy guy any day. Unfortunately, he only came out at nights, when he knew he could give you nightmares.

"Okay! Fine!" I grabbed her wrist before she could touch the knob. "I'll talk!" I would have made a lousy spy. If I were ever captured, all the bad guy would have to do is threaten me with country music and I'd sing like a canary.

She didn't actually smirk — my mother didn't do that — but there was a satisfied tilt to her lips as she sat back and waited patiently for me to begin.

I faltered in my explanation. Every thread I grabbed proved to be the wrong way to start. My jumbled emotions kept knotting up inside me like yarn, tying up my tongue, making every attempt to speak impossible. Mom never interrupted me. Maybe because she knew how hard it was for me to talk about things I didn't understand myself. I knew she would sit there, for hours if she had to, waiting, never breaking my concentration, until I was ready to speak. Just so long as I told her, she would wait.

"I had another dream," I finally said, staring down at my lap as if the rest of my courage was somehow sitting there, waiting to be plucked up. But the only thing there was my hands, clenched together between my jean-clad thighs. Sweat squished between my palms. I wiped them on my jeans.

"What was it about?" she asked, casual with a tense undertone she was failing miserably to conceal.

Her knuckles blistered white around the steering wheel and there were slight pinch lines on either side of her lips. She stared with such fierce determination out the windshield that I half expected there to be scorch marks on the glass.

Mom was very pretty, much like those old black and white movie starlets they showed every so often on basic TV. She had beautiful cinnamon-colored hair that was naturally wavy when she didn't cut it pixie-style and it always carried the lingering scent of citrus from her shampoo. She also had beautiful hooded, viridian-green eyes that seemed to always be shimmering like sunlight over a lake. Her complexion wasn't as pale as mine, but porcelain, and she was willowy, not gangly like me, but… graceful, like a dancer. No one ever believed Erin Braeden was my mother. We were as different as night and day physically. My hair was thicker, curler and the highlighted with streaks of blue and it hung to my waist. It also had a life of its own, constantly creeping into my eyes when it was down, catching on things, and when the wind blew through it, the whole thing was one giant bird's nest. I tried cutting it more than once, but it had a maddening way of growing back, longer and thicker than before. I eventually gave up and kept it in a tight braid down my back.

"Fallon?"

I averted my gaze. "I don't remember."

Liar, liar, pants on fire! But it was either lie or tell her about Amalie. Lying was safer.

The dreams had begun six months before and I could never remember more than a few seconds of it. It was always dark with flashes of light, like someone spinning around and around with a camera in a room full of candles. Every so often I would see a flicker of a hand holding a pen over a faded journal, but the image would always dance away too quickly for me to read what was written. There were only two instances where I actually caught a glimpse of something tangible and both times it was a name:

Amalie Nicolette Dennison

I didn't know who she was or why she kept popping into my dreams every night, or why I would wake up in the morning, dizzy with the salty scent of sea breeze hanging thick in the room, but I wished she would stop. I wasn't sure my brain could take any more sleepless nights.

"Where are we going?" I asked, needing a change of topic.

Thinking about Amalie always creeped me out and I didn't like it. I refused to believe that I was some pod for spiritual communication as I'd heard it once called on a TV show somewhere in Alberta a few months back. The whole show had been ridiculous. Spirits from the beyond had better things to do than wander into the minds and dreams of the living. Besides, Amalie hadn't left me any subliminal messages or announced the name of her killer — assuming she was murdered. She just kept trying to make me nauseous with the spinning and the lights, or she was trying to drive me crazy from lack of sleep.

Honestly though, I blamed the whole thing on my mom. Would it have killed her to spend *one* night somewhere that didn't *look* haunted? It was no wonder I was getting crazy dreams. My subconscious was begging for a hint of normalcy. But Mom wouldn't see it that way.

"I was thinking we could just drive west for a while," she answered, rhythmically tapping her unpainted fingernails on the worn leather of the steering wheel in a way that meant she was in deep thought but was answering because she believed children should always receive an answer when they ask a question. "What do you think?"

I thought I would like to head back to Nova Scotia, rent an apartment and stay there. But that answer would only earn me a deep sigh and a long speech about firsthand experiences and how every teenager in the world would have loved to be in my shoes and how I should enjoy it and blah, blah, blah. I'd heard it all before.

So, instead, I replied dryly, "West — fun. Nothing there we haven't seen a million times before."

She either didn't pick up on my sarcasm, which was unlikely, or she chose to ignore it, which I was sure of, because nothing ever passed over her head.

"Actually, there's a school I called the other day—"

Reflexively, I groaned. "Not another one…" I was ignored again.

"—they teach Latin and French."

"Wow! Latin! That should come in handy, oh… *never!*"

She spared me a glower from the corner of her eyes. "You will like this one and it's only for a little while!"

Every time our funds began to decrease, Mom would stuff me in the most heavily guarded private school she could possibly find, while she worked herself silly earning more travel money. She claimed it was a good opportunity for me to make new friends and learn something new. It also gave her a chance to do what she needed to get done without having to worry about leaving me alone in a motel. But what I never confessed to was that I stopped trying to make new friends after leaving the fourth grade for the sixth time in one year. I learned everything I needed to know from the mountain of textbooks, worksheets and notes I carted around with me from all the schools I had left behind over the years, and there were tons of those. The number was mindboggling so I never kept count. But she always insisted.

"Can't we just use the money dad left me?"

I knew it was useless to ask, even before she speared me with a dark scowl. Mom never touched that money, except to pay for all the high priced schools she thought I needed. I think it was her way of making it up to me for missing out on so much of my childhood to the open highway. Not that being stuck behind towering walls and iron gates was any better and I was sure dad would have told her so as well, had he not died when I was four.

"That money is for you to start your own life one day."

One day. I knew my dad would have wanted Mom to use the money instead of working herself to death, but Mom refused to touch a penny of it in any way that didn't involve my education.

"How long are we staying there?" I sighed heavily.

Mom shrugged. "I don't know yet." In other words: until she had enough cash to keep us afloat for a few months. That could be anywhere from three to six months.

Well, maybe it would be different this time. Maybe Amalie would behave for once. Maybe she'd go away. I believed that nearly as much as I believed the sleek, black motorcycle racing to catch our fender was on its way to rescue me.

The sun gleamed off the rider's black helmet, and as I watched, he raised a hand and gave me a two-fingered salute.

My lips twitched and I raised a hand and waved back through the side mirror. Deep down, I stifled the mindboggling pulse of familiarity that warmed in my chest. I didn't know him, yet the pull was unmistakable, As was the distinct sense of déjà vu at seeing that exact bike a few days ago at a gas stop in Nova Scotia and then again periodically for as long as I could recall, but always from a distance and always gone when I tried to get a closer look.

I must have been waving for too long, because my mother's voice broke through my train of thought. "Fallon? What are you doing?"

I quickly stuffed my hand back between my thighs. "Nothing."

But Mom wasn't fooled. She took one glance into the rearview mirror and lost all coloring in her face. She cursed under her breath and floored the gas pedal.

Somewhere on highway 1 heading west, four sets of jagged burn marks mar the asphalt where the Impala had all but ripped through the concrete. Black smoke billowed, choking the clear sky with the stench of burned rubber. The motorcycle screeched, swerving under the attack. But where most would have shaken a fist and thrown a few curse words, the rider righted himself, leaned over his handlebars and sped up.

We were doing a hundred kilometers, and climbing. The needle quivered as we accelerated to speeds the Rust-Bucket was not accustomed to; the Impala groaned and shuddered, but kept pace.

"What's going on?" I shrieked, partly out of soul chilling terror, partly to be heard over the clashing roar of two engines battling, one ours, the other the speeder behind us.

"Get down!" Mom shot back, hunched over the wheel, eyes narrowed on the road.

I wasn't given time to follow orders. I was thrown back into my seat as the acceleration jumped nearly off the radar. I didn't even think the Rust-Bucket could go that fast.

"Hold on!"

Jagged gashes scarred the leather dash where I clawed for bearing as I was smashed against the door. My skull ricocheted off the glass with a sickening thud, sending a burst of light exploding before my eyes. My spleen slammed into my ribs when Mom suddenly hammered down on the brakes. My heart had already taken shelter in my throat, thrashing like a captured bird struggling for escape. I would have been panicked, but I was already having trouble reminding my lungs to breathe and my brain not to explode.

The Rust-Bucket nearly flipped. For a split second, that's *exactly* what I was expecting, and in that second, my heart forgot to beat. I watched, paralyzed from the brain down, as the car skidded as though on ice, rolling dangerously close to the ditch on the side of the road. The world seemed to clash, swirling in smears of greens and blues. I might have screamed, but even that seemed unlikely when I'd forgotten how.

Behind us, the motorcycle screeched, sounding like a desperate cry before it swerved under the rider's erratic attempts at trying to miss the back end of the Impala. I was twisted in my seat before it even registered that I was no longer frozen. The leather headrest tore under my nails as I scrambled into the backseat, over duffle bags, blankets and fast food wrappers to watch with crippling horror as the bike squealed once more before disappearing over the edge, into the ditch.

My soul screamed before the sound tore through the soft tissues of my esophagus and exploded from my lips. Time screeched to a halt. Everything froze, except the loud cracking of my heart, and the bike doing a nosedive over the lip and crashing.

"No!"

"Fallon!" Only when my mother's blunt nails peeled the skin on my arm did I realize she'd stopped me from throwing myself out the door.

I kept screaming. My insanity raged against reality. The world spun and dipped, andflashed crimson. Everything roared, swallowing the animal-like howls tearing through my lungs. I felt deranged, completely unhinged, like someone losing something so utterly precious to them that the very idea of living was unbearable. It was inconceivable. I wanted to die. I wanted to throw myself out of the car and dive into the ditch and… and what? *What was wrong with me?*

"Fallon? Fallon, calm down." Although soothing, my mom's tone did nothing to calm the hysteria eating me up inside.

"Don't leave him!" I pleaded, only just then realizing I was sobbing like my heart would cease beating if I stopped. "Don't leave him! Please!"

"We have to go," she said, still holding on to me as she used her free hand to maneuver the Impala back onto the road.

"No!" I shrieked, renewing my thrashing, throwing myself against the door. "Don't leave him!"

But she didn't stop and I was taken away; away from the other half of me.

END OF PREVIEW

For more, visit Airicka's website for book info!

http://airickaphoenix.com/Author/?cat=10

Now enjoy an excerpt from

Flutter

Melissa Andrea YA Fantasy Available Now!

ALEJANDRO BURST through the double doors of the nursery chambers.

He stood there, his arms widespread, his chest rising and falling rapidly, trying to drag air through his deprived lungs. His breathing was loud and haggard; and shouldn't have been the only sound to fill the room. Especially not with the chaos erupting outside the nursery windows. Dropping his arms from the door, Alejandro gave his horror stricken wife a once over where she stood in the middle of the room, clutching their sleeping baby girl closely to her chest. The spirit, the fire, in her eyes that she claimed proudly, was no longer existent.

The straight, silky strands of her long, black hair cascaded elegantly down the length of her back, brushing against her curves. There was a slight tremble to her curvy figure, and he could tell by her clenched muscles that she was desperately trying to control the unwanted convulsion underneath her formal, floor length gown. The soft shade of champagne material complimented her naturally tan skin, and flattered her shape in a way that appealed to Alejandro's eyes.

She was nervously chewing her bottom lip, making it red and slightly swollen from the edges of her teeth. Her flawless complexion had been drained of its color and he knew that, like their kingdom, his beloved Queen was also holding onto her final thread. She was staring back at him with wide, wild eyes. The unique blend of green and brown tones, tinted with warm golden hues, no longer shone brightly. Untamed and free, her vivacious eyes reminded him of the jungle that surrounded them.

Though their very existence was crumbling down around them, the desperation and pain that pulled at the corner of her eyes and lips didn't alter her devastating beauty one bit.

Alejandro knew that if he didn't live past tonight, her flawless perfection would haunt his spirit for eternity.

His eyes traveled just past his wife, to the window behind her. A warm sunset rippled across the sky, leaving everything it touched in a glow of pink, blue and purple hues. Walking to the window, he stopped in front of it, looking at his wife as she faced the opposite way staring at their daughter. As the two stood shoulder to shoulder, Alejandro brushed his fingers against hers. She turned her head in his direction, and without looking up, linked her fingers with his.

Turning back toward the window, Alejandro rested his arm against the frame, letting his forehead rest against his forearm. The King gazed over their entire kingdom, leaving nothing untouched by his greedy eyes. His mind was busy, working to burn the image before him into his memory forever.

The small village below was peaceful, quiet. He knew that, if only by deception, they were the only three on the island right now. The ocean that surrounded their small island had never looked calmer. Small waves were rolling in, washing over the beach and melting into the sand.

Even from here he could see the small diamonds reflecting off the water, like the perfect illusion of twinkling light above the water.

Dragonflies

"It's beautiful."

Even though the words had been whispered, the pain in his voice was evident.

Everything they had built, the world they had created for their daughter, was being destroyed out of anger and greed, and it was his fault. Though he had known the consequences of his own selfish actions, he just couldn't find it in himself to regret the decisions he had made. He didn't regret the love he had found, or the daughter that love had created. He only regretted the burden his daughter would have to carry when the time came.

Alejandro turned his attention back to the room; he had been so lost in thought that he hadn't realized his wife had moved toward the center of the room. After a few minutes of watching her privately, she turned around and their eyes instantly connected. She could no longer hide the anguish that was burning inside the enchanted irises he loved so much.

Reyna took one look into her husband's eyes, and the tears that she had managed to keep from forming, pooled regretfully. They filled her eyes like liquid emerald pools, clouding her vision, until she could no longer see the man standing in front of her clearly.

"Reyna," Alejandro's voice cracked in agony.

At the sight of her distress the King rushed to her, desperate to make her feel safe; desperate to make his daughter safe. Before he could get close enough to pull them into his embrace, Reyna put out a shaky hand, stopping him short. Roughly, she wiped away the unshed tears with the back of her hand. She was furious with herself for showing her fear and anger; making his torment worse. Nothing was going to change the outcome of tonight, no matter how many tears she shed.

Her eyes fell to her sleeping daughter, her innocent Princess who would soon be safe from the imminent threat that would be storming the nursery any minute.

Lost in thought; Reyna hadn't realized Alejandro's presence, until she felt the warm pressure of his hand on her back. His other hand came around to rest atop their daughter's soft, black hair. Together they watched as she slept peacefully within the sheltered arms of her parents; both of them knowing this would be the last time they would all be together again. Making soft sighs in her sleep, the Princess's smooth cheek nestled snugly against her mother's breast, her heartbeat a sweet lullaby.

"My Queen-" The urgency in the statement ended in an exclamation of awe. "Wow." He breathed, looking all around.

At the sound of the interruption, the King and Queen turned toward the sudden addition to the room.

Following closely behind Alejandro, had been Andres, their most trusted Watcher and truly loyal friend.. Their kingdom was gone, their people were dying, and Andres was still devotedly by their sides; ready to die for his King and Queen.

Together Alejandro and Andres had barely managed to climb the steps of the tower leading to the nursery wing without tripping on each other, as they had raced to reach Reyna and the Princess. After securing the entire floor of the Princess's quarters, Andres had returned to join them.

Now, as he stood just inside the room, frozen in surprise - he was afraid to move in any closer. He could see the visible tremble of the simulated sunset, the peaceful depiction of their world beyond the castle grounds, and he knew it was taking all of the Queen's energy to hold onto the bitter-sweet illusion.

"My Queen, they're coming." He finally said with a slight bow to his head.

At his words, the last of Reyna's restraint was defeated, and just like that, her trance was broken. The transient illusion had been weak and fragile under the circumstances. The muffled screams just beyond the created deception could be heard, and the entire scene wavered. Colors ran and blurred together, forming a rainbow of mist that faded away around them; leaving in place, the harsh reality of her kingdom, her people and their families being torn apart. Her posture slumped; she was completely worn out. The reality of what was happening was like a splash of cold water.

She couldn't save her kingdom.

She couldn't save her husband.

She wouldn't save anyone… but she *would* save her daughter.

Even if that meant dying.

Noise surrounded the small tower, and all at once she could hear the crackle of fire as it consumed the small village that formed their kingdom. She could hear the angry stomping of the rider's horses as they rummaged through the streets of *Encanto*, and tormented the innocent people who lived there.

As more armies of intruders surrounded the castle, the royal family's hope was diminished; the attack had caught the castle unprepared and defenseless. The frantic voices of soldiers shouting below and the sounds of tortured howls echoed loudly, finally snapping Reyna aware of what needed to be done.

Running to a beautifully carved, cherry-wood armoire, she pulled out her favorite blanket. Clear crystal beads created a diamond pattern on the shimmery, olive green material. She wrapped the Princess snugly inside as she tried to calm the excruciating pounding of her heart, caused by the knowledge that the time to escape had come.

Staring down at the sleeping child, overfilling her arms, she begged time to stop as she tried to memorize every feature of her daughter's face. She combed her fingers lightly through the child's soft hair, smiling as the midnight black curls clung, coiling around her fingers. She traced a line over the baby's dark eyebrows, down the curve of her nose, and over the silky skin of her closed eye lids. Her long, black lashes kissed the russet colored skin just below her eyes, fluttering softly, as her mother's finger tickled the graceful curve of her plump cheek, and down the side of her neck. Reyna watched the gentle rise and fall of the Princess's chest as she took each peaceful, sleepy, breath. Emotion squeezed the breath from Reyna's body. She suddenly doubted her ability to let go of what was most precious to her. She held the child tighter to her chest, receiving only a small protest from the sleeping Princess.

"Alejandro," she whispered, looking up at him with eyes glistening like green gems.

She clutched his arm, squeezing until the skin of her knuckles stretched and turned white in protest. Alejandro ignored the sting of her nails as they cut into the skin of his forearm.

She shook her head frantically.

"I can't do this. I can't let her go." She pulled the Princess up so that her head was nestled against the warmth of her neck. "I thought I could go through with it," she rushed on, "but I can't. I can actually *feel* my heart breaking in half. There has to be another way. We have to find another way. Please, please," She begged. The tears she had so desperately tried to contain spilled uncontrollably, running along the curve of her cheeks.

"I can't do it, I can't, I can't, I can't." She repeated over and over, until her words became muffled by the King's chest as he pulled her to him, pressing Reyna's head against his chest.

"Shh," Alejandro whispered into her hair. His fingers found the back of her neck, under the weight of her hair, and he rubbed the soft skin hoping to calm her.

When she was no longer chanting, he spoke. "Reyna my love, listen to me," he soothed, catching her face and gently holding her cold cheeks between his hands, the pads of his thumbs tracing the smooth lines of her jaw and neck.

"You can do this. I know you can." He said fiercely. He peered deeply into her eyes, as if he were trying to channel the confidence she needed to continue with the plan they had formed.

"*I* believe in you." He said, pouring all the emotion he could into his words. "Sara is depending on you. You are the strongest women I know, and you have passed down that amazing strength to our daughter. I need you; I can't do this without you my wife." He pressed his forehead to hers, and her eyes squeezed shut letting free more tears.

"We knew this was coming. *He* will take care of her for us, and when it's time, he will do what he was destined to do for her."

Reyna pulled her bottom lip through her teeth a few times, before slowly nodding her head. He sighed, knowing they were accepting a future without their daughter. He kissed her roughly on the mouth before slowly releasing his wife and daughter from his embrace. Reyna looked down at her daughter one more time, and kissed her lips, her nose, her forehead; inhaling her sweet scent.

The shouting was getting louder, closer. She knew they were running out of time; they would be ambushed if they didn't hurry. She rubbed her fingers over her daughter's cheek one last time and looked to her husband.

"You have to take her from me." Her voice trembled as she spoke. She couldn't describe the gut wrenching feeling that consumed her, as she held the Princess out to her father. "If you don't, I won't be able to let her go." She confessed.

Alejandro took a step closer, and tenderly scooped the child into his arms, protectively tucking her head to his shoulder, and resting his cheek against her hair. Tiny, chubby, arms immediately encircled his neck, curling herself closer to his familiar warmth, before her breathing became a sweet sound as she settled back to sleep.

The pain Reyna felt the second her baby girl was no longer in her arms was unbearable and overwhelming. The intensity of the anguish nearly brought her to her knees, and she clutched her stomach gasping for breath; but she knew she had to continue, and she began to move around the room quickly.

She picked up a pre-packed bag, which had been sitting on a rocking chair near the crib, and handed it to Andres. He was standing there, feeling helpless and confused throughout the entire scene. He frowned as his fingers closed around the straps of the bag. Puzzled, he looked at her, taking the bag from her shaky fingers.

Alejandro, who had been talking very softly to his daughter in his native tongue, walked over to Andres. Looking away from his daughter, his eyes reflected a pain so visibly strong, Andres wanted to turn away from the force of it.

Alejandro slowly lifted his daughter toward Andres, staring at him, waiting for him to understand what he wanted, what he *needed* him to do.

Hope you enjoyed the excerpt of
Flutter

This paperback interior was designed and formatted by

www.emtippettsbookdesigns.blogspot.com

Artisan interiors for discerning authors and publishers.

CPSIA information can be obtained at www.ICGtesting.com
Printed in the USA
LVOW12s1449170114

369894LV00018B/1020/P